AMANDA'S RETURN

Hunter's Find II

By

June Kramin

Pau Hana Books

For my cousin, Kellyann, with the golden eyes.
Thanks for all the help, God-sister.
You rock.

CHAPTER ONE

After she was given the doctor's news, Mandy leaned into Hunt, heavy with relief. There was no medical reason she wasn't getting pregnant.

"Hunt checked out just fine, same as you. Don't stress over it, Amanda. These things tend to have their own schedule. When you least expect it is when it usually happens."

Hunt stood. "Thanks, Doc. Sorry to have wasted your time on unnecessary tests."

"Don't be ridiculous. This is the kind of news I like to give my patients. You need to relax and enjoy each other."

Mandy couldn't help but laugh.

The doctor turned red. "You know what I mean."

Now standing at Hunt's side, Mandy said, "Thanks again, Doc. I hope to see you again soon." She rubbed her belly. "Just a little fatter next time."

He reached for her hand. "It'll happen. Give it time."

A slight smile was the only response she could give him. As they left the office, she leaned into Hunt's chest and softly cried. Already the good news was pushed aside, and her doubts came back.

"Hey," he said as he wrapped his arms tight around her. "What's that for? That was good news."

Mandy sniffed. "It's been almost three years, Hunt. What if he's wrong?"

"Shhh, babe. From what we've been hearing, that's nothing. My insurance premium tells me he knows what he's doing."

"Do you think we should try the fertility clinic?"

"No. No more cups."

Mandy's lip trembled.

"Shit. Come here." Hunt backed toward a loveseat in the sitting area and pulled her to his lap. "We have to do what he says and stop fixating on it. Of course I want to expand our family, but I refuse to see you get upset over trying, babe." He reached to the coffee table for a box of tissues and offered her one. "How about we take a vacation? Maybe time away will do you some good."

"Because my days at home with Hannah are so stressful?"

"Don't sell yourself short. I know staying at home is no picnic. Granted, she keeps you on your toes, but that hardly compares to your finger-breaking days with the Menuscos." Hunt laughed as he held up his fisted hands, making a breaking motion.

Mandy scowled. "I never would have told you that—"

He placed his finger over her lips, cutting her off. "Where do you want to go, babe? I'll make it happen."

"New York."

"Now I know you're off your nut."

"I'm serious. I want to wear a nice evening gown and go to a show that doesn't involve cartoon characters. I want to drink champagne until the restaurant runs out of the good stuff. I want to walk down the street in stilettos until my feet are killing me."

Hunt scooted her aside and stood. "I was afraid of this." He walked away. Mandy hurried after him. Their truck was on the street, and Hunt had already climbed in. He usually waited and held open her door. This wasn't good.

After he peeled away from the curb, Mandy dared speak. "Don't be angry. It's not what you think, Hunt."

"The hell it's not. You've been acting like you were content to play housewife when all this time you've wanted to be donning a firearm, not a diaper bag."

"That's not true. I want to get pregnant again. If I can't, then I want to have a little fun."

"And you can't do that anywhere else? You want to put yourself right back in the heat of things with the Menuscos? I didn't move down here and give up my name so I could waltz you back into firing range, Amanda."

"Amanda? You are pissed. Why have you never complained about your name before? You didn't have to change it."

"Like hell. Change it or risk you being found easier. It wasn't a tough call."

"I don't want to fight with you. You asked where I wanted to go, and I answered."

"You need to stop and think for a minute. What you're asking is insane. You know there is no way in hell we're allowed to go back to New York. I'm not about to break the rules of protective custody because you want a night out on the town."

"You pick somewhere, then. Let's go to Vermont and visit your friends."

"You know we can't go back to Vermont either." Hunt stared straight ahead. They were silent the rest of the ten-minute drive home. Hunt put his truck in park without going in the garage. Hannah was already running out to greet them.

As Hunt leaned down to pick her up, Hannah asked, "Am I going to have a baby brother or sister?"

"Not yet, baby girl. Soon, though. You keep saying your prayers."

Mandy reached their side and rolled her eyes.

Hunt frowned.

Religion was a subject they tried not to get into if they could avoid it. After giving her daughter a pat on the back, she walked toward the house. Hunt's parents were walking out as she reached the front door.

"Thanks for watching her."

"Our pleasure, dear," Hunt's mother said. "You know we'll come any time you need us." She placed her hand on her cheek. "It'll happen. Just give it time."

"Thanks, Mom." Mandy received a hug from both of them and entered the house.

Hunt joined Mandy by the pool with Hannah in her swimsuit and water wings. "Stay on the stairs, Peanut. I'll be in after a second."

"Okay!" she squealed, then ran off.

Mandy was lying down on a lounge chair under the shade of an umbrella with her eyes closed. Hunt sat down and took her hand. She didn't open her eyes but softly said, "I'm sorry."

"Me, too. You know I'm not pissed about the name thing."

"I know. I'm just..."

"Stressed. Will you settle for Paris?"

Mandy opened her eyes and sat up. "Really?"

"Really. I know you can take the girl out of the city—"

"But you can't take the city out of the girl." Mandy beamed. "I'm sorry I brought up New York. I know we can't go there. Paris sounds great. I just need some big city life. It'll be a bonus if we can hook up with Sue."

He leaned back. "Sue is in Paris? Since when?"

"Didn't I tell you?"

"Gee, babe. You only have one ex-mob sister-in-law in hiding that I'm aware of, and you can't even keep me up to date with that one."

Mandy laughed. "She's only doing what I told her to do. She keeps moving around and keeps herself safe."

"So, Paulo is out?"

"You have to keep up, my love. Actually, I haven't heard from her in a while. I couldn't get her last time I tried. She hasn't called me with a new number. Maybe she's not even in Paris anymore."

"But you've decided? Should I make reservations for Paris?"

"Yes. That sounds great."

"Okay then." He picked her up and, despite her wiggling and protests, dropped her into the pool.

Hannah squealed. "Me next, Daddy!" Hunt hurried over to her before she tried to swim out on her own.

Mandy was lying beside Hunt in bed, listening to his heavy breathing when she heard a rustling outside. Strange sounds had woken her before. After they'd moved, it had taken her a long time to get used to the noises of life outside the big city. The lack of sirens, cars, and people milling around was something she didn't think she'd ever get used to. Too many nights she got out of bed and picked up her revolver, only to discover it was a stray cat or raccoon.

They had moved to Celebration, Florida, and changed their names after the arrest of Vince Menusco, a New York mob boss and her former employer. She'd been an undercover agent and called him "boss" for almost a year, but Craig Abbey of the FBI had been her real boss. A final shoot-out in an isolated cabin in Vermont left her shy one boss and Vince Menusco behind bars. She'd met Hunt during that case, and nine months later she'd brought their daughter Hannah into the world.

Although they had changed their names and were in the witness protection program, Hunt stayed a police officer. This left Mandy uneasy for the most part, but he loved what he did, and she would never take it from him. Celebration was filled with nice families and easy access to Disney World. Not too much went on by way of heavy crime. Hunt hadn't seen a lot in Vermont, anyway, so the transition wasn't too rough for him. He had joked many times that Mandy was the only exciting thing to come along—ever.

Their relationship had had a hell of a start. Mandy smiled at Hunt's sleeping face as she reminisced about their first days together. She was beginning to feel silly about her fears, writing it off to old job jitters, when the rustling happened again. She carefully slid out of bed and managed to get her gun from the nightstand without waking Hunt.

She cautiously descended the stairs, hugging the wall to avoid creaking them, and went to the sliding kitchen door. It sat directly under their bedroom window. She checked the door to make sure it was locked and peered outside. Satisfied that there was nothing there, she turned back around.

A silhouette of a man was now in her sights. She jumped and pulled her gun up.

"For God's sake, don't shoot me, Mandy!"

She lowered her gun and leaned into her husband's chest. "You scared the shit out of me, Hunt."

"Yeah? Well, you don't want to take a look in my shorts right now, either. Why the hell didn't you wake me if you were freaked enough to grab your gun?"

"I didn't want to worry you."

"Right. This is so much better."

"I knew it was nothing."

"That's why you took your gun out?"

She leaned back. "I don't know, Hunt. Old reflexes die hard, I guess."

He removed the gun from her hand, and then they walked arm in arm up the stairs, checked on Hannah, and crawled into bed.

"You think it was a raccoon again?" Hunt asked.

"Probably. Maybe you should go get some more live traps. Just don't let Hannah see it if you catch one. She'll want to keep it."

Hunt became serious. "Don't ever let me catch you getting out of bed with a gun again, babe. I don't care what you think it is. If you're that scared, I'm going." He cut off her protests by putting his hand over her mouth. "Or going with you. I know you're a toughie, but let me play man of the house, okay?"

She nodded her head, and he dropped his hand. "I'm sorry. I guess my imagination got carried away. You'd think after all this time I'd be used to this peaceful lifestyle."

He pulled her closer to him. "We'll get you a room right off the worst part of Paris. With a little luck, you'll get your fill of enough sirens and gunshots to make you appreciate our home."

"Sweet talker." After leaning over and kissing him, she maneuvered her way on top of his chest. "I'm really not sleepy anymore."

"I think I'm up to the challenge of wearing you out."

"Put your money where your mouth is, lover."

He changed positions with her and let out a growl. "I hope you don't ever learn to sleep through those little backyard noises. I live for your two a.m. horny attacks."

After Hunt left for work the next morning, Mandy's mind wandered to their vacation. She was getting excited about the hustle and bustle of a busy city. Unlocking the glass door, she slid it open to let the fresh air in. She'd take the heat as long as she could before turning the air conditioner on. Hannah would be up soon and, as usual, would want to go for a swim before breakfast. Even at the age of four, she didn't like to go out in the afternoon heat, but Mandy didn't want her out in the harsh sun in the middle of the day, anyway.

A floating ring in the pool caught Mandy's attention. She took the net off the wall to retrieve it. After fishing it out, she spun around and let out a scream.

"Dad! You scared the hell out of me!"

He chuckled. "Sorry to scare you, dear. Everything okay?"

She gave him a kiss hello. "Everything is fine. A raccoon woke us out of bed early this morning. I guess I'm shy of a little sleep." *And I didn't mind it one bit,* she thought.

"Is that what's been trampling your hostas?" He pointed by the screen door.

"Damn rodents! I swear I'm going to tell Hunt to hell with the live trap and shoot the bastards!"

Again he laughed and shook his head. "Mom made a coffee cake this morning. She wanted to bring it over here while it was good and hot. Did we miss Hunt?"

"You just missed him. He'll love it for tomorrow morning. I have coffee on. Come on in."

He took the net from her hand. "I'll hang this up for you and be right in."

"Thanks."

Mandy found her mother-in-law walking down the stairs with Hannah.

"I went in to check on her, and she was up. I promise I didn't wake her."

Mandy laughed. "That's okay if you did. She was due up any second."

"See right through me, don't you, dear?"

"You're like a window, Mom." Mandy kissed them both then went to get coffee and plates for the cake. She never minded Hunt's parents popping in unexpectedly. They had already given up spontaneous kitchen and couch sex, anyway, once Hannah was crawling around.

Hunt's parents wanted to live nearby after they went into witness protection. They already had a winter place in the Keys, so it was an easy decision for them to make their retirement official and move permanently to Celebration. Give up seeing their granddaughter or change their names. It wasn't a tough call. Normally something like that wasn't allowed, but after what Mandy was put through, the FBI owed her at least that. Not having any family around of her own, Mandy welcomed grandparents who wanted to be an active part of her child's life.

After serving them, she asked about the vacation she and Hunt had been discussing.

"Of course we'll watch the peanut. You mind if we take her to our house? You know how that pool worries me," Hunt's mother said.

"That would be fine. She's used to your place. I know she'll be okay."

Hunt's father spoke up. "Well? You going to ask her?" he said to his wife.

"Ask me what?"

"We wanted to take Hannah to the circus this afternoon."

"There's a circus?"

"It's about an hour away. I'd love to take her, dear. I know how you feel about the circus. I didn't think you'd mind us doing it."

"Personally, I can't stand it anymore, but if you want to take her of course it's okay." She turned to Hannah. "Sweetie? You wanna go with Grandma and Grandpa and see some tigers and elephants?"

Her eyes lit up. "Yes!"

"Go wash your hands, I'll be up to help you get dressed."

"I'll help her," Hunt's mother said. "Thanks for letting us take her."

"Of course you can take her. You know that, anytime. And don't think I didn't know your coffee cake came with an ulterior motive."

"Damn window again, huh?"

"Absolutely." Mandy laughed and gathered the empty plates.

After waving goodbye, Mandy set about her daily routine. She wasn't as unhappy as Hunt thought. She didn't mind the mundane, everyday chores of being a housewife.

She had enrolled Hannah in an early childhood class and made some friends, but she didn't have a lot in common with the other women. Growing tired of Pampered Chef, Princess House Crystal, Naughty Nightie, and various candle parties, Mandy really wanted some time away. She needed more for adult conversation than breast feeding, toddlers sleeping through the night, and the new series on Nick Jr.

More than once she'd looked into the different martial arts classes in the area, but she worried what Hunt would think, so she stuck to her various workout videos while Hannah napped. Maybe she didn't give him enough credit. After they got back from vacation, she'd talk with him about it. She was more than qualified to be a martial arts instructor, but of course she could never admit to that. Being a part of the class would be rewarding enough.

She flipped through her recipe book, hoping to find a meal that would make Hunt melt in her arms tonight. He was trying hard to make her happy; she wanted to do the same. Amanda usually steered away from pasta dishes. Anything Italian reminded her of the days when she worked for Vince Menusco and ran around with his son, Angelo. Restaurants they'd gone to were always Italian and owned by someone actively involved or under protection, willingly or not. They were usually private to Vince and his gang. Tie optional, guns not.

Amanda couldn't help but laugh out loud at the memory of questioning Willy the Face over a meal and having the attention of the whole restaurant. She couldn't believe he'd had her fooled about being a double agent.

She hadn't thought of him in ages. Last she saw of him was at the hearing. At the time, she was more concerned with avoiding Hunt than with Willy's sentence. She was sure he was locked away for good. The FBI wouldn't let him out. That, of course, was if he survived prison at all. When the word got around prison that he'd two-timed the mob, he was sure to be killed.

Mandy shuddered. "One strange sound and you're back to tough girl status. Chill out."

She returned to her dinner preparations, hoping Hunt would get home early and they could enjoy an empty house. After checking her temperature this morning, she was sure she was ovulating. She hoped last night had done the trick, but once more wouldn't hurt. Or twice. She grinned as she chopped carrots.

CHAPTER TWO

After hanging up the phone and returning to the table, Mandy smiled wide.

"You can read my mother like a book, babe."

"I knew what packing a change of clothes 'just in case' meant. I never mind when they want her overnight. She loves them."

"They have bragging rights with their friends, that's for sure. No one sees their grandkids as much as my folks. Have I said how much I love you for putting up with them?"

"There's nothing to put up with, Hunt. I love them." She grinned.

"I know that grin. You love them more for keeping Hannah overnight. Table or couch?"

She slid herself onto his lap and kissed him fiercely. Wasting no time, she undid his shirt buttons slowly. He moaned as he pulled her hips tighter to his. As she kissed down his neck, Mandy was certain there was a noise coming from the patio again. She stopped kissing abruptly and looked up.

"What is it?" Hunt asked her.

"Did you hear something?"

"Just my pants getting tighter."

"Must be the neighbors." She returned to kissing down his neck then went back to his lips. They were lingering over a long kiss, tongues entwined, when suddenly she was pulled off Hunt's lap. She kicked backward at her attacker and screamed.

Hunt tried to stand, but a rope was thrown around his neck. Someone was pulling against it, holding him down. He struggled with it until there was a click. Within a second, a gun pressed at his head. He faced Mandy, who had given up her struggle. She was held captive by a very large Italian man who had one hand around her waist and one over her mouth.

"Get your filthy hands off my wife."

The man grinned and gave Mandy a kiss on the cheek. That got him an elbow to the stomach. She took his arm and tried to wrench it around but stopped when another gun clicked. Another man entered the kitchen and took a few steps closer to Mandy. She shook herself free, stepped forward, and kicked at the hand holding the gun. When the man that held her took a step closer, she kicked at his knee, sending him back a few steps. Hunt hollered, "Mandy stop!" when the man holding the rope at his neck aimed his gun her way.

Another man entered the room. He wasn't holding a gun and was far too calm for the situation. Hunt figured he was in charge of whatever this was. "What do you want?"

"Where's the kid?"

"With my parents tonight. They aren't coming back. What do you want with us?"

"You? Nothing. Amanda we need to borrow for a few days."

"Over my dead body."

The man reached in his coat and pulled out a gun, aiming it at Hunt's head. "That can be arranged."

"No!" Mandy screamed and stepped forward. "Eddie, you touch my husband and so help me, I'll kill you with my bare hands."

"Eddie? You know these guys?"

"Ugly Italians. What do you think?"

Eddie backhanded her across the face. Again, Hunt tried to stand. This time he was hit in the head with the butt of a gun. He wasn't knocked out, but it hurt like hell. The rope was let go and Mandy ran to him. She flew onto his lap again and threw her arms around his neck.

"I'm so sorry, Hunt."

"This isn't your fault, babe. How many times do I need to ask what the hell you thugs want? I know you're not here to visit Mickey Mouse."

Mandy turned around but stayed on Hunt's lap. He held her tight.

The man who had been holding Mandy hobbled over to the table. He picked up the serving fork and helped himself to the meal.

Eddie spoke again. "We have ourselves a bit of a situation. We'd like the little lady's help."

"What can she do? She's out. Been out for years. Both from the FBI and your little family organization. There's nothing she can do."

"I beg to differ."

"If she were to step foot in that neighborhood, she'd probably be killed within five minutes. Anyone who wasn't busted or killed would have it out for her. You know better than I do the things she saw."

"Don't forget the things she did herself."

Mandy stood and addressed them both. "Quit acting like I'm not right here."

Eddie pointed the gun at her and motioned for her to sit back down.

"What's the matter, Eddie? You've never been such a pussy before. If you're going to shoot me, shoot me already."

"Just sit still. I don't want to have to take either one of you out. I told you, I need your help." He scratched his head with his gun. "To back up just a little, cop, it wasn't made common knowledge that Amanda was a fed. You know she was kept out of the papers when the bust went down and Menusco was hauled off to jail."

"He's out now, though," Mandy said. "I was mailed an article."

"You were what?" Hunt shouted.

"It was from the FBI, Hunt. I didn't think it was worth mentioning and upsetting you. We're safe here."

"I currently beg to differ."

"You two shut the hell up. Vince hadn't said a word about you to anyone. Those of us who knew what you were kept it to ourselves. No one else knows shit."

"Why would you keep that a secret?" Mandy asked.

"Vince didn't want it to look like the feds, or a broad, got the best of him."

Hunt spoke up again. "It still doesn't make it safe for her if we go back. There has to be people who will remember her, and not in a good way."

"It ain't about being safe for her."

"The hell it's not. Why don't you come out and say what you want?"

"It's not what I want. It's who I want."

It was Mandy's turn again. "Who? What kind of pull do you think I have anymore that I can find anyone for you? I have no loyalties left for Vince."

"Vince is dead."

"What?" Mandy stood again.

"Last week. Things became pretty bad shortly after he was released from jail. We did what we could, but you know how stubborn he was. There was no covering him all the time. Someone got a lucky shot."

Mandy walked over to the kitchen window. Hunt wasn't sure how to take her reaction. Her heart couldn't be bleeding for this man. She turned back around and leaned on the sink.

"How's Angelo taking it?"

Now Hunt stood. "Excuse me? You really want to know how his son is doing?"

"Don't give me grief, Hunter Blaine. You know how close we were. He saved our asses back at that cabin."

"I know, but you know what he is. He's not someone you can be pen-paling with, babe. This life is past both of us. I thought we'd left it all behind." The situation was finally registering. These men here and now made Hunt's blood boil. His face reddened with anger as his hands balled into fists. He spun around facing Eddie, voice in full authority mode. "Just how the fuck did you find us anyway? Dammit all to hell! I don't want this shit in my life!"

"You chose her, old man. Should have stayed away after the trial."

Hunt lunged for him but was again stopped by a pointed gun and Mandy's scream.

"I'll tie your ass up, Blaine. Better just cool off." He pointed him toward the chair with the gun. Hunt obeyed. He put his arm out to Mandy, wanting her with him. Once she was on his lap, Eddie started up again.

"It's funny you should ask about Angelo. He's who we want."

Mandy was confused. "What do you mean it's Angelo you want? Where is he?"

"If we knew that, we wouldn't be here. Angelo disappeared the night Vince was killed."

"Who took him?"

"I don't have a clue. That's why I'm here to get you. You know who his enemies are better than I do."

"I've been gone a long time, Eddie."

"It's still the same punk-ass groups."

"Why would they take Angelo?"

"You know why. Same reason they killed Vince. Gain more territory."

"But you'd think they would have just killed him, too."

Eddie dropped the gun. "Angelo isn't the same man. He's been slipping ever since you left. Drinks most of his life away. I think he misses you."

"Go to hell, Eddie. This isn't about me. You know we didn't have that kind of relationship. He simply didn't want that life anymore."

"No. You didn't want him to have that life anymore. It's in his blood, sweetheart. You don't up and leave the family business. Especially not someone in his position."

"Well, it looks like he might one way or another."

"You have any idea who would take him and where he may be held?"

"Two punks come to mind, but they don't have the brains for this alone."

"I can't give up until I know for sure. You know what his disappearance would mean to the business."

"And what do you think I can do?" Mandy asked.

"Get in there and get him back."

"What if he's dead?"

"Then confirm it. I can't move forward on a rumor."

Against Hunt's protests, she stood again. "I don't see how you think I can help or why you even think I would help. This isn't my life anymore. That was never my life. I was undercover. You forget my job was to get you all behind bars."

"You thought that was your job."

She shook her head. "Right. I thought that was my job. I didn't know I was just a pawn to keep exactly that from happening. Why do you even think I'd want to help? You don't even know if he's alive. Why would I risk my life to find a corpse? He could be at the bottom of the Hudson in a pair of cement shoes, for crying out loud."

Eddie closed the gap between them. "I didn't want to have to play this card, Mandy."

He handed her a handkerchief. Mandy opened it slowly then dropped it with a scream. Hunt stood so fast his chair flew backward. He held it up, not needing to ask the question.

"It's his." Mandy choked back a sob.

In the handkerchief was a pinky ring that belonged to Angelo. Unfortunately, it was still attached to his pinky.

With guns finally put away and everyone sitting around the table, Hunt spoke up. "I still don't see how you think Mandy can help you."

"I already told you, no one knows she was a fed. People listened to her when she went places with Angelo. She was, or at least seemed to be, more serious than he was. She ran most of the show."

Hunt gave Mandy's hand a reassuring squeeze. "I'm dying to see where this is going."

"We need to get her back on the streets. They'll buy what story we want them to buy. It's believable that she was just let out of jail. We could set her up as the one they placed to be the 'Patsy' and had the longer sentence. She did kill her husband."

Hunt glared at him.

"Sorry. Ex-husband."

"You want me to take charge of the streets again?" Mandy said with great shock in her tone.

"I've seen you in action, sweetheart. Don't even begin to tell me you didn't enjoy it."

"It wasn't a fucking tea party, Eddie. I did what I had to do from both ends."

"And I still say you would make one hell of a mobster."

"I'm supposed to get out there and pretend I'm in charge with Vince dead and Angelo missing? Who's going to buy that?"

"Everyone."

"Hasn't whoever has Angelo made demands to set up his release?"

"Yup."

"Well, when the hell were you going to share them?"

"I just did." Eddie patted the finger he placed back in his coat pocket.

"Getting me back is part of the deal?"

"I'm supposed to be with Lou expediting your release right now."

"Who's Lou?"

"Your new husband."

"Wait a second!" Mandy stood and slammed her hands on the table. "I'm not bringing Hunt into this."

"Like hell you're not." Hunt stood and faced her. "There is no way I'm setting you loose in the middle of all this crap in God-knows-where backstreet New York." He turned to Eddie. "I'm in. Whatever this is, I'm in."

"That's not what I meant. Lou took over where Gerard left off. I figured if she had the balls to bone one lawyer, she could do the other."

Mandy reached for a gun that was lying on the table and aimed it toward Eddie. Before anyone else could pick theirs up, she fired.

Mandy brushed past Eddie to the body that had come through the sliding glass door with a sawed off shot gun aimed at her. She gasped when she recognized one of Willy the Face's men. She spun around and aimed the gun at Eddie.

"Why is Ray here, Eddie? You jerking my chain with this?" She cocked the hammer back and held the gun aimed squarely at him.

He showed no fear at all and reached into his pocket.

"Get your hands where I can see them!"

Eddie didn't stop his task. Instead of a gun, he pulled out a cigar.

"I didn't even know the bastard followed us." He lit his cigar, still showing no emotion.

Hunt took the man's pulse, even though he knew it was useless. "He's gone. How does he fit into all of this, babe?"

Mandy grumbled, "Shit," as she gave Hunt the gun and walked out to the pool. A neighbor was peeking over the fence.

"Sorry, Jimmy. I didn't realize Hunt had a round in the chamber."

"Finally *off* the old man?" he said with a chuckle.

"I grabbed it too fast, trying to move it out of the way of a hot dinner pan. Luckily all it hit was the trash can."

"I'm surprised at Hunt."

"It's my fault, actually. He'd never leave it sitting around loaded. Hannah is at her grandparents tonight. I was going to stake out that stupid raccoon that seems to be terrorizing the neighborhood."

He laughed harder. "You housewives are a scary breed these days. All you need to go with that gun is a string of pearls."

"I'll tell Hunt you said so."

He laughed again. "Good night, Mandy."

"Good night, Jimmy." Mandy walked back in and returned her attention to Hunt. "He was one of Willy's men."

"Willy the Face?"

"Yes." She let a small smile show. "You really did pay attention."

Hunt closed the gap between them. "It involved you. Of course I did. I have to admit I never expected things to come back into play, though."

She turned back around, glowering at Eddie. "You get your goons to load this thing up," she said as she kicked the body. She knelt down and removed a ring from his middle finger. After putting it in her pocket, she stood. "And you'd better check in at work, Hunt, so no patrol cars show up. Someone else could have called in after hearing the shot."

"I'm on it."

Mandy glared at Eddie. "You know I have no ties left at the agency."

"Ain't a bunch of feds going to help us anyway."

"I just murdered a man as a Joe-blow citizen, not an agent with a license to kill. This already stinks ten ways from Sunday, Eddie."

"I don't know what he was doing here. That's the truth. He's not with us, and I don't know why he would have followed us."

"Just fucking great," Mandy said with a sigh.

CHAPTER THREE

After calling the department about the shot, Hunt called his parents and explained that they found a last-minute deal on a trip and had to hustle to the airport. He said there was a bag packed by the door for Hannah, but they weren't able to drop it off.

Hunt had more than enough vacation time and the pull to get the time off work. After speaking to his parents and making sure Hannah was taken care of, he called the station again to ask about taking a leave of absence.

"You want to do a drive by and do a visual on my wife, so you don't think I was lying about that shot and am fleeing the country?"

The officer on the other end laughed. "You're good to go, Sheriff. You're lucky the spring breakers are long gone or I'd never let you split."

"I'd never ask if it was a busy time. I really appreciate this, Greg. Thanks." Hunt hung up and spun around, glaring at Eddie. "It's taken care of."

"You do this mobster 'bug out' thing pretty good. You sure you've never been on the take?" Eddie asked.

Hunt closed the gap between them. "If anything happens to my wife, know that I *will* kill you."

Eddie didn't react, he just re-lit his cigar.

His two men loaded Ray's body in the car while Mandy did what she could to clean up the floor. She was never so grateful that she insisted on ceramic tile. She was filled with a strange sense of how cold she could be. He hadn't bled much. At a time like this, all she could feel was happy that she wasn't going to have to re-grout. *What a bitch.*

Once that was done, she joined Hunt upstairs. He was packing for Hannah. "I'll finish. You go pack yourself."

"I think I'm done. Give it a once over. It's not like they can't come grab anything when they need it."

"I'm sure you did fine." Mandy walked closer and wrapped her arms around his waist. "Are you sure you want to come?"

"You're shitting me, right? You think I'm going to sit back while you take off at gun point to rescue Angelo? You're more insane than I thought, woman."

"I can handle this, Hunt."

"And I can't?"

"No. And before you get pissed off, it's not what you think."

"What is it, then?"

"If we walk in somewhere and I get slapped, what would you do?"

"Easy. Kill the guy."

"See. That's what I can't have. You have to let me deal with things in my own way, and you have to sit back and let me do it."

"You mean to tell me if someone slapped you in front of Gerard, he'd stand there and watch?"

"No. They would have been killed. But no one would do that in front of him. What Angelo and I did was a different story."

"I can't imagine he'd watch it happen, either."

"It's more to make a point, Hunt. Whatever role they're going to have you playing here, I need to know you are going to let me do what I need to do and not get in the way."

"Why do you assume I'll be in the way?"

"Because I don't want you there in the first place. It's bad enough having Angelo held somewhere. I don't want anyone getting the upper hand and having you, too. Don't you get that? It almost killed me last time I thought you were dead, Hunt."

He pulled her head to his chest. "Nothing is going to happen to me. I have my big bad mobster wife to protect me, remember?"

"This isn't a game."

"I know." He leaned back and took her hand. "Let's go pack. Don't forget the evening gown and stilettos. When this is over, we have a date in the big city.

They drove until one a.m. without much conversation. There was no point trying to find out what Willy's man wanted with her. If Eddie knew, she wouldn't get an answer anyway. When the exit for rest stops and hotels came into view, Mandy told them she was tired and refused to be driven another mile without sleep. Vern, the man with the now-sore kneecap, pulled over at the first hotel they found. It was a small no-name place with a single row of rooms. Hunt arranged for three rooms; two were adjoining.

When they reached their rooms, Eddie said to Hunt, "I'll be in here with Amanda. You bunk with Verne."

"The hell we are," Mandy said as she swiped a key from his hand. "We're already going with you. We're not going to make a run for it, asshole. Besides," she said as she reached for Hunt's hand, "I'm ovulating. Get your goons to get rid of Ray. I'm not driving through another state with that body in the car." They walked in the room with their luggage and closed the door without any more fuss from anyone.

Mandy was naked as soon as the door closed and had her hands at Hunt's belt. She had it whipped off before he grasped her by the wrists.

"Are you serious?"

"What? I'm sure I'm ovulating, Hunt. I don't want to miss the chance."

"We have Handgun Harry next door, and you want to have sex?"

"I'm not letting them be the cause of me wasting a month. Since when don't you want sex?"

"Since about a few hours ago when there was a rope on my throat, a gun at my head, and you killed a man. Jesus, Amanda. Are you so hell bent on getting pregnant you're not thinking straight or what? These guys mean business."

"So do I!" she shouted as she unbuttoned his pants. Hunt held them closed and sat down.

"Well, I'm sorry if I'm not aroused by the scent of gun powder and killing a man like you are."

"I'm going to pretend to ignore that. Get off your ass and have sex with me, dammit."

Hunt sighed. "I'm tired."

"I don't care. The drive was long, and I'm tired, too, but we're having sex."

"Not the drive, babe. This." He motioned back and forth between them. "I want to have sex because we can't keep our hands off each other, not because you're trying to get pregnant. You're making it a chore, and I don't like it."

"You sure as hell seem to like it to me." Angrily, she unzipped her suitcase and pulled out a bikini.

"The pool is closed."

"I don't care. They can throw me out if they want."

Hunt stood and went over to her as she rushed through getting changed. "Don't leave pissed. You have to cut me a little slack here, babe. Hearing the stories is one thing. Sitting in the middle of it is another. I can't take the 'get me pregnant' shit on top of it."

She turned away and left without responding. The pool gate was locked, but it didn't take much effort to climb over. Everything was dark, but she could see Eddie sitting in a lounge chair smoking a cigar. "Trouble in paradise?"

She only said, "Fuck you," before diving in the pool. She swam a few laps without looking back. When she finally glanced up, Eddie was gone and Hunt was standing by the stairs with a towel.

"I don't want out. I'm getting in the Jacuzzi."

He walked over and turned on the jets as she got out of the pool and climbed in.

"I'm sure the manager isn't going to do rounds and check on things by the looks of this place. Other than us, it looks pretty empty." He slid in next to her, but she still wasn't speaking to him. He pulled her onto his lap. "You know I love this suit."

"So, it's the body in it that you don't want anymore, then?"

"Dammit, Mandy. Knock it off. You know what I'm asking. Do you see me pulling a pout fest, saying you're not interested in me? That all you want is sex and my best swimmers?"

She rested her head on his neck. "I'm sorry. You know that's not all I want."

"Then let's stop with the drill sergeant stuff. Stop with the temperature taking. Let's get back to normal and have sex for love's sake, babe. You know I love you, need you, want you every minute of the day and would take you any chance I can. Can't that be enough? We have a great family. I want more, but not at the price of losing you in the process. I want you to be happy where we are."

"I am happy."

"So, start acting like it."

She reached down and placed her hand at his crotch.

He laughed. "That's not what I meant." Meeting his lips, she passionately kissed him. "This isn't fair, babe. Now I want you so bad I can't stand it."

"Your point?"

"Look where we are."

"We're alone and it's dark."

"Yeah, well, we should also make the most of this, and I don't think heat is the best thing for my boys to do their job."

"I don't care on either account," Mandy said as she worked his swim trunks down and slid on top of him.

Eddie watched from the window of his room. He ground out his cigar then dropped onto his bed. "Look out New York. She's back."

The group was up and gone early the following day. Eddie pulled the car to a stop at an airport in Atlanta.

"I thought we were driving to New York?" Mandy asked.

"We're flying," Eddie said.

"So, why didn't we just use Miami's airport?" Hunt asked.

"I don't like it. Georgia is the next hub."

"I'm not even gonna ask," Hunt said as they walked to the gate.

"You're smarter than you look." Eddie started to light up a cigar but stopped and put it away. "I miss the old days of smoking on planes."

No one spoke during the flight. There wasn't anything to say that would remotely resemble normal conversation, and there were too many people on the plane to discuss their situation. The last thing they needed was to attract attention. Mandy rested her head on Hunt's chest for the short, uneventful flight. A limo was waiting for them when they landed.

"I forgot what a life of luxury you guys lead," Hunt said as he climbed in.

Mandy leaned toward Hunt when they were settled. "Stop being so smug, Hunt. Nothing is stopping one of them from plugging you for being an ass."

"I was merely stating an observation."

"Well, stop it."

Obviously irritated, he immediately began pushing buttons, messing with the window and stereo controls. Mandy scooted away from him. When a button lit up the bar, he slid over and helped himself.

To Amanda's surprise, the limo pulled up at Lonny's house almost an hour later. "We're staying here?"

"You want a crap-ass hotel? The house has been vacant since the shootout. It was technically Vince's. We use it here and there when we need a safe house. You'll be fine."

Mandy walked through the door and stood at the entry. The memories were too fresh for her. Sue's daughter, Darci, standing on the couch, excited to greet her. The window shattering and Darci's little body falling over, shot. She turned to the side and envisioned Lonny dropping from his wounds, seconds after her. Mandy turned to Hunt, and he wrapped his arms around her.

"Do we have to stay here?" he asked Eddie.

Eddie strode past them. "She'll get over it."

"Look, asshole—"

Eddie pulled out his gun and pointed it at Hunt. "I've taken all the shit from you two that I'm going to." He pulled on Mandy's arms, separating her from Hunt. "Take the master bedroom and go get settled. Call for whatever you want for dinner. There's cash under the phone." He pointed to a phone on a small stand with a drawer. "Tomorrow morning, we go visit some old friends, Amanda."

"I'm not going anywhere without my husband."

"Take his sorry ass with you. I don't want to sit here and look at him. Just keep the sex noise down, doll. You're going to drive Jeremy crazy. He never could stand listening to you and Gerard goin' at it."

Gun or not, Mandy punched his chin hard. He snapped back and aimed it at Hunt again. "Touch me again, and your kid will grow up without a father."

Mandy hurried over and stood in front of the gun. "Take it out on me, Eddie. Not Hunt."

"You, I need. Him, I don't. I'll do what it takes to keep your ass in line."

"Then you leave him alone."

He waved the gun upstairs. "Get out of my face. I don't want to hear a peep till I call you down in the morning."

Mandy took Hunt's hand and led him up the stairs. As soon as they walked in Lonny and Sue's old bedroom, Mandy opened the large window.

"What are you doing?"

"We're splitting."

"We're what?"

"I'm not staying here, Hunt."

"Don't you think there is a better way to go about it? I mean, if you're upset because of Darci—"

"That's not it. I'm not waiting around here until morning."

She put one leg out the window, and he grasped her arm, stopping her. "I really don't think this is a good idea."

"I know you don't. If I had a pair of cuffs, I'd cuff you to the bed to keep you safe."

"Keep me safe? Oh, no, you don't. You are not doing any disappearing acts on me. I'm with you, like it or not."

"Not, and I know. Come on," she said as she tugged at his sleeve. "Jackasses will be too busy farting around with Lonny's stuff to notice us leaving."

Mandy and Hunt made it down the trellis and across the yard. They walked around the outer hedge to the end of the driveway where they climbed into one of the cars. Mandy reached under and was about to hotwire it when keys rattled by her head.

"Nice try, Freddie Fingers, but I think these will work better. They were in the center console."

She ripped them from his hands and took off. After a few blocks of watching their backs, she was certain they had made a clean get-away.

"You want to tell me why we just did that?"

"I don't trust Eddie, Hunt."

"There's a big surprise."

"I don't think he'd bring me all the way here to save Angelo. I wouldn't put it past him to let Angelo be killed."

"Would that put him in charge?"

"With Vince gone...I'd have to say yes. Angelo is all that's left in the way of family. Eddie would be next up if he wanted to take it. I'm sure of that."

"If your plan was to escape, why did you let us come this far?"

"Because I'm going after Angelo."

"You're what?"

"I have a good idea where he is. I'm going to get him."

"Not like these guys are on my Christmas list or anything, but don't you think we would have been better off taking them with us?"

"He'll have one or two people on him, tops. If he's where I think, it'll be an easy in, easy out."

"It's never as easy as that."

"Just trust me, okay?"

"The last time I trusted you, I was shot. Twice."

"You wanted to come along."

Hunt was quiet for a minute. "I don't like this."

"I understand that. Do you think I'd do something, and risk Hannah being left without a mother?"

"I think you're on an adrenaline high, and you're not thinking straight. What are we supposed to do for weapons?"

Mandy pulled over at a park and popped the trunk. When Hunt joined her, she picked up the carpet used to hide the spare tire. There was no tire, but there were enough firearms to start a small war.

"Oh," was Hunt's only response.

The drive took almost an hour. The traffic was as lovely as Mandy remembered it. Always a detour or two for road construction. Always someone wanting to wash her windshield for a buck. She finally pulled up to the warehouse.

"Lovely establishment," Hunt said.

"It's gotten worse since I've been gone."

"You're sure he's here?"

"Not positive, but I have a nagging suspicion. We dealt with the Cornellas a lot here."

"Do you have a plan, or are you going to just shoot your way in?"

"The second one."

Hunt raised an eyebrow.

"Shouldn't be much shooting to do. My guess is Kermit and Axle are in the back, drunk as usual."

"Kermit and Axle? Are we attacking Sesame Street?"

"I'm pretty sure the puppets are smarter, but there is a hand up their asses, too."

Hunt took in the state of the dilapidated warehouse again. "They actually live here?"

"It doesn't look like this on the inside, Hunt. They actually have quite the setup. Besides, the deals were conducted in the main warehouse area; the back is a five-star crib."

"Crib? I love it when you talk ghetto, babe."

"Stuff it, Blaine."

"Blair."

Mandy chuckled. "We were so super-secret there. No wonder they found us."

He shrugged. "Could have gone with Lane."

She leaned over and gave him a quick kiss before getting out. "I would have changed my name to Lois, and you'd be my Superman."

"Nice try."

"Come on, lover. Showtime."

CHAPTER FOUR

Mandy walked by the front door of the warehouse, fighting to show no fear. Trying to get her mindset back into this life was a tough stretch after a few years of playing stay-at-home mom. She wasn't afraid for herself so much as she was distracted with Hunt there. Letting her mind wander to Hannah wouldn't do her any favors, either.

The scents were the same. Sweat, gunpowder, money. Remembering the horrible things she'd witnessed and did here helped keep her focused. Get in. Get Angelo. Get out.

They marched down the alley to the apartment door and gave it a hearty knock. Hunt stood close to her side.

A boy in his twenties opened the door. When his drunken gaze fell on Mandy, his eyebrows arched and his jaw dropped.

"What the hell are you doing here, bitch? Thought you was in jail."

"I was, now I'm out."

"Who's this jerk-off?"

"Hammer. I don't think you want to mess with him in his mood."

"I thought Hammer was black."

Mandy took a step closer. "You want to tell him he's supposed to be black?"

"Get out of my face. What do you want?"

"You have something of mine, and I want it back."

"I ain't got nothin' of yours. Scram."

He tried closing the door, but Hunt put his foot forward, blocking it.

"You want to move your foot, butt munch?"

Mandy grasped him by the throat and took him a few steps back before Hunt could do anything she'd regret. Another boy stood and pulled a gun from a shoulder holster.

"What in the hell are you doing back here? I thought we'd seen the last of you."

"Likewise, I assure you," Mandy said. She let go of the kid she was holding and gave him a not-so-gentle shove back. "How's it hanging, Axle?"

"Just peachy, Mandy. What brings you here?"

"You know why I'm here."

"We ain't got him."

She pulled a handgun out of her waistband and shot the kid that had answered the door in the arm. She had chosen a small caliber gun and was careful to only nick him. By the way he screamed, you would have thought she'd shot him in the balls. Aiming the gun back at Axle, she said, "Bullshit."

Hunt took a few steps toward the kid that was now lying on the ground. "Lock him in there," she said as she motioned toward a small closet. Hunt did as he was asked and returned to her side.

"Jesus, Mandy!" Axle put his gun down and held his hands up.

"Where's Kermit?"

"My brother's not here."

Mandy shot past him, so close he was sure to feel the breeze. A TV screen blew out behind him.

"Goddammit! That was brand new."

She aimed at a bottle on the bar and fired again.

"Enough! He's in back!"

"Kermit or Angelo?"

"Both, man. Quit shooting. My beef isn't with you."

"It is when you have my man."

"We were gonna give him back."

"In a body bag, no doubt."

"It wasn't like that."

"I don't want your excuses. Let's go." She waved the gun in the direction of the door to the back room.

As he turned to walk away, a door past the bar opened. They were fired at. Hunt dropped to the ground, drew his gun, and shot back. He only had to fire once. The kid that had opened the door went down. Again, Axle stood with his hands in the air. "I didn't call that! He heard the shooting!"

"Who else is here?"

"No one. Ah, man..." He hurried over to his brother on the ground. Hunt had only grazed his forearm—that was all. Mandy was grateful Hunt had followed her lead.

Mandy walked over, aiming the gun between the two of them. Hunt was beside her and kicked away a gun that Kermit dropped. She took zip ties out of her pocket and handed them to Hunt.

He attached both boys to the brass poles of the bar while she held her gun on them. "Gotta love your foresight, Mandy."

"This isn't my first time."

After the boys were secured, Mandy led Hunt through the door Kermit had come out of and locked it behind them.

"How do we get out?" Hunt asked.

"There's a back door." She went past two doors before she opened a third. Angelo was in the middle of a bedroom, furnished completely in black. He sat in a black desk chair with his hands secured behind his back. "Angelo!" Mandy rushed to his side.

He picked his head up slightly. His face showed signs of having been beaten. His head lolled as if he were drunk. "Mandy? Fuck me. They killed me, and now I'm seeing angels." His head dropped to his chest. He was out cold.

Mandy cut through his restraints as fast as she could and examined his hands. He had all his fingers. Whoever sent the ring to Eddie wanted to make a point without really hurting Angelo. She didn't waste time wondering whose finger it was.

As soon as he was free, Angelo fell forward, but Hunt caught him. He knelt in front of Angelo, draped him over his shoulder, and stood. "I have him. Get us out of here."

During the escape out the back door, down the alley, and back to their car, they didn't encounter any more trouble. Hunt had placed Angelo on the back seat, and Mandy sat with him, resting his head on her lap. He hadn't budged or so much as groaned the whole way.

"Where to now?" Hunt asked.

"I'll direct you to the office building. I'll bet he still has an apartment there."

Hunt spun around. "Are you insane? Didn't we just escape those guys?"

"Eddie and his goons, not everyone else. We can hardly go strolling in the Waldorf with him looking like this. I need to call the house doctor. I can trust the people there to take care of him."

Staring at her, Hunt asked, "You sure you know what you're doing?"

"It's not like I can go to the FBI, Hunt. You'll have to trust me."

"What about the guys we shot back there?"

"Axle will already be loose and making calls. They'll be fine."

After pulling away from the curb, Hunt said, "I didn't expect any of that."

"I didn't take guns because I missed the accessory, Hunt. You must have had a clue."

He was silent for a minute then sighed. "I suppose I did, I just didn't want to believe it."

"Nice shot, by the way."

He dared a smile. "You need me."

"I still wish you hadn't come along."

"Because you could have carried him out by yourself?"

"If I had to."

"Mandy..."

"Let's not, okay? We're here now, and we need to figure out where to go from here. I didn't want to let him sit where he was. I don't know what Eddie has planned, but I'm disturbed he didn't ask what I thought and offer to let me go in and do what I just did. If I thought of the Cornellas right away, he should have, too."

"Are you sure you'll be welcomed back at this office building?"

"I think Eddie was right about one thing. Vince wouldn't have made it common knowledge about me being a fed. At least not to anyone who didn't already know. I think showing up with Angelo will put any ill feelings to rest. At least initially."

"And after 'initially?'"

"I don't really have a choice, Hunt. I need to get him home."

"I really want to get home, too."

"I'm working on it. Take a left at the next light."

Mandy directed Hunt to the offices above the little corner grocery store where she used to work when she was undercover for the FBI.

"Will you stay in the car with Angelo, please? I'll go in first and let them know we're coming."

"All right, just be careful. Any sign of trouble and you get the hell out of there fast."

She sighed before stepping out. "I must be insane coming back here, but I don't see that we have another option."

As the elevator dinged and the doors slid open, she stiffened her shoulders and walked toward what used to be Vince's office.

A secretary sat outside his door. That was new.

"Can I help you?"

"I need to speak with someone about Angelo."

"This is in regard to..."

Mandy put her hands on the desk. "Him being found. Now you call whoever you need to and get me some help."

"I'm not sure Mr. Menusco—"

"Vince is dead. Cut the crap. Who took over when Bennett was killed?"

"I'm sorry. You are?"

Mandy pulled out her gun and placed it on her desk. "Get someone out here now."

The woman finally got in gear and picked up her phone. Within a minute, the door was opened. Knowing she wouldn't get a welcoming hug from whoever opened it, Mandy stood firm. She was surprised at who showed up, but didn't skip a beat.

"Hello, Eddie."

"What the hell are you doing here? I told you to stay at the house."

"I have Angelo in the car. I need a path cleared and some help getting him to his room."

"What the hell have you done?"

"Got him free. That was the goal, right? Stop busting my chops and grab his apartment keys. Call Doc Chu while you're at it. He's taken a bad beating."

Hunt declined help from the goons who came down with Mandy and carried Angelo up to the penthouse by himself. No words were spoken through the length of the elevator ride. Once the two guards led Mandy and Hunt into the bedroom, she asked one to stand guard outside the front door and one outside his bedroom. She closed the door while Hunt gently placed Angelo on the bed.

"I want to get him undressed, Hunt. I need to see what they did."

"I'll do it. You go get a washcloth and towels to clean him up. You have a doctor you can call?"

"He's on the way."

Angelo didn't move while Mandy carefully cleaned his face. He smelled of alcohol. She couldn't figure that out. Torture him after they'd shared a few nightcaps? None of this made sense.

The bell rang and Hunt went to get the door. He expected it to be the doctor but was surprised to see Eddie's face glaring back at him instead.

"If you're here to make trouble, I'd leave now before I let my wife know you're here."

"That's not why I'm here. Where did you find him?"

"The first place Mandy went to. With those Muppet brothers."

"She's the one that shot them up?"

"She had a little help. Man, good news sure travels fast around here."

"Who did you think they would blame for this little rescue of yours? Of course I heard about the shooting." Eddie paced the room. "Why did you sneak out? Couldn't this have waited?"

Hunt crossed his arms. "Not by the looks of him, no. If you knew he was with those two, why the song and dance to get Amanda here? Why didn't you just go there yourself?"

"We didn't know he was there."

"But you didn't even bother to look? For crying out loud. If Mandy drove straight there, why couldn't your guys have done that? What is this shit, Eddie?"

Their argument was interrupted by the doorbell. Hunt opened it and was glad to see a doctor and not another goon with a previously broken nose and an ill-fitting suit. He led the doctor to Angelo's room and closed the door behind him. He thought it was best if Amanda handled this alone, even if it meant he had to return to Eddie's company.

Eddie had poured two drinks by the time Hunt joined him. Hunt accepted what was offered him. He didn't care much what it was.

After a long silence, Eddie finally spoke. "I honestly didn't think she'd pull this."

"Pull what? Save the kid? What did you expect? She loves him."

"I didn't think...hell. I don't know what I thought. It's been a long time. I had no idea..."

"No idea what?"

"That she'd look for him, let alone find him."

"So, you didn't want him found?"

"Hell yes, I wanted him found, dammit. That boy is as close as any son could be."

"If she found him so easily, explain to me why didn't you send your people to him."

"It was too easy going over there. I never thought they'd be that stupid."

"But you didn't bother to check before you barged into our lives?"

Eddie got in Hunt's face. "Don't you tell me how to run my business!"

"Wouldn't dream of it. I'd have to make all kinds of protective body armor and bullet suggestions."

"Screw you, cop."

Just then, Mandy walked out.

"You two knock it the fuck off! I can hear you through the walls!" She turned to Hunt. "Doc wants to start an IV on him. Come help me rig something up."

Hunt put his drink down and followed her in.

The doctor explained Angelo's condition. "He's taken a good beating. I'm pretty sure there are a few ribs busted or cracked. I'll have to X-ray him to be sure, but I wouldn't go moving him just yet."

"You think he has internal bleeding?"

"I don't see any cause for alarm there. He is pissed drunk, that's for sure. I bet he'd blow double the legal limit."

"I don't understand," Mandy said.

"You've been gone a long time. If my liver were this kid's, I'd be dead. If you hadn't found him tied to a chair, you'd've found him in the street. We would have written it off as a bar brawl. Wouldn't be the first time."

"Eddie didn't call me here because he thought Angelo was off on a bender. It doesn't make sense to kidnap him and get him loaded."

"Makes perfect sense. Like I said, they could have ditched him in this condition, and we would have been none the wiser."

"Shit. I'm running on nothing here, Doc. I guess you're right." She motioned her head toward Angelo. "I can't do any good here. I'm going to head back to Lonny's and catch some sleep."

"I'll call you if anything changes. I'd hate to add much by way of meds on top of the booze. He'll be out till morning would be my guess. I'll give him something for the pain, then. You did good finding him, Amanda."

"Thanks. See you, Doc."

Mandy walked out of the room with Hunt and faced Eddie. "I'm going to get some sleep. Keep a guard on him."

"No shit."

"Someone you can trust dammit, Eddie. Is Earl still around?"

"Already called him. He's been a little on edge with Vince gone. This will give him something to do."

"I have something I need to do tomorrow, and I want no grief from you about it."

"You keep me in the loop about everything. We ain't done here."

"I'll check in with you tomorrow, Eddie. When I'm damn good and ready." She grasped Hunt's hand and stormed away.

Mandy walked into the FBI building like she owned the place. Her thoughts went to how she'd sauntered in all those years ago: pink high-heel sneakers, cut-off top, pierced belly button showing. She hadn't believed Craig Abbey wanted her as an agent, so she'd tried to project how much she didn't want to be there when she showed up. She was tempted to do the same now but didn't want to take the time to shop for a get-up or get her belly button pierced again just for the effect.

Her attitude must have worked. Two guards immediately stood at attention.

"You're back?"

"Damn straight."

"You know that Abbey—"

"Yup." She snapped her gum. "I'm the one who killed him. You going to let me in or what?"

"I'll need to call you in to Sherry, Ms. Smith."

"You do that, Ernest."

After ten minutes, Mandy was escorted up a few floors and over to a familiar office. The guard left after he motioned for her to go through the door.

The secretary smiled. "Good to see you again, Agent Smith."

"Mrs. Blaine."

"You mean Blair."

"Right. Can I go in?"

She grinned. "This could be fun. I don't think I'll announce you. Go right in."

"Thanks. I'd actually prefer you didn't."

As Mandy strolled through the door, James Stoner quickly stood. "Amanda. To what do I deserve this honor? You here to ask about getting your old job back?"

"Not even in my wildest nightmares do I come back here."

"Yet here you are."

"I want answers, I don't want a job."

"What can I do for you?"

"You have a guy inside with the Menuscos again?"

"Are you serious?"

"Do I look like I'm kidding?"

"No, I guess not. We don't. I can promise you that. You were the last man we had in there, figuratively speaking. We got around to that shipment you botched and tracked its source. It may not have made the news, but we cut the coke import business by about ten percent. That may not sound like a lot to you—"

"I know what the figure means."

"We'll never stop all the gangs and mobs, Amanda. We have to go after the source. Just because we don't have anyone in there anymore doesn't mean we aren't making a dent in their corner of the world."

"This is one of the reasons I wanted to run for the hills when Abbey tried to recruit me. All the political bullshit that goes along with this is insane. You see a bad guy doing something wrong, you should lock him up. End of story. Instead we watch them for a year, spend a fortune in resources, and do jack-shit even after we hold the cards."

"I'm not going to lecture you on things you already know. We may not have someone there, but we are making headway. Your problem isn't who we are watching. It's who we aren't."

"What do you mean?"

"I mean there is some kind of vigilante out there and frankly it has everyone scared."

"Vigilante?"

"Someone is out there trying to mop up the city, Mandy. It isn't us."

"Oh, bullshit. It was someone I knew who took Angelo. There's no vigilante."

"I know nothing about anyone taking Angelo. What I do know is that over the past few months things have gotten crazy, and we don't have a clue who it is."

"You have to have an idea."

"We don't. You think the mob is going to let us in there and investigate? One of theirs is killed, and they kill back. They don't even particularly care if it's the ones responsible. They get even. End of story. People out there are dropping like flies in retaliation, only they aren't sure who for anymore."

"And you're just going to sit back and watch this happen?"

He leaned back in his chair and laced his fingers, dropping his hands in his lap. "My uncle had a small farm upstate. He could hear coyotes all the time and always feared for his chickens. One summer he went on a hunt with some buddies and killed twenty of them."

"I'm dying to see where this is going."

"You'd think, after killing the coyotes, the chickens would be safe, right?"

"Of course. He removed the problem."

"Wrong. He lost everything in a week."

She stared at him dumfounded. "More moved in?"

"That's right. He had coyotes surrounding him, but they had their boundaries. For whatever reason, they hadn't gone to his farm. A new batch came in, and without the others to stop them, they wiped him out. You remove one, Mandy, and another will take its place. Chances are the one who replaces it is worse than the first. You think we're not policing, but trust me, we are. It may not be the best system, but it's the best we have, and it works."

"I'm not really buying this bullshit analogy of yours, but let's say for a second we put it aside. We still have a vigilante out there, but you're not going to worry about your chickens?"

James laughed. "I'm not going to risk my men to hunt down someone, or a group of someones, who want to clean up the streets."

"So much for what you just fed me."

"I said it couldn't be done on a grand scale. I didn't say I gave a rat's ass if someone else decided to take the law into their own hands."

"Perfect."

"You're out. You're never coming back. Why do you care? Especially if it means a few less mob men running around."

"They aren't all bad."

"Who? This Angelo you're so fond of? Still, Mandy? I thought you'd moved on."

"I did. That doesn't mean I want to stand by and watch him be killed if I can help it."

"He's Vince's son."

"You know I'm aware of who he is."

"I'm just saying, unless you expect us to stick him in protective custody, which I'd have a hard time selling anyone, he doesn't have a snowball's chance in hell."

"Right. Witness relocation? 'Cause it worked so well for me?"

"What are you talking about?"

"What in the hell do you think I'm doing here? They walked in my house and dragged my ass here!"

"Who did?"

"Eddie, dammit!"

"Christ! Why the hell didn't you say something earlier?"

"You were a little busy with coyote stories."

James picked up the phone. "Sherry? Get Joel in here. Pronto."

After he hung up, Mandy asked, "Who's Joel?"

"Our resident computer geek. I'll have him look into it. See why you were compromised. We'll need to relocate you."

"No."

"What do you mean, no?"

"I mean no. I'm not doing this again. They found us once. If they wanted to, they'd do it again. I'm not going to continue to run. As odd as it sounds, I don't really think I have to worry about Eddie or any of the mob."

"How so?"

"If Eddie wanted me dead, he would have killed me. He has something in mind. I can only ride it and figure out what it is."

"That's not the smartest thing I've ever heard you say."

"I don't really have a choice. They've involved Hunt."

"How's he taking it?"

"His smart-ass meter is set to high."

"Shouldn't you be worrying about the vigilante? If word gets out you're back, you could be in trouble. You were pretty high up there when you were in. Someone won't take kindly to you back on the street."

"I don't see why I'd be of any concern to a vigilante, if there even is such a person."

"You will be a concern if you show up again. Don't fool yourself."

"I can't even think about that. My worry is for Angelo."

"What are you proposing?"

"You've already said you're not going to help. I'll take care of this myself." She turned to walk out.

"Wait. Walk with me for a bit. I want to talk to you."

CHAPTER FIVE

James walked Mandy down the familiar corridors. "Can I buy you a cup of coffee at least? I'd really like to talk."

"Is it still that same lousy shit?"

"They put in a pretty decent machine, actually."

She hesitated for a moment before agreeing. "I suppose."

After they got their cups and settled at a table, James reached over and placed his hand on Mandy's. "How are you really doing, kid?"

"Aside from being kidnapped from my own home and dragged back to New York? Great."

He leaned back in his chair. "Really? You trying to sell me on the fact that you're happy playing Suzie Homemaker? You were the best student I'd ever had. I only wish I'd known what Craig Abbey was up to. Maybe you'd still be on the team."

"I can't say I regret any of it."

"Killing a man you once loved and another you once respected?"

"You trying to get added to that list?"

"I'm just saying, Mandy. You could have really been something."

"I am something. I'm a mother. If anything had gone down differently, I wouldn't be with Hunt or have Hannah. I wouldn't change anything."

"I wish you'd reconsider coming back."

She sighed and stared into her coffee cup.

"You have thought about it, haven't you?"

"Not really."

"Bullshit. I know that fighter in you is still dying to come back out."

"Maybe it is, but I still won't put myself in the situations I have in the past. I won't risk Hannah growing up without a mother."

"You could get hit by a bus tomorrow."

"Thanks for the reminder. At least I'm not going to wear a 'hit me' T-shirt."

He smiled at her then chuckled.

"What?"

"You used to kick my ass on the courses."

"I still could. Even in these heels."

"After we talk, I am so making you put your money where your mouth is."

After outshooting James on three body targets and completing the obstacle course, coming close to the record she'd set that still held, Mandy dropped to the gym mats. He caught up and dropped at her side, dripping with sweat.

"Pit stains are a bitch to get out of dress shirts. I wish you let me change first."

"Hey, if I have to do it in heels, you have to do it in Dolce."

He turned to face her. "You need to consider relocating. We can set you up again, and I'll make sure it's done right. If you like Florida, there is a new training facility out of Naples. I'd love for you to come back any way I can have you. I think you'd make an excellent trainer."

"I don't know, James."

"You'd be nine to five, and I can personally guarantee you no field work."

"I'll think about it, but I won't make any promises. Let me live through this first."

The sound of a throat clearing made them both jolt upright. "Hey, hon," Mandy said as she stood.

"So, this is him?" James asked as he joined her side.

"This is him."

James extended his hand to Hunt. "James Stoner. Nice to meet you. I've heard a lot of great things about you."

"Wish I could say the same about you."

James laughed. "I admit to not being her favorite instructor."

"A story or two came up," Hunt said with a grin and pulled Mandy close to his side.

"You asshole!" Mandy shouted as she stuck a finger through the tear in her favorite pink sweatshirt. She was four months into her training. The hardest of all her instructors was James Stoner. He was tough on her, but she knew he felt she needed the extra pushing. She'd never admit he was right. "You did that on purpose!"

James laughed. "It's your own fault. You always keep your right side wide open."

She threw down her sword and reached behind her back for a gun. She held it up to him for a second before firing at the target that was a good twenty feet away.

James turned around and squinted. "Damn, gorgeous. I think that's a bullseye."

"That's what I'll be doing out there, shithead. How many mobsters do you think are going to engage me with swordplay?"

He swiped at her left side, adding yet another hole. "Don't act so helpless. I read your record. You fenced in college. I don't get a lot of practice around here. Humor an old man. Besides, it's good for your reflexes. I may make it mandatory. Come on. Show me what you got."

Angrily, she threw down her pistol and dove on top of him. He rolled her once and lay on top, but she managed to roll him again then flip herself so she had him pinned by the shoulders in a wrestler's hold.

He could only laugh. "Uncle."

Mandy pressed hard against his shoulders. "You owe me a new sweatshirt."

"As soon as you disarm me."

"Bring it on."

She let him go and stood, then picked up her sword. The swordplay lasted for almost five minutes. Mandy was in a full-bore attack mode, leaving James in defense. He never had a chance to get the upper hand. Mandy backed him up against a wall and disarmed him within seconds. For good measure, she flicked her sword and tore his shirt.

"Eat that, Stoner."

"What are you doing here, Hunt? Everything okay?"

"You told me to come back in an hour. I did. Then I drank crappy coffee in the lobby for over an hour before they finally let me in and told me where to find you."

"It's been two hours? I'm so sorry."

"It's okay. Unless this guy is trying to talk you into coming back." Hunt was teasing, but he could tell by the looks on their faces, he was right. "You're shitting me, right?"

"I asked, but she shot me down cold, buddy. Honest."

Mandy jumped in. "Actually, you showed up right as I was about to tell him we were trying to get pregnant again, so there is really no way I'm even going to consider it. James, accept that I'm happy, and a civilian is kicking your ass at the course."

James chuckled. "Can't blame me for wanting the best."

Hunt pulled Mandy to him even tighter. "Guess I can't. Come on, babe. We're about overdue to work on that 'trying' thing you just mentioned." He waggled his eyebrows for effect.

Mandy blushed and elbowed him. "We'll see ourselves out, James. Thanks for the workout. I was afraid I was out of shape."

"Oh, wait!" James called as they turned to walk away. "There is one last, quick thing I'd like you to do."

Together they walked down a series of hallways and closed doors. When James opened one up, Mandy stopped him. "Just what is it that you want me to do?"

He smiled wide. "Trust me, you'll enjoy this one."

They entered a room with two-way glass. James excused the man who was in there. Once he was gone, James flipped a light switch. They could now see who was in the interrogation room.

Mandy lit up like a Christmas tree. "No way. He's back here again?"

"Way. We drag him back from time to time. This is your lucky day. Care to have a little talk with him?"

"Would I ever!" She laughed hard. "What do you want out of him?"

"Anything you can get."

She rushed over to the door as Hunt stood back.

"What's she going to do?" Hunt asked.

"Just watch. Abbey put her to the test with this guy to see what she'd do the first day she showed up. She was in some getup; he had no clue who she was. He's just a two-bit loser, but every now and then he offers something useful. He goes by 'M.' I use her first interrogation tape with him for training. She's kind of a legend here. Abbey thought she'd use her fancy degrees and talk something useful out of him."

"And what did she do?"

"Kick his ass."

The man frowned when she walked in. "No way. You?"

"Hello, Melvin," she said before shutting the door behind her.

Hunt and Mandy didn't talk much on the way back to the house. Mandy couldn't tell if he was angry or not, but she wasn't going to ask and risk starting an argument.

"Did you call your mom?" she finally asked.

"I did. Everyone is fine. She said Hannah is having a blast with them."

Mandy rested her arm on the door and leaned her head into her hand. "It's not like she would tell me if she was crying the whole time."

"She loves Mom and Dad. She's fine, babe."

Sighing heavily, Mandy moaned. "I suppose."

He placed his arm on her leg and gave it a squeeze. "Kind of fun watching you in action today."

She forced a smile and shrugged.

"You do miss it. Don't you?"

Her hands fell to her lap. "Do we have to do this now? My plate is a little full with frustration. I don't want to fight about this again, Hunt."

"I don't want to fight, either. You have me seven ways from horny watching you handle that dealer. I want to pull this car over and do you right here."

She placed her hand on his crotch and discovered he wasn't lying. "You can't wait till we get back to the house?"

"I'm not sure I'll function with one of Eddie's men breathing through his mouth, listening outside our door."

Mandy pondered it for a moment. "So, let's find a pit of a motel. You can do me in a filthy dive for old time's sake."

Hunt grinned. "You're the boss."

The place they stayed in was a bit of an upgrade from their back-road escapades a few years ago, but it was close enough. Where before they'd had only the sounds of nature serenading them, they now had traffic and an occasional backfire or gunshot.

Mandy lay flat on top of Hunt, still breathing heavily. "I was so lost in thoughts of how much this was like the motel Hannah was conceived in, I almost paused there for a second, worrying about your side." She snuggled into him. "I can't believe you wanted sex with a gunshot wound."

Hunt laughed. "You didn't seem to mind at the time." He wrapped his arms tighter around her. "I love you."

She rested her chin on his chest and met his gaze. "No regrets for the color I've brought into your life?"

"You're shitting me, right?" He gave her a playful swat on the behind. "Books aren't as entertaining as my own life. You spoil me, babe."

"Spoil you? I'll write down 'get kidnapped by mobsters' for our tenth wedding anniversary present if this is what floats your boat."

He rolled her over to her back. "As long as you're there with me, it's a date."

She kissed him then let her gaze roam around the room. She grimaced.

"Hey. I would have sprung for something better. You wanted a pit."

"By the hour is cheaper. Besides, we'll have to get back before Eddie blows a vein in his head."

"Tough shit. I paid for two hours."

Mandy rubbed her belly and said, "I guess it couldn't hurt."

"Ah-ha."

"Ah-ha what?"

"You thought we had a magical touch with a dive. You're hoping to get pregnant, aren't you?"

"Hey, now. You're the one who said you had to have me right now. And hello, of course I want to get pregnant. That's no secret."

He gave her a kiss before lowering his weight onto her body. "Second time's a charm?"

"Couldn't hurt."

They showered together before heading back to Vince's office. "Okay. Third time is a charm," Hunt said as he offered Mandy a towel. "Worth the extra hour."

"These dives really do turn you on."

"Nope. All you, my love."

Eddie was sitting at his desk when they walked in. He tapped his pen on the arm of his chair as he rocked it side to side.

"You mind telling me why I don't shoot you right now myself? What were you thinking going there?" He stopped his tapping and threw the pen on his desk.

"Can it, Eddie. If I wanted the FBI here, they'd be here."

"Who are you in bed with now, Amanda?"

"Hello. I'm right here," Hunt said as he crossed his arms.

"I'm not buying what you're selling, Eddie. I'm not so sure I'm buying what they're selling either."

"And that is..."

Mandy dropped herself into a chair. "They seem to think they have on a good source that there is a vigilante out there."

"A vigilante?"

"That's what they said. You guys are killing each other off for no reason."

He chuckled. "There's never a bad reason to off another mobster. Have you forgotten everything we taught you?"

"This isn't funny, Eddie." She slid her chair back and stood. "I'm wasting my time here. I miss my daughter. You said you needed me to get Angelo back and I did. I want to go home."

"Sit back down."

"Kiss my ass."

Eddie picked up the gun that was sitting on his desk and pointed it at her.

"You're not going to shoot me, Eddie."

"Maybe. Maybe not. But I will shoot him." He pointed the gun at Hunt.

"Not if you want your dick you won't. Put the fucking gun down."

He refused.

Giving in, Mandy sighed heavily and sat back down. "How is Angelo doing?"

"Better. You can see him when I'm done with you."

"Done with me? Keep talking like that, and I *will* leave. I don't owe you anything, Eddie. Let's get that straight and cut the shit. I'm here for Angelo. I don't need your permission to take him away from this and neither does he. Things aren't what they used to be. Stop watching old mob movies. You need to get a life and move on. I bet you have enough money stashed away to live ten lifetimes."

"It's not about the money."

"Then what? The power? You getting your rocks off bossing around brainless thugs and selling drugs to kids? Extorting money from hard-working businessmen?"

"Now it's you who watches too many movies. You know what we do. Things aren't going to change any time soon."

"Unless you get killed."

Eddie finally put the gun back down and laced his fingers behind his head. "Tell me what you know."

"Nothing more than hearsay. The FBI isn't going to waste any manpower figuring out who this vigilante is."

"Color me surprised."

"If you want their help, I'm sure there's someone new you can pay."

"What makes you think I'm not already?"

Mandy paused. "Good point. Remind me again why you have me here against my will?"

"Because I know a thing or two that you don't."

"And that is?"

"Angelo isn't an only child."

"Of course he is." Mandy paused and stared at Eddie. "Oh, shit."

"You see my dilemma."

CHAPTER SIX

Hunt finally joined the conversation. "Wait a second. You're not going to tell me this old story. Let me guess. Scar wants the crown and offs Mufasa and Simba, so he can have it. Talk about too many movies. Now you jackasses have me quoting The Lion King."

Mandy laughed. The new and not-so-improved smart-ass Hunt was starting to grow on her. She turned to Eddie. "Let me guess. Vince wasn't faithful to his wife."

"You know of a man that is?"

"Again, right here," Hunt said.

"Okay. Aside from the beaming love of your life. Come on, Mandy. Every dame in the area wanted a piece of him. He was the leader of our little corner of the world. Of course he was swatting them away like flies. Only a few made it in his bed. Only one stole his heart."

"And he got her pregnant," Mandy said with a sigh.

"He wouldn't let her move in after his wife died. Vince knew she would never have Angelo's love, and he would have probably never forgiven his father for the affair when he found out."

"Does Angelo know about his brother?"

"Brother?"

"Isn't that what we're talking about here?"

"Vince's other kid was a girl."

"A daughter?"

"I know you're not going to belittle the power of a woman dead set on revenge. Look at the size of you. One of my men will walk with a limp for the rest of his life because of you."

"He should have listened to me."

"Women like you are the reason there are battered women in this world."

"Lucky for me Hunt prefers his women raw." Mandy leaned back and crossed her arms.

Hunt chuckled in the background.

Eddie's face froze as he processed her comeback. He allowed the slightest grin.

"You can steal the line," Mandy said to him.

"I just might."

"Can we get back on track now? So, you think this daughter has something to do with what's going on?"

"Well...that's kind of hard to say at this point."

Mandy was getting more frustrated with each passing second. "Then why bring her up? Dammit, Eddie! Where is she?"

Eddie stood. "You need to follow me."

"Where now?" She stood with a huff.

"Back office. It'll only take a second."

The back office had been vacant for as long as Mandy knew of it. It was set up with nothing more than a desk, chair, and couch. She wasn't sure who was supposed to fill the office. It was just there and had come in handy for an afternoon tryst or three with Gerard. Eddie opened the door and Mandy gasped. The office now held a young woman who was barely twenty, secured to a chair.

"You kidnapped her?" Mandy rushed over to ungag the girl.

"We didn't kidnap her. We collected her to keep her safe."

"And you couldn't treat her any better than this?" As Mandy undid the gag, the girl glared at them all.

"You son of a bitch, Eddie!" she screamed.

"Uncle Eddie, sweetheart."

The girl gave Mandy a good once-over. "Who the hell are you?"

"That's a long story." She went to the back of the chair to take care of the bindings. "Throw me a knife, Eddie."

"She'll only run."

"You can't keep her against her will."

Hunt removed a pocketknife from his pants pocket and tossed it to Mandy. "Here, babe."

Mandy caught it but paused before cutting through the ties. "I'm cutting you loose, but I'm going to beg you to stay and talk to me for a minute. After that, you're free to go."

The girl still scowled.

"I'm begging you, not telling you. I'm on your side. I'm not a part of this bunch any more than you want to be. Okay?"

"All right."

Mandy cut her free.

The girl stood and rubbed her wrists. She took a stance as if she were going to attack Eddie.

Mandy was grateful when she walked to the window instead. She wouldn't have particularly cared if this girl gutted Eddie, but that wasn't going to help any of them.

After turning to Mandy, the girl asked, "What do you want?"

"I don't want anything, although your name would be helpful for starters."

"Angie."

"Do you know why you're here?"

She glared at Eddie. "No. I know what my father was, but I don't understand what that has to do with me and why you have me here against my will!" Angie shouted the last bit in his direction.

Mandy turned to him. "What were your plans for her exactly?"

"Exactly? I didn't have any. She's your problem now."

"My problem? She's a young girl, not a problem, ass wipe." Mandy didn't want to push it with Eddie, but she needed to establish some trust with Angie. If she could show Angie they had a common enemy, it would be a good place to start. "Honey, I don't know your story, but if you'll let me, I want to help you. Did you get to pack a bag?"

Angie pointed to a corner where there was a suitcase sitting.

"Will you come with us?"

"Anywhere is better than here."

Mandy turned to Hunt. "Hon? Will you grab Angie's bag and wait outside with her for a minute? I need to speak to Eddie."

"Sure, babe."

Once they were outside, Mandy moved closer to Eddie. She didn't want to be overheard. "Did you have to tie her up?"

"I didn't know what the hell to do with her."

"Did you grab her from her home to protect her or is there some kind of plan here?"

"She wasn't safe. I promised Vince if something happened to him, I'd keep her safe."

"How much does she know?"

"Her mother told her who her father was before she died. Vince had never been an active part of her upbringing, and she'd never had a steady stepfather. Her mother never married."

"Was her mother afraid of Vince? How unfair was that to the poor woman?"

"She wasn't afraid of him. She loved him. He took care of them from afar; he just wasn't active in her life. They died loving each other and stealing minutes together where they could."

"When did she die? Is this related to what's going on now?"

"No. She died a year ago in a car crash. And no, it was an honest accident. That was before this shit. No one was out to get her. Very few people knew about her."

"You think Angie will run?"

"Maybe. Stubborn little thing. I think you need to put the scare on her and keep her close."

"Until what?"

"Until we get this business figured out."

"Dammit, Eddie. I have a life, you know."

"And if you want any peace in it, you'll take this one step at a time. Get her back to Lonny's place. Convince her to stay. Besides the two bodyguards already there, I'm sending one to be on her at all times. If you get any more funny ideas to take off and visit old friends, I want to know about it first. From you, not secondhand."

"How can I watch her and do what you want from me?"

"You'll figure it out. We're not done by a long shot, but for now, concentrate on her."

"Can Angelo know about her?"

"I suppose he's going to have to."

"And I suppose I'm the one to tell him."

"You ain't just a pretty face, after all."

Mandy stopped at Angelo's room, but the doctor held up his hand. "I'd rather you didn't go in, Mandy. He's resting pretty soundly right now."

After getting the update on him she said, "Let him know I'll stop back in the morning, Doc."

"Will do. I think it'll do him some good to have a visitor. He's been an ornery cuss."

"He in a lot of pain?"

"Yes, but an even bigger pain in my ass. He needs to get up and moving."

"I'll come by around eight and see what I can do."

"Bless you."

Hunt and Angie were waiting out front in the car. She climbed in, and they headed for Lonny's home, which for now was their "home away from home."

"Eddie said someone has supper ready at the house," Hunt told her as he pulled away from the curb.

"Milo, no doubt. He's quite the chef."

"Do we get maid service with this, too?"

Mandy ignored him and turned around to face Angie. "How are you doing?"

She rubbed at her wrists again. "For a hostage? Fine."

"You're not my hostage, but until I can get to the bottom of whatever is going on, you will be a lot safer with us."

"Safer than with Eddie or the world in general?"

"Eddie is rough around the edges to say the least, but he's not your worry. Despite how he handled this, he was looking out for your safety. So yes, I suppose the rest of the world. Most of the wrong side of the street of New York, anyway."

Angie crossed her arms. "Exactly who are you?"

"For all intents and purposes, I'm nobody as far as this family goes. You deserve the truth, though, if we are going to be spending some time together. I was undercover FBI a few years back and dealt with Vince."

"FBI? You're *that* Amanda?"

Mandy grinned. "I suppose if there's a *that* Amanda, that would be me."

"Holy shit." She slid forward. "And you're that sheriff. You two should be dead."

"Well, I guess small town know-how overrides mob muscle," Hunt said. He turned to Mandy. "This Milo know who you really are?"

"No. We need to assume no one does unless I say otherwise. Understand, Angie?"

"Yeah, sure."

Hunt spoke to Angie again. "You going to share your story? How do you know about Amanda and me if you weren't involved?"

"After mom died, I became curious about my father. I started seeing someone who was in deep and tried to learn what I could."

"Who?" Mandy asked.

"Darin."

"Earl's son?"

"Earl?" Hunt asked.

"One of Vince's bodyguards."

"I take it you know him," Angie said.

"He was a piss-ant when I was around. What are you? Around eighteen?"

"Nineteen in December. He's only twenty. That's not that big of a deal."

"You have your whole life ahead of you, and you decided you wanted to get in with the mob to catch your thrills?"

She shrugged. "You can't blame me for wanting to know my father. That's what started it, anyway."

"Then what? Why stay?"

"I really like Darin. The gifts are nice, too, and I figured what the hell. It is the family business, right?"

Hunt scoffed. Mandy shot him her "you'd better quit while you're behind" look and turned back to Angie. "Did you let Vince know who you were?"

"I didn't get the chance. He was killed before I was brave enough to approach him. When Darin told me about him being killed, I broke down. That's when I told him who I was. He ran to his dad, his dad ran to Eddie. That's how I got locked up."

"But Vince was killed a few days ago."

"I hid for a while, but they found me."

"Where's Darin?"

Angie shrugged. "I don't know. He wasn't around when they took me. I bet he's worried."

"I'll call him."

"Can he come over? Wherever it is we're going?"

"I don't think that's possible. I don't know who's trouble and who isn't. You may think you sought after him, but it could be the other way around. I can't say I trust anyone right now."

"No. I found him. He really didn't know who I was. I may have started off wanting to find some stuff out, but I really like the guy. I know what this is, but I don't want out. My place is with Darin and whatever happens...so be it."

Again, Hunt scoffed. This time, Mandy hit him in the arm.

"Sorry. I guess I forgot how irresistible these mobsters can be."

"Keep it up, Blaine."

"Blair."

"Whatever." She crawled in back with Angie. His smart-ass meter was set to high. That was not one of his more charming personality traits.

"That's not asking for a ticket," Hunt complained.

Again, she ignored him. Mandy took Angie's hand. "Honey, look. I know you're young, and you may think this is some kind of glamorous life, but you couldn't be more wrong. These people are dangerous."

"I'm not an idiot."

Mandy glared into the rearview mirror almost daring Hunt to make a sound. Lucky for him, he didn't.

"Well, stop acting like one. You don't put yourself in this situation on purpose."

"You did."

"It was my job."

"And then it was for love. You of all people should understand how I feel. You can't stop me."

"No, but I can sure as hell try to make you come to your senses before you get killed."

The rest of the ride was quiet until Hunt said, "Honey, we're home," when they reached Lonny's.

Mandy let herself out and leaned against the car. Hunt joined her. "You okay?"

"This house still gives me the creeps."

He wrapped an arm around her. "Come on. Let's call Mom. She'll get Hannah on the phone for you. You'll feel better."

Angie walked over to them. "I heard about Darci, too. I'm sorry."

Mandy blinked back her tears. "Let's hope I don't have to leave you in a pool of your own blood while we're here." It was harsh, but Angie needed to understand the danger she was in.

Angie swallowed hard and followed them into the house.

Milo lit up when Mandy approached. She walked over and gave him a hug. As strange as this was, she took comfort in familiar faces.

"How is Angelo today?" he asked.

"I didn't get to see him. Doc said he was asleep. I'll go back in the morning."

"I'll send you off with eggs Benedict in your belly and a plate for him."

Mandy laughed. "Are you camping out here?"

"Eddie's an asshole, but he wants you on top of your game. I'm yours for the duration."

After introducing him to Hunt and Angie, Mandy went to draw a bath. She was settled in the large tub with soothing bath beads, surrounded by bubbles and scented candles with a glass of red wine, when Hunt joined her.

"I'm sorry for the wisecracks."

"Do I need to say again that I didn't want you here?"

Hunt said, "Tough shit," as he sat on the side of the tub. Mandy didn't realize a tear escaped her until Hunt wiped it away. "You that mad at me?"

She shook her head and held up a rubber duck.

"Darci's?" he asked.

Mandy nodded.

Hunt leaned in and hugged her, not caring that he was getting himself half drenched. After just a moment, her sobs became heavier. It wasn't enough to hug her the best he could at that angle. Fully clothed, he slid in and shifted positions with her, wrapping himself completely around her and holding her tight while she cried herself out.

CHAPTER SEVEN

Hunt tucked Mandy into bed and went downstairs to make excuses for her. Milo wasn't happy, but he said he'd make up for it in the morning with a big breakfast.

"I can imagine what being back in this house does to her. She really loved little Darci."

Angie walked up to them. "She's not coming back down?"

"To say she's under the weather is an understatement. I hope you're not planning on pulling any surprise punches or trying to take off. She really wants to talk to you."

"I'm not going anywhere. Not really anywhere to go, anyway."

"I've been told I'm a pretty good sounding board."

Angie shrugged. "I don't know that I have much to say."

Milo approached them. "You two sit. Dinner is ready."

Hunt and Angie encouraged Milo to join them. The conversation was kept to simple pleasantries. Hunt didn't want to get Angie upset about anything, not that he had much input on the situation.

After dinner, they went to a sitting room. Angie found a cribbage board while snooping around.

"You play?" she asked.

"I do."

"Care to have your ass handed to you? I'm not ready for bed."

He chuckled. "Set it up. I'm going to have a drink."

"Get me one, too."

"Hell no. You're not old enough."

"I do all the time."

"Not on my watch."

"Sheesh. Whatever, Dad."

Just as the game was about to end, Mandy came downstairs. Hunt stood and walked over, meeting her halfway into the room. "You okay, babe?"

"Just not tired enough to sleep. That or overtired. Is he treating you all right, Angie?"

"He won't let me have a drink."

"And he shouldn't." Mandy took Hunt by the hand, sat them both back down, and motioned toward the game. "You two done?"

"You'll save me, actually," Hunt said with a grin. "Allow me to walk away with a little dignity, anyway."

"Told you," Angie said before she removed the pegs. "I had him in one more hand anyway."

"I'm lying up in bed with my mind racing, Angie. I guess that's why I can't sleep."

"My fault?"

"Of course not. I have to say, I didn't expect you to be so agreeable. To see you two down here playing a game has thrown me for a loop."

"Eddie never even gave me a chance to not put up a fight. They snatched me outside of my home, tied me up, and packed a bag. End of story. Darin is going to be pissed."

"He'll get in trouble of his own for just knowing you, so don't expect a hero out of this situation."

"Why is he in trouble?"

"Even with Vince dead, there's that whole 'dating the boss's daughter' thing to consider."

"But he didn't know."

Mandy motioned to Hunt, and he took the cue to speak. "I'm not sure that it's going to make a lot of difference."

"That's not fair."

"You wanted to get involved with the mob. Exactly what part of that did you think would be fair? The drugs, the extortion, or the bodily harm?"

Angie sighed. "So, what now? Am I in some kind of protective custody? You going to ship me off to Mexico or something?"

"Until I can get to the bottom of whatever is going on, I can't say we know what we're going to do with you," Mandy explained. "I know you're safer here. Word is going to get out about you, and that will raise hell from all kinds of angles."

Angie picked up a throw pillow and played with the fringe on it. "Will I be able to meet my brother?" She all but pleaded with her big brown eyes.

Hunt melted. Even with Hannah at only four years old, he already couldn't resist that look. Angie was a stranger, but still, his fatherly instincts kicked in.

Mandy took her hand. "I think he'd want to know about you. I'll talk to him tomorrow."

Angie stood. "I think I'm going to shower and go to bed."

"Want me to walk you?" Hunt asked.

"The house is plenty big, but I'm all right. Thanks, though."

After she left, Hunt turned to Amanda. "Can I get you something to eat?"

"I don't think so. I'm really not hungry."

"I'm ready to turn in." He stood and took her hand, helping her to her feet. "Maybe you needed me in bed with you."

"That's probably it." She rested her head against his chest. "I want to go home."

"Me too, babe. This will be over soon."

They cuddled together that night without making love. She was exhausted, and he had to admit that he was, too. Funny how time plays tricks on marriages. Not that long ago, a bullet wound couldn't stop them from having sex. Now, however, he was content to just hold her.

Mandy could play mobster tough when she needed to, but she was still all woman with a heart of gold to him, no matter what. He loved playing the comforting husband role. Resting his hand on her belly, he gave the back of her head a comforting kiss. He longed for a life to be growing inside her as much as she did, but he had to play patient, or it would only make her crazier.

Now wasn't the time for baby-making. They had enough on their plate as it was. He never dreamed he'd see the likes of these people again. He drifted off thinking about removing anything remotely related to mobs from their DVD collection.

After breakfast, Mandy told Angie they would be going to see Angelo.

Not much was said in the car. Angie was silent and fidgety throughout the ride. A few blocks before his apartment, she finally spoke up.

"What if he hates me?"

"How could he hate you? He doesn't even know you."

"He's bound to blame me for his father's affair."

"That's plain silly. You couldn't help that."

"I'll be some kind of competition in his life."

"Competition? For what? His father's affection? His father is dead. Maybe he'll welcome family. Seems to me you two are about all you have now." Angie fiddled with the buttons on the door, rolling the window up and down. "Are you having second thoughts?"

"Sort of."

"I'll talk to him first. If there is any sign he'll be angry, I won't let you in. Okay?"

Angie let out a heavy sigh of relief. "Yes. Please. That would be great."

Once they arrived at Angelo's apartment, Hunt walked with Angie to a sitting room while Mandy went in to see Angelo, carrying the breakfast Milo sent along. He was sitting up with an empty tray next to him on the nightstand. Not being able to help herself, she ran to his side and threw her free arm around him.

He held her tightly in return. Mandy was certain he was choking back tears, although she knew he'd never shed them. She gave him a minute to compose himself before she leaned back and slid the breakfast from Milo onto the tray.

Angelo smiled. "Eddie sent Milo to you?"

"Yes. He wanted you to have his eggs Benedict." She motioned to the empty tray. "I see you ate already. Want me to put this away?"

"Hell no. I'll eat it. I'm still hungry."

"That's a good sign." Brushing the hair out of his eyes, she said, "You need a haircut."

Angelo chuckled and took her hand. He gave it a long kiss. "I've missed you."

"I've missed you too, Angelo." Her free hand went to his cheek, not believing he was really in front of her after all this time. "How are you doing?"

"Okay now, I suppose, thanks to you."

"Do you know what happened? Or why?"

"I haven't a clue as to the why. Axle and Kermit haven't been so bad lately, truth be told. We were actually having a few drinks and talking when I had a burlap bag thrown over my head. I was knocked out, and when I came to, I was tied to that chair."

"Why were you so drunk?"

"That's all they fed me. Forced it on me was more like it. Every time I came to, they poured another fifth of some cheap ass bourbon in me."

"Why?"

"To help with the pain of them beating me? Hell, I don't know, Mandy. There are far worse ways to torture a guy than keeping him drunk."

"I hear you've been doing a little self-torture yourself lately."

He shrugged. "So?"

"So? What's gotten into you?"

"What? How is this new?"

"Come on. You weren't that bad when I was here. Except on the anniversary..."

"Of my mother's death. Yeah, well, I guess my misery was worth more than once a year."

"Stop it."

He stared at her. "When I last saw you at the cabin, I didn't think I'd ever be seeing you again. Why are you back?"

"Wouldn't we both like to know."

"What do you mean?"

"Eddie brought me back, claiming he wanted me to find you." She glanced behind her then leaned in closer. "Only I didn't get the reaction I thought I would when I actually showed up with you."

"Huh?"

"I know your father trusted Eddie with everything, but you know we've never clicked."

"There's an understatement."

"He said he needed me to hit the streets and find you, but I knew where you'd be. When I found you, he said I still can't go but won't tell me what it is I'm supposed to do next." Mandy reached in her pocket and pulled out two rings. She gave Angelo his.

"Why do you have this?"

"That ring had a finger attached to it. Any idea whose?"

"There was no one else with me. It could be anybody, Mandy. Whoever it is, I bet he's not missing the finger anymore."

"That was my thought."

"Who does the other one belong to?"

"Ray."

"Ray? Why do you have his ring?"

"He showed up at my place after Eddie."

"At your house?"

Mandy nodded. "I took care of it. Don't worry." She placed the other ring back in her pocket.

Angelo put his ring back on then winced and held his side.

"Are you okay? Want me to get Doc?"

"I'm fine. I have a few fractured ribs is all."

"You want some more pain meds?"

"Naw. I'll take a drink, though."

"Angelo Enrico Menusco! It's not even ten o'clock."

"Don't you mother me, Amanda. I fucking hurt."

She stood. "Then take some more pain medicine. You shouldn't be mixing that with alcohol."

"Did you come here to fight with me?"

"No, you spoiled little shit." She turned her back on him and crossed her arms. After standing a minute, she turned back. "How can I love you so much, yet you infuriate the crap out of me?"

"It's 'cause we never banged. We'd've gotten that tension out of our system if you had let me do you when I first asked."

Mandy was about to have a horrible fit before she caught Angelo grinning. She sat back down and held his cheek again. "You sure you don't want more pain meds?"

He shook his head. "I never did like fighting with you."

"So, let's not. I need to find a lot of answers, Angelo."

"I don't know how I can help, and I really don't feel up to doing shit right now."

"I understand. We don't have to do it now. I have someone here I want you to meet, though."

"You setting me up?" His eyebrows waggled up and down.

She playfully smacked his arm. "No. Honestly? I'm not sure how you'll take this."

"Take what?"

"You have a sister, Angelo."

He flopped backward against the headboard. "Angie from Queens. Yeah, I know."

"You know about her?"

"Of course I know about her. What did you think? My dad was a lousy liar."

"He told you?"

"Of course not, but I found out."

"You never told him you knew?"

"He seemed to want to keep it a secret, so I let him. That's not who you have, is it?"

"Angelo, this girl is your sister. Aren't you the least bit curious about her?"

"Why would I be? She's the product of my dad's affair. We didn't share bedtime stories and cuddle up together while Mommy and Daddy were fighting. She's no more my sister than you."

"She's your father's flesh and blood. She's your blood relative, Angelo. She's also all you have left."

His arms were now crossed. "Why are you being such a hard-ass about this?"

"Because you're all she has left. Her mother died, and she came in search of her father, and now he's dead, too. She's out there scared to death you're going to hate her."

"I don't hate her, I just don't care."

"Well, start to care, dammit. She may be a little screwed up right now, but she wants to meet you. She needs to know she belongs somewhere."

"This is hardly a family to jump in with."

"We'll work on that. Just meet her and be nice. Please. For me."

Mandy helped Angelo clean up and put on a fresh shirt. She chose a casual button up that she could pull on without hurting him. He declined a shave.

"Like I'm letting you near my neck with a straight blade."

She laughed and held his chin in her hand then gave him a gentle kiss on the cheek. "Punk ass kid."

He caught her hand as she dropped it and held on tight. "I never got to say thanks for what you did."

"Hell, Angelo. I'm making a fuss about Angie, but I feel like we're family, too. You have no idea how much it tore me up to think you were lying somewhere dead."

"You'd never know it by the way you neglected to contact me over the years."

"You know that was impossible for me no matter how much I wanted to."

"Was it Hunt's doing?"

"No. It was mine. I can't have this old life be a part of my present one. This was a job for me. I was supposed to get something done and move on. I never expected it to turn into what it did. I'll give you that Hunt wouldn't be pleased if I kept in touch, but it was my doing. Besides the fact it would have broken every rule of witness relocation."

He let out a heavy sigh.

"You can't tell me your father would have been thrilled if you tried to keep me in your life."

He answered like a scolded child and dropped his head. "No. He wouldn't have been happy. Jesus, Mandy. I protected you, and he was shot. That was hardly a fair statement."

Again, she took his chin and picked his head up. "But I'm here now."

"How long will you stay?"

"Just as long as I have to. I don't know what Eddie wants with me, but I'll do what I can as long as it benefits you. I want to get home to my daughter, Angelo."

"I didn't know you had a baby." He grinned. "It's hard to picture you with a baby."

She playfully punched his arm. "Don't change your opinion of me. I could still whoop your ass."

He rubbed his arm and laughed. "I know you must miss her. I'm sorry."

"It's not your fault." A knock on the door interrupted them. Mandy called out, "Come in."

Hunt poked his head in and gave the slightest of pleasant smiles at Angelo. "You look a lot better."

"Thanks. I feel a lot better."

"I really hate to interrupt, but you have a girl going crazy out here."

Mandy turned to Angelo, silently asking for permission.

Angelo pulled the blanket up a little bit. "Send her in."

CHAPTER EIGHT

Angie entered the room hesitantly. She stopped halfway to the bed, waiting for an invitation to go closer.

"How about we leave you two alone?" Mandy took Hunt's hand and walked out without waiting for an answer.

"Pull up a chair," Angelo said as he pointed to one at a small desk.

She did as she was asked and sat there quietly. After a minute, she finally said, "Mandy tell you who I was?"

"Yes, but I already knew about you."

"You did?"

"For a few years now. I figured I needed to heed my father's wishes and leave you alone."

"Why would he want that?"

"Why do you think?"

"This whole thing was really dumb. I only just found out, and now I'm robbed of ever getting a chance to know him."

"I really don't think he would have been quite the father figure you would have been looking for."

"What do you know what I would or wouldn't be looking for? Maybe I needed to know him. I don't care what he did for a living."

"Well, you'd be the only one who didn't care. You really would have been better off just staying away."

"You've obviously never heard about a woman and curiosity. I couldn't let something like this go by. Do you even care that you have a sister?"

"Of course I care. Right now, though, it makes things more complicated."

"Well, I met Darin, and things seemed like the perfect time."

"Darin? You're who he's dating?"

"Yes. Why?"

"I officially know more than I want about my sister's bedroom habits." He chuckled, but Angie blushed. "I'm sorry. It was a joke. I didn't want to make you uncomfortable."

"So, he talks about me?"

"Are you kidding? He's crazy about you."

"Mandy thinks he's in trouble now because of me."

"He didn't know. I honestly don't think it will be that bad, although I do see him being told to stop seeing you."

"That's not fair."

"You know...I'd really hate to go all big brother on you already. For starters, you're too young to think he's the last guy you'll love."

"And B?"

"What the fuck are you thinking, purposely trying to get yourself involved with the mob?"

She stood fast, not hiding her frustration. "You're a fine one to judge me. I suppose you never date."

"The girls I'm with never know what I am. I keep it simple. I'd never ask anyone to jump into this mess."

"So, you're going to live your life screwing one girl to the next and never settle down?"

"Probably. I was born into this. I didn't have a choice. I know a lot of guys have wives, but I would never ask that of someone I loved. You're making a poor decision if you ask me."

"Well, I'm not asking you, and F—Y—I, I was born into it, too."

"No, you weren't. You were kept out of it. What you're doing now is stupid."

She dropped herself back into the chair. "I didn't come here to fight with you."

"I don't want to fight, either, it's just the way it is. You showing up now is the worst possible timing. I can't explain what's going on out there, but it's bad. I was taken because of who I am. I shouldn't be alive right now. If word gets out about you, there's no telling what will happen."

"But Mandy's here to help. This will get sorted out."

He laughed hard. "Sorted out? Even if we get a clue as to what is going on now, there's always someone out there after you for something or another. People respected my dad and a certain chain of command. Some things were always understood and a way of life here. Someone broke the rules, and all hell has broken loose. I don't know what will happen from here, but I do know I don't want you a part of it."

"That's really not your call."

"Really, it is. Despite my current state, what I say now goes around here."

"So, what now? You're going to have your goon, Eddie, tie me back up?"

"Don't be ridiculous. I like the fact you're under Mandy's wing for now. Wait. He tied you up?"

She crossed her arms. "Yes."

"I'll deal with him about that. I'll also have to decide what to do with you soon."

"Decide what to do with me? I'm not your possession to do anything with, Angelo!"

"Wrong!" He sat tall. "Like it or not, you're my baby sister and all I have left for family. I'm not letting you get hauled off and killed."

After a staring contest, Angie's features softened. Angelo reached a hand to her, and she accepted it. She rested her head in his lap. "I'm sorry about your dad."

"And I'm sorry about yours. I'm sorry you never got to meet him." He gently stroked her hair.

"Will you tell me some good things about him?"

They spoke for over an hour, getting acquainted. Despite initially feeling awkward about the meeting, Angelo was more relaxed and laughed more than he had in months. There was a knock on the door, and he said, "Come in."

"How are things going?" Mandy asked. "You two learning a little bit about each other?"

"We're doing great," Angie said.

"Glad to hear it, but Doc wants us to skedaddle. Angelo needs his rest."

Angie stood and reached for his hand. "Can I come back sometime?"

Angelo accepted her hand and gave it a gentle squeeze. "Sure. I'd say anytime, but for now you only come with Mandy. I don't want you showing up here alone. At least until we get things figured out."

"All right."

"I need a minute with Mandy, okay?"

"Sure." She walked out and closed the door.

"Thanks for that," Angelo said.

"I've been away too long. Is that sarcasm?"

"No, I mean it. She's a great kid." He leaned back into the pillow, finally allowing his tiredness to show. He'd played tough with Angie, but he was hurting.

"I'm sorry. I should have interrupted sooner."

"No. That's okay. I'm fine."

Mandy sat on the bed next to him. "You never could lie to me."

He reached and gently tugged on the chain around her neck until the locket came out from under her shirt. Angelo grinned. "You still wear it."

"Of course. You bought it for me." She opened it up. "It has my daughter in there now, too."

Angelo smiled up at Mandy. "She's lucky she takes after you."

Mandy laughed and slapped his hand away. "I think she looks like her daddy."

"You are really happy, aren't you?"

"Yes, Angelo. I really am. What I had when I was here wasn't real. Not by a long shot. I see that now. It's time for me to play grown-up."

Angelo closed his eyes. His words came out barely above a whisper. "That's funny because when you were here, that was the only thing that was real to me."

As Mandy shut the bedroom door, there was a commotion going on in the entryway. Removing her revolver from the small of her back, she rushed out there. She took the corner with her gun drawn but lowered it when she found what was causing the disturbance.

Angie stood behind Darin. He had one arm wrapped around her while the other was straight out, with his hand open in a "stop" pose, toward Hunt and the other guard, Charlie.

Mandy put her gun back. "What's this, Darin?"

"I heard she was here. I needed to see her."

"How did you hear?"

"How do you think? It's not like you used a secret entrance, Mandy. Someone called me. I've been worried sick. I swear to God if what they tell me is true, I'll have Eddie's balls in a vice myself."

"You'd best watch that talk," Charlie threatened.

Mandy held her hands up to him. "He's just hot right now, Charlie. Give me time with him. Your job is to watch Angelo, and he obviously isn't here to hurt him. Let me deal with this."

"I don't recall I'm supposed to be taking orders from the likes of you."

Mandy squared herself off. "Then get Eddie on the phone or get out of my face!"

He glared at Mandy before going back to his post at the bedroom door.

"Come in and sit down for a second, Darin. You can't take off and do anything half-cocked. You know you won't get far."

"I don't want to sit down. This is total bullshit."

Angie came out from behind him. "Total bullshit, but you're the one who sold me out."

"I didn't sell you out, baby. I was scared. I had to tell them who you were. It was for your own good. I had no idea they would react that way. I'm sorry."

He reached for her, but she pulled her hand back. It was only a few seconds before she flew into his arms, sobbing.

"I was so worried about you," she cried.

"Me? Hell. I was worried about you." He held Angie tight then faced Mandy. "Why are you back?"

"Wouldn't I like to know? Come on, let's go sit."

They settled in the sitting room and were silent for a few moments. Hunt sat next to Mandy on a loveseat, while Darin chose a recliner and held Angie close to him on his lap. He spoke first. "So, what now?"

"She's mine to watch for now, and I don't know that the plans will work to include you," Mandy said.

"Then make it part of the plan."

"Darin...would you stop and think with your head instead of your dick for a minute, please? We're lucky to have Angelo back and alive. Whoever killed Vince is sure to want him dead, too. What do you think they'll do if they discover he has a daughter? Invite her for tea and crackers?"

"Kermit and Axle wouldn't have killed Angelo. They ain't got the brains to carry out that kind of plan. If they were in a tiff, it would have just happened by accident. They never would have planned something that extreme."

Hunt jumped in. "You think maybe these two knew something was going down and in their own way were protecting him? You know—keep your enemies close?"

"Right. While they near beat him to death." Darin scoffed.

"No. Wait a second." Mandy stood. "I bet Hunt is on to something. Angelo said they haven't been that bad lately. They were drinking together before they took him then kept him liquored up."

"While they beat him," Darin added.

"More likely, while someone hired them to beat him. Maybe they were doing as they were told, keeping him off the street and continuing their version of a party while helping him with the pain in the only way they could."

"You sure can stretch it, Mandy."

"It is a stretch, but it makes sense. It's the only thing that makes sense. You've never gotten someone drunk after he was in a fight? Dull his senses a little?"

"Sure, but—"

"But nothing. Maybe you haven't had the pleasure of digging a bullet out of someone yet, but I'll tell you this, you'll give the man a bottle of booze to suck on first."

Now Hunt stood. "And I can personally vouch for that one. So, we shot up the two boys who were helping him?"

"I'm not going to feel bad. They still had him hostage. Who knows what their orders were going to be next. Those two don't do any thinking for themselves. Keeping him drunk could have had nothing to do with helping him, either. In their pea brains it could have been one big party. You're not in that kind of position unless you enjoy what you do."

"You've now talked yourself into a complete circle, Mandy. Are they the bad guys or not?"

"Well they're not the good guys, just not the brains behind this, either. Indirectly, they know what's going on. They either held Angelo for someone to deal with him later or helped hide him to keep him safe, so they could hold the cards later."

Hunt spoke again. "It's obvious someone wants to replace Vince. The only one I see gaining from this immediately is Eddie. I hate to say it, but I know you're all thinking it."

"He could have killed me instead of giving me to you two," Angie said.

"Except it's highly unlikely you'd step up and accept the crown."

"So, I can go with Darin, then, if I'm not accepted as part of the mob family. You have no reason to keep us apart."

"Wrong," Amanda said. "You could still be held for a type of ransom to get what they want, or they could kill you out of spite. You're far from safe." She turned to Hunt. "I have questions about Eddie, too, but I don't think he'd be behind any scheme to harm Angelo. That much I know for sure."

A bullet shattered a window nearby, and everyone hit the floor. Hunt removed his revolver, but Mandy grabbed his hand. "Just stay down. No one is going to start anything here."

Charlie came running into the room, and Mandy shouted at him to get down. "We're fine. Stay low. Go back and check on Angelo. Don't leave his side, you hear me?" He nodded and crab walked back out of the room. She turned to Darin and Angie. "You two stay put. Hunt and I are going downstairs." Mandy stood and went over to Angie. She was pressed as close as she could against Darin's chest, his arms holding her tight. Mandy placed a hand on her shoulder. "Just stay here with Darin. And Darin, don't think about any heroics. Just watch her."

"Got it." Darin removed his gun and chambered a round. Angie buried her head deeper into his neck.

Hunt and Mandy went downstairs. They took one of the guards from the front door with them. Earl was there waiting in the lobby. Mandy paused for a moment but didn't bother with introductions.

"You see anything?"

"Black sedan tore off after the shot."

"That's a help," Mandy said as she placed her gun back in her waistband. "You have anybody after them?"

"No point. They're long gone, Mandy." Earl shook his head in Hunt's direction. "This your sheriff?"

"Hunt—Earl, Earl—Hunt."

The men gave a brief nod then Hunt spoke. "This is Darin's father?"

"Sometimes I wish you weren't so good with names. Yes, he is." Mandy turned and addressed Earl. "Are you who called Darin and told him Angie was upstairs?"

"Boy has a right to know. He's been worried sick. There's no reason he shouldn't be able to date who he wants. I was obligated to let Eddie know who she was. I didn't expect him to snatch her up like that."

"He went about it the wrong way, but he was trying to protect her. I need to keep her with me for a while."

"What about Darin?" Earl asked. "You're not being fair to the boy."

"Initially I wanted him out of it, but I think under the circumstances I'm changing my mind."

"How's that?"

"I want Darin with her. No one will protect her like he will."

"I'm glad you see it that way. I was about to duct tape his ass to a chair, with him so hell-bent on getting to her. I'm not saying I'm thrilled about who she is, but there has to be a way around all of this. He thinks he loves her, for crying out loud."

"Their love life isn't my concern right now. I need to keep her alive. I want them up at the cabin, not in the city."

"The cabin? Why?"

Amanda stopped talking as Eddie's limo pulled up. She waited until he reached them.

"What the hell went on? No one has ever fired at us here before."

"I want everyone upstairs, now," Mandy said. "I'm only going to say what I have to say once, and I want no lip, or I go the fuck home."

CHAPTER NINE

Once Mandy had everyone's attention in Eddie's office, she moved to Hunt's side then began to explain her plan.

"First of all, Darin, I want you to know I've changed my mind about you being with Angie."

"That's good, because I wasn't about to be a part of any plan that kept us apart."

Eddie spoke up. "You'll do what you're told, boy. You're in no position to demand anything."

"I'm not—"

"You'll shut up," Earl interrupted. "You have what you want for now, so shut the hell up and listen."

"Yes, sir."

Mandy continued. "I can't do what I plan on doing and play glorified babysitter, Eddie. I want Angelo and these two moved up to the cabin in Vermont."

"Back to Vermont?" Hunt yelled. "Why do you want to put them back where this all started?"

"That cabin has no connection to anyone. I want them out of the city, and that's the best place I can think of. Vince never made deals there, it was his retreat. Should I know otherwise, Eddie? Do I need to pick another safe house?"

"No. I think the cabin is a good call."

Mandy turned to Hunt. "I don't think you need to notify anyone in Vermont about this, but if you feel better having Roy on stand-by, that's your call."

Roy was the deputy back when Hunt and Mandy first met. He'd saved them on two occasions. Hunt had him promoted to Sheriff before they relocated.

"I don't think I'm going to involve him unless I have to. Please don't make me have to, baby. I still don't like this."

"But it's okay?"

"I'd hate to agree with Eddie, but I guess it's a good call."

"Okay then." Mandy turned back to Eddie. "I want four men out there in shifts, not including Darin."

"I thought I was going?" Darin asked.

"You're going, but I can't trust you not to be distracted. You're to protect Angie with everything you have, not just take a honeymoon and screw yourselves senseless." Directing her attention to Angie, she softened her tone. "I'm sorry, but you two need to understand what's at stake here. You came into this with delusions that being a part of the mob was a grand affair. How's it treating you so far, sweetie?"

"Honestly, you're kind of scaring me."

"Me or the bullet that flew over your head?"

"Both, I guess."

"Good. What Eddie did was nothing compared to what anyone else would do." Mandy's focus returned to Eddie. "You haven't even said what you're keeping me for, so now I'm telling you. I'm running the show."

"You think so?"

"Yes, I think so. I want to flush out whoever is doing this, and I'm the new bait."

Hunt stepped in front of her. "Oh, no, you're not!"

"I have to, Hunt."

"You don't owe these people anything."

"Maybe not, but we're not going to get any peace until this is over. I refuse to go home and wait to be snatched up again. Eddie? You find any connection to why Ray was on to us?"

"I told you. I don't have a clue. This wasn't our doing. If it's related to the killing here, they shouldn't have gone after you."

"But he just happened to show up when you did."

"So, he followed us. I'm not sure I like what you're getting at here, Mandy."

"What I'm getting at is you've already made me a target. Vince is gone, Angelo was temporarily out of the picture, and they came after me."

Eddie finally got it. "You and Angelo went everywhere together."

"Exactly. Someone already pegged me for his sister."

"What?" Hunt shouted.

"It's all I can figure. Word is out about Angie, and someone pieced together that I was her."

"How is that possible? You have ten years on her."

"They don't know specifics. You know how rumors fly. All they knew is that Vince had a daughter. I had a lot more say than I should have when I was with Angelo. I was married to the lawyer. I guess anyone looking in could easily assume that."

"So, what are you willing to do?" Eddie asked.

"I'm not playing house with Leo if that's what you're asking."

"Then what?"

"I'll spread the word that Angelo is dead, and I'm in charge."

"Not if I have any say in this." Angelo stood at the doorway, leaning on it for support. Charlie tried to help him, but he shook his arm free.

Amanda walked over. "You shouldn't be out of bed."

"Then you should be having this little meeting in my room. I have a say in what's going on around here, in case you've forgotten who's really in charge."

"I didn't mean to exclude you, but I really don't see another way around this, Angelo."

"I'm not going to sit and hide out in some cabin while you run around the city by yourself, trying to flush out whoever is after us."

"She's not going to be alone," Hunt said. "There is no way in hell I'm letting you do this alone, babe. I don't care what I have to do. But you're not leaving my side for anything. You fight me on this, and we go home right now."

"Hunt. Everything about this goes against everything you are. You're a hero, not a gangster."

"And you were FBI. You can break a finger, but I can't?"

"These people know me. New faces they aren't so fond of."

"You were a new face once, too."

Arguing would be pointless. When his mind was made up, there was no changing it. "I don't like this."

"You don't have to like it, but I mean it. I'm there, or this conversation is over."

"I think I like this guy," Eddie said. "I don't think I've ever seen you take anyone's shit before, Amanda."

"This isn't shit, asshole. You may have forgotten, but I have a daughter I don't want to leave an orphan. I can't believe I have to get involved in helping the fucking mob. You should be taking care of your own dirty work. This has to be one for the books."

"You joined us to help Angelo. You're not fooling anyone." Eddie stared at Angelo. "I know you went soft ever since the shoot-out at the cabin. Your father dying only made things worse. This life isn't yours anymore. You want out, get the hell out. You're only keeping the rest of us in danger. I'll do you one up, Mandy. Settle this, and I'll allow you to take Angelo and move him. I don't care where, and I don't want to know." He motioned toward Angie. "Take her too. I don't need the estrogen around here. I just got the stink out of here from when you left, for fuck's sake."

Darin opened his mouth but must have thought better of it. It closed as quickly as it had opened.

Eddie continued. "You deal with your son, Earl. Frankly I don't care if he goes or stays, but I won't have that girl dictating the show because Vince couldn't keep his dick in his pants. He's dead, and despite the war going on and what people think, I'm in charge here."

Angelo glared at him but said nothing.

"You know I'm right, boy. You'll stay at the cabin until Mandy gets this wrapped up. If she does what she says, you'll be free to go. I don't want you back here." He turned to his men. "Help get his ass back to his room before he falls over."

Hunt left with Darin and Angie, so they could pack a few things, because Amanda didn't trust them not to run off. She stayed back with Angelo, who was fuming at what Eddie had said. He tossed things on the bed angrily while he kept an arm close to his side.

"It's true, isn't it?" she asked, packing his bag.

"What?" He flung a sweatshirt at her hands. The force caused him to wince in pain.

"You okay?"

"I'm fine. What's true?"

"You do want out, don't you?" Silently, he walked from his closet to a six-drawer dresser. "Angelo?"

"What do you want to hear, Mandy?"

"Try the truth for once. I knew this life wasn't you. I knew that from practically the moment we'd met."

"Funny how that works, isn't it? I was born into it, and it's not me, but you show up and take charge and tell me what I want."

"I'm not telling you what you want, Angelo. Why are you fighting with me on this? If I'm wrong, go in there and tell Eddie to shove it. I'm happy to let you duke it out and get home to my daughter."

He leaned against the wall and slid to the floor. "I don't want this. I never did, but I'll be dammed if I'll let you fight my battle."

Mandy kneeled in front of him. "I'm not fighting your battle. I screwed up somewhere along the line, and I need to fix it. I need Eddie out of my hair once and for all. He couldn't make me stay if I didn't want to. There is no way I'm going to spend my life running from him."

"He's not going to just let me walk."

"Yes, he is. He won't have a say in it. When things are over, I'll get you taken care of."

"Witness protection? And how is that working out for you?"

"Someplace deep inside, I knew this wasn't over for me."

Angelo met her gaze and chuckled. "You little shit. You still love this, don't you?"

She pinched her lips tight together. "You tell Hunt, and I'll neuter you."

He laughed hard then took her hand. "We made a great team. You sure I can't stick around and help?"

"Absolutely not. You're in no shape to crash warehouses with me."

"Can Hunt handle it?"

"He held his own saving you just fine. I'm not worried about him doing the job. Physically he's able do it, I only worry about what will happen when his morals kick in."

Angelo held his head low. "They didn't force me to drink, Mandy."

"Who? Axle and Kermit?"

"Yeah. I wanted to get good and drunk, and I wanted to stay that way."

"Why?"

"I wanted to be numb. I figured it was over for me, and I wanted to be drunk through the ordeal. It became a game with them."

"A punch for a shot?"

"Something like that. You know I've been pretty much drunk since you left."

"Pretty long drunk. That's not much of a life."

"It wasn't much of a life, anyway."

"You done now?"

"Yeah, I think so." Angelo reached for her locket and opened it. "Are you in touch with Sue?"

"I'm not supposed to let anyone know."

"Tell her I said 'hey' next time you talk with her."

She took his hand again. "Maybe you'll get the chance to tell her yourself soon."

They stood and finished packing. Angelo needed to rest when they were done. It worked out well; Mandy needed to make a call.

When everyone was loaded into the limo, Mandy gave the driver one last set of instructions before sending them on their way.

They were quite the sight. One blonde nineteen-year-old girl and her Italian boyfriend, two bodyguards (one black, one white), one Asian doctor, a Hispanic driver, and one handsome twenty-six-year-old Italian who pretty much melted any woman of any age.

Mandy never admitted how handsome Angelo was. He was just a kid to her, even though they were close in age. She always saw the boy first, but she knew there was a man fighting to get out. In agreeing he wanted nothing to do with the family business, he was maturing. It took more courage to leave than to stay. Hopefully she could end this quickly and get him on his way.

Angie would probably take a few years to realize leaving was best for her, too. Darin was nothing like Angelo. He loved what he did and would stay in, there was no question there. Angie would stay with him as long as he'd have her or until his usefulness ran out. She was certain of that.

Mandy waited until the limo was out of sight and turned to Hunt. She leaned into him, and he held her tight.

"Will you pinch me and wake me up from this nightmare," Hunt said softly.

"It'll be over soon."

He held her face with both hands and gave her a long kiss. "What's the plan now?"

"I'm not starting anything tonight. Let's get a good night's sleep and have at it in the morning."

"You have some kind of game plan?"

"Get back out in the game and let it be known I'm back."

The next morning, Hunt and Mandy added lightweight bulletproof vests to their attire. Hunt stood next to Mandy and fastened the last Velcro strap. He had an unsure look in his eye.

"Hunt, I do know what I'm doing. You'll need to trust me or go home."

"I know you think you know what you're doing, but you can't blame me for worrying."

"We're not having this discussion again."

He shoved his gun into his shoulder holster a little too harshly.

"Careful. You'll shoot something I want later."

"Later?" He brought his eyebrows together and twisted his lips into what Mandy called his "wounded puppy" look. Nothing snapped them out of a fight quicker than the mention of sex.

She crossed her arms, pretending to be put out by his reaction. "It's been twenty-five minutes since we had sex. You really want to pull that look now?"

He took her by the hips, pulling her close to him. "Come on. You know anything over eighteen and I'm good to go again."

She wrapped her arms around the back of his neck and drew him in for a kiss. "I know, but we need to get going."

"You also know I'm still upset."

"I know. Thanks for pretending to be distracted for a minute. Fighting isn't going to get us anywhere. I know these streets, and I know my people."

"Your people?"

"You know what I mean. I did this for a year, Hunt. Sometimes it was hard telling which was the act: the FBI informant or the Mob lawyer wife. I know I can do this."

"I love you, dammit. It's my job to give you grief and worry about you. I was on the other end of your shtick, remember? I know what you're capable of; I don't have to like it, though."

"No, I guess you don't." She pulled on her jacket and tucked her gun where it had always been most comfortable, at the small of her back. She had never used a holster. Even in the middle of summer, she preferred a dress jacket.

"We do need to make one stop first."

"Where's that?"

"My old job."

"I thought this was your old job."

"My first old job."

Hunt finally understood what she was talking about. "Oh that. Fine. I could use more coffee, anyway."

They arrived at the little corner store where Mandy had worked. She'd taken the job when she was undercover, as directed by Craig Abbey, and thought for weeks that it was a waste of time. As time progressed, she was dealing drugs passed off as cartons of cigarettes for the mob. Slowly, she earned the trust of the men in charge then became Angelo's "right hand man." Of course it seemed strange to her, but she stayed in, thinking she was making headway and sending the FBI the information needed to shut Vince Menusco down. She had been clueless Vince was on to her and that her contact at the FBI had no intentions of letting her succeed. He'd hired her to fail, and she refused. Vowing not to fail now either, she strode into the little shop like she owned the place.

They sat at the counter and waved over the young girl working there. Mandy fought a smile. She reminded her of herself. A lot. Or at least the part she played while she worked here. The girl cracked her gum.

"What can I get you?"

"Two coffees," Hunt said as he slid the container of sugars toward Mandy. When she came back, there was another crack of her gum. "Anything else?"

"How's PLU number ninety-nine looking today?" Mandy asked.

The girl hesitated for a moment. "We're out."

"When will it be back in?"

"Not sure."

"Is your boss around?"

The girl leaned forward on the counter. Her ample breasts and low-cut top were enough to make Hunt turn away and pretend to be interested in a paper a few chairs over. He stood and walked away. *Smart man.*

"You a cop?"

Mandy laughed hard. "Not even close. I used to have your job."

"You did? Well, shit. You look okay, but honestly that dude you're with reeks of cop."

"Yeah...don't I know it. They had to go and give me Pretty Boy Floyd here for back up."

"Doesn't look like a Floyd to me."

Mandy sighed. "It's an old expression. Goes by Hammer."

"I thought Hammer was black?"

Crap. Mandy forgot about that when talking to Axle. "Obviously not this one," is all she could say in recovery.

"He's a hunk, anyway."

Mandy had to not let her jealousy show. "I'm not here to talk about my man."

"Your man—your man, or your man as in *your* man."

Mandy blinked and stared at her, wondering how this girl could even operate a cash register. "We're not a couple if that's what you're asking."

"So...is he available?"

"No."

"Bummer. There's no ring."

"There's no what?" Mandy spun around then quickly caught herself. She shouldn't react that way in front of someone else. "No, there isn't. But he still has a gal at home that would shred you in two if she caught wind of you. Can we get back to business?"

Hunt joined them again and pretended to be reading the paper. Mandy was sure he overheard. He gave her knee a squeeze under the counter. Now that her breasts were out of Mandy's face, she read her name tag. Terri.

Terri took one last look at Hunt and let out a heavy sigh. "Right. I really don't have anything. My last runner was plugged, so things are late by a few days. Should be later today, though, if you're desperate and want to stick around or check back."

"They killed Buck?"

"Buck? No. Must be someone you don't know. Todd something. I don't think I was ever given his last name. He was the delivery and messenger guy. I guess they killed the messenger." She laughed until she snorted. "I'm sorry. That wasn't funny."

"No, it wasn't."

"Ummm...you still want the boss? He really ain't here, either. Want me to tell him you stopped in?"

"Sure. Tell him Mandy's back in town, and I'm going to fix whatever this is."

"Holy shit. That's you?"

Hunt jumped to his feet when Terri swayed forward as if she was going to faint. She took a step back and gathered herself.

"I'm sorry. I didn't realize I held a reputation here."

"Are you shitting me? Angelo doesn't stop talking about you."

"You mean used to not stop talking about me."

"What do you mean 'used to?'"

"Angelo died this morning."

"No!"

Terri managed to faint after all.

CHAPTER TEN

"What did you do that for?" Hunt asked as he jumped over the counter and picked Terri up.

Mandy whispered. "How was I supposed to know she'd faint? She should have thicker skin than that with this job. We have to tell everyone he's dead, Hunt. We can't pick and choose. When this is over and he's relocated, everyone has to think he's dead."

"I think Suzie D cups here had a crush on him."

"Well, she has one on you too, so there's no accounting for taste."

He grinned.

"Take her to the office in the back. There's a couch. She'll snap out of it soon enough. Where the hell is your ring, anyway?"

"You really think we need to be walking around with matching bands?"

"Oh. Good point. You could have warned me."

He shrugged. "Just thought of it as we walked out. Are you afraid I thought if you could play mobster, I could play single?"

"Jackass. I was worried you lost it."

Hunt leaned over Terri and gave Mandy a kiss. "Never. I'm afraid the tan line will make it look like I'm hiding it, though."

Mandy scoffed. "That'll only make you that much more mysterious."

"You're right. A total turn on."

Just as they parted, the chime from the door sounded. Mandy hurried behind the counter. She smiled at the familiar face. The man was carrying a box filled with cartons of cigarettes.

"Hello, Buck."

"Mandy? You have your old job back? Is that your punishment for getting caught and going to jail?" He laughed as he dropped the box on the counter.

"Looks like you were demoted, too."

"Yeah. It's temporary. The other driver was capped."

"So, I heard."

"I thought you would be promoted after saving Angelo."

"You heard, huh?"

"Of course. Rumor has it you and some white Hammer shot up the place good. Where's Terri?"

"She passed out. I'm not actually back. Not here, anyway. I stepped up while she comes to."

"Comes to? What happened?"

"She kind of fainted."

"Fainted? What'd you do that made her faint?"

"I guess I let it blurt out, and I shouldn't have. I should have taken more care with the news."

"What news?"

"Angelo's dead."

"What? When?"

"This morning. We didn't think he was as bad off when we brought him back. They just couldn't pull him out of it."

"Damn. That's some serious bad news."

"Feel free to let everyone know. I'm back now in every sense of the word, and I mean business. With Vince gone and now Angelo, that leaves me."

"You? Why you? Weren't you like his assistant or something?"

"That's what we were selling, but I'm also his sister. That leaves me in charge."

His jaw hit the ground. "His sister?" he asked with a squeak.

"Right. Vince never wanted anyone to know. Angelo promised never to tell anyone. That's why we were together. He insisted on keeping an eye on me. I refused to listen to Vince and play Susie Homemaker, staying put in some mansion and getting married off. Being with Angelo was the compromise."

"Holy shit. You do know what's going down around here, right? Things ain't good, beautiful."

"I'm aware of that. I intend to fix it."

Hunt walked out of the back office. "Let me guess. Hammer," Buck said with not too much emotion behind it.

Hunt stopped and frowned.

"That's right. And we need to split. Will you go sit with Terri until she's okay?"

"Got it. Dammit, Mandy. Nice to see you, but I'm really sorry to lose Angelo. He was a good friend."

"We're going to miss him. There will be no services. We can't risk any kind of gathering right now. Do spread the word, though. People need to know."

"Got it." He nodded to Hunt as he walked by.

Hunt joined Mandy. "Hammer?"

She shrugged. "My spontaneous name-making-up sucks. Take it out on me in bed later."

After they were on their way, Hunt turned to Mandy. "So, was making the new girl faint the reason we were there?"

"Of course not. I really wanted to see my old boss. I guess Buck showing up was good enough. I needed the rumor mill to start spreading the word about Angelo."

"You sure he's really okay with you telling everyone he's dead?"

"I talked with him more while you were packing Angie and Darin. He holds no ties to anyone here and will make a clean break without any problems."

"We're not adopting him, are we?"

Mandy laughed. "He's a big boy, you baby. I know what you think about my feelings for him, but I really don't see the need for us to become pen pals once he's out. He'll need to move on, and that includes saying goodbye to me. We've done it before."

"Exactly."

"Exactly what?"

"You've done it before, but wild horses couldn't keep you away from coming back and helping him."

"I knew you were upset."

"I'm not. Honestly. You'd think you could drop your defenses for once and read me like I know you can. I know he's important to you. I wouldn't be here otherwise. I think—" He slammed on his brakes as a black sedan came to a sudden stop in front of him. When the driver got out, they both reached for their guns.

Mandy recognized him and said, "Put it away, Hunt. It's okay." She rolled down her window.

"What gives, James?"

"Good news travels fast, Mandy. You're going to play kingpin now? What's this shit?"

"If you're not going to do anything, someone has to."

He leaned on her window and sighed heavily. "I knew you were going to be trouble the second you stepped into my office."

"So, look the other way. It's never bothered you people before."

"This isn't the same department with Abbey gone, Mandy. You go rogue agent on us, and you won't be protected."

"Well, lucky for you, I'm not an agent anymore."

"You'd go to jail as a vigilante. You'd be no better than who you're looking for."

"I have to do what I have to do, James. You know this."

He glanced over to Hunt as if asking for help. "Don't look at me. I'm afraid of her, too."

James reached in his pocket. He tossed two leather items between them that resembled wallets. Mandy and Hunt both picked one up. Mandy opened hers and met James's gaze.

"I don't want my badge back, and I'm pretty sure I speak for Hunt when I say he doesn't want one, either."

"Well, tough shit. You go out there without them and I can't help you when all hell breaks loose. At least it'll keep you out of jail."

"I can't report to you."

"I'm fine with that. Throw me a crumb or two when you can. Just stay safe, dammit."

He turned and walked away, but Mandy climbed out of the car and hurried after him.

"James?"

He stopped and turned around. "What is it?"

"Just thanks. I know you had to take some shit for this."

"Not yet, but I will when I get back. Don't worry about it. I'll deal with it."

"I mean it. I can't have any interference if I'm going to do this."

"I know. Keep your head down."

When Mandy got back in the car, she buried the badges in the glove box. "I don't know if I feel any better with these or not. If the wrong person finds them..."

"No one will. It's like a 'get out of jail' free card. You must really have some kind of pull, baby."

"You know I wasn't anyone in the time I was in, Hunt. I was Abbey's puppet and nothing more."

"Well, it seems to me you made the right friends, anyway."

"Don't let it fool you. If something goes wrong, they won't claim any responsibility."

"Well then, here's to nothing going wrong."

Mandy smiled at him, then returned her focus out the window. *Fat chance in hell.*

When Hunt pulled up at the warehouse, Mandy instructed him where to park.

"Is there another bitchin' crib in this shithole?"

"Stop it, Hunt."

"If I can't pick on you, this won't be any fun at all."

"Hunter Blaine! This isn't a game."

He reached for her hand. "I know. I'm sorry." He leaned in for a kiss, but she backed away.

"We can't. What if someone is watching?"

"Will I get some 'Hammer time' later at least?"

"You're horrible." Mandy got out and slammed the door.

"You picked the name," Hunt called after her. He caught up to her as she went in the metal side door without knocking. Two men standing inside reached for their holsters then stopped when they recognized her.

"Mandy?"

"That's right."

"You have balls."

"That's Hammer, Jeff."

"You know what I mean. What are you doing, showing up again?"

"I have business. Same as before."

"Heard you two shot up Axle and Kermit's."

"Good news travels fast. Nice to know some things never change."

"So, it was true?"

"They had something of mine, yes. You want to exchange recipe cards, or are you going to take me to the office?"

"Gimme your weapons first."

"Am I stupid?"

"I don't know. Are you? Either way, you're not going in with them."

Mandy hesitated before she removed her gun from her back. She slapped it into Jeff's hand. Hunt lifted his jacket, revealing his gun. Jeff reached in and removed it.

"After you," Jeff said, motioning forward.

Once they reached the office, everyone went quiet. There were a few men standing around what used to be Willy's desk. Gunner, the man she'd had a hard time with when she had first been brought here with Angelo, was behind the desk. He had given her grief, and she'd pinned him on the ground. If he was in charge now, this was not going to go well.

Mandy wasted no time in getting to the point. She wasn't going to let any fear show. "Where's Face?"

"You crazy? Face is in for a few back-to-back life sentences."

"He's still in?"

"That's usually what that means. I kinda hoped that was your fate as well."

"Sorry to disappoint. You in charge now, Gunner?"

"I guess you could say that."

Mandy had to stay in control. She had to summon up her worst attitude. "I'm not even going to beat around the bush here. Did you sick Ray on me?"

"What are you talking about?"

"May I?" Mandy asked as she reached for her inside coat pocket.

He motioned for her to continue.

She removed her hand and tossed the ring at him. Gunner caught it and squinted at her.

"Where did you get this?"

"Off of his cold, dead hand. He tried to kill me, and I beat him to it. I want to know what the hell is going on here."

"What do you mean tried to kill you?"

"What does it sound like? He broke into my house in Florida and tried to kill me. I want to know why."

"It wasn't my orders. Hell, Mandy. We thought you were long gone. I didn't even question him not showing up the past couple of days. He's been really off lately."

"Does he go to visit Face much?"

Gunner paused. "I know a few times that he went, but I ain't his babysitter. I don't ask what he does on his own time."

Mandy rushed to the desk and slammed her palms on it. "I want to know what the fuck is going on around here! I just told you I killed one of your boys, and you have no reaction to it? What's happening, Gunner?"

He continued to glare at her. "Why do I need to tell you shit? Where the hell is Angelo? I don't talk to no skirt. Without him here, you ain't shit. I took your crap when I had to, but no more. You were gone for too long, and I took you for dead or in jail. I was kinda hoping for the first one. I don't need to answer anything. Get the fuck out of my office and take your...tool with you."

Mandy kept her stance firm. "I guess you haven't heard yet."

"Heard what?"

"Angelo is dead."

"Bullshit."

"Died this morning. I think you know more than you're saying. The boys had a little more fun with him than they planned on. That, or it was the plan all along."

Gunner sank in his seat. His voice was softer now. "Angelo's dead?"

"Yes."

"Aww, fuck. I heard Axle and Kermit had him and that you rescued him. There's no way they were trying to kill him."

"Well, they did."

"So, what now? You sending someone after them?"

"I'm not really in a forgiving kind of mood, but no. I know they didn't mean to kill him, and I find it very hard to punish stupid. They'll get what they have coming one way or another."

"Then what?"

"I need to get to the bottom of who hired them to take Angelo and why. I'm back, Gunner. I'm in charge now. You're the lucky bunch to be the first to know."

Hunt finally spoke. "Second."

Mandy spun around and gave him a glare for all to see. She wasn't really mad and was sure Hunt knew it.

"Second. I had to hit up the shop earlier. Terri didn't take the news too well."

"Wait a minute. You're in charge? Who the hell are you to decide you're in charge?"

"Vince's daughter."

"No way! That's total bullshit."

"What do you think I was doing during my time with Angelo? Making him an afghan?"

"Where the hell have you been, then? There is no way Vince's daughter spent any time in jail."

"When her husband is the lawyer she happens to kill, it's been known to happen. My father wanted me out, and he figured a little jail time would help seal the deal. Well, it didn't, and he's not here to stop me now, is he?"

"I went to see Face in prison, too. He said you were a fed."

"And you bought that? A fed who married a mob lawyer then killed him? You think Vince is that stupid to let a fed be right under his nose? Face would have said anything to cut a deal. I guess he had his deal cut then tried to find a way to get even with me, anyway. Too bad he couldn't convince someone smarter than Ray."

"I'm not sure I buy he's dead. You've given me a ring, not a finger."

"Maybe I don't work that way. He's buried somewhere in Georgia. You want a map to his body?"

Gunner's head lowered to his hands with his elbows on the desk. "No."

"Then we need to get to business. I'll have to figure out what the hell Ray wanted with me after all this time. Maybe he figured out who I was and that I would come back and take over after Vince's death. Maybe he's not linked to Face at all. I don't know. What I do know, and you need to understand, is that your orders now come from me and only me. I want you to call a meeting with everyone you have out there A—S—A—F—P. This bullshit with 'who's running the show' is going to stop. I'm here, and I'm it. If you don't like it, kiss my tiara." She turned to Jeff. "Now give us back our fucking pieces."

CHAPTER ELEVEN

Mandy stood there with her hand outstretched, but Gunner stopped Jeff from retrieving their guns. "Hold on a second. I heard rumors about Vince having a daughter. I think you're a little old and a little 'not Italian enough' to be her."

"Ever hear of a daughter favoring the mother? What do you want Gunner. A DNA test?"

Gunner turned to Hunt. "Your boy here sure doesn't speak much."

"He speaks when he's told to speak."

"You banging him, too?"

Mandy stormed over to his desk and slapped him hard.

Gunner stood and backhanded her. Hunt flew across the desk, tackling Gunner. He sent one solid punch to his chin then held him by the tie, ready for another. Hunt held his fist high, ready to swing again.

Mandy shouted, "Stop it! Let him go."

Hunt lowered his fist but still held on tight to Gunner's tie. He pulled him closer to his face. "Touch her again, and I'll fucking kill you. Understand?"

Gunner nodded. As Hunt stood, he showed no fear at the four guns pointed at him.

Mandy wasn't surprised at the reaction from the men. Hunt's mere stare said enough. She'd forgotten how intimidating he could be.

"Drop 'em," Gunner said, and everyone complied.

Hunt offered Gunner his hand to help him up, and he accepted. He dusted himself off once he stood. "I think we've established a pecking order here."

"Sorry it came to that. I tried to be matter-of-fact about it," Mandy said.

"I would have liked this to come from Eddie first."

Mandy pulled out her cell phone. "You want me to get him here? Prepare for more of what Hammer gave you. You know Eddie hates being on the street."

"No. We're good."

"All right then. You stop worrying about who my legs are spread for and concentrate on work. You'd best straighten up whatever rumors are going around about Vince's daughter."

He eyed Hunt. "No disrespect, but you know how word on the street goes. I have to ask. Does that include the rumors that you're doing Darin?"

"I've heard the rumors and dealt with it the best I can. Darin and I are on the same page about this. He'll do what he can from his end, too. Now can we get back to my original question? What the hell is going on around here?"

Gunner excused his men then pointed at Hunt. "Does he need to be here?"

"Consider us attached at the hip," Hunt said.

"Amanda?"

"He stays. He may be a new face for you, but I can tell you nothing will be going on without his knowledge. If you see him without me, know he's speaking for me. Understood?"

"Yeah, yeah." He closed the door and went back behind his desk. "You want to know what's going on? I can't tell you."

"Can't or won't?" Hunt asked.

"Can't explain it," Gunner said at a growl. "People are getting capped left and right. It's like nothing we've ever seen before."

"What's your take on this? I know you're not dumb enough to think we don't have enemies."

"Of course not, but that has always been there. No one has ever acted out like this. Remember back when you were hanging with Angelo, and we thought there was an undercover fed?"

"I do remember. They wanted to cap Face for it, and I stopped them."

"I didn't know that."

"He was good to us. I couldn't see him go down on a rumor. I actually stopped Gerard from killing him."

"Guess he probably would have preferred that to life in prison." He motioned his head toward Hunt. "Can I ask again exactly who this is? Without getting hit?"

"He's with me. That's not enough?"

"With what is going on? No. Just when did he step into the spotlight?"

Mandy turned to Hunt. The question had caught her off guard. Hunt spoke up, saving her from stammering.

"Vince had me protecting her from the day she was released. She's a feisty cuss to say the least, but I do my job. Just because Vince isn't here to answer to doesn't mean I can walk away. I may not be family, but I owe him my life, therefore, I owe Amanda mine. Good enough answer for you?"

Mandy held back her smile. She wasn't sure how she felt about Hunt being able to lie on the spot. In this case, it was a good thing.

"So, you did know Vince."

"He hired me personally. Said he wasn't going to take someone off the street here. I'm military trained if you need to know. Special Ops. I hold no regard for the law if you think that's an issue. I was dishonorably discharged. Attitude problem."

"Now that makes sense."

"Vince thought it would be a good fit, knowing his daughter's reputation. He didn't want her back here anymore than you do."

"That's enough, Hammer."

"Yes, ma'am." Hunt resumed a stance as if he was awaiting his next order.

Gunner laughed. "Military. What the hell next?"

"You satisfied yet?"

"He ain't my problem. What's out there is my problem."

"So. Theories. Let's have it."

"It ain't the feds."

Mandy played along. "You sure?"

"You know how they work. They watch us for a year, and then decide to start thinking about doing something. They don't start killing."

"Cops?"

"We own too many of 'em."

"So what? A vigilante?"

"What does the average Joe give a shit for?"

"Someone's kid was killed in a drug incident. Someone's daughter was involved with one of our boys. It wouldn't take much."

Mandy was suddenly slammed to the ground by Hunt. Before she even hit the carpet, a shot hit the wall behind her. She turned her attention to Gunner. He was fine. His gun had been drawn, but he was already putting it away.

"You sure make enemies fast, Mandy," Gunner said as Hunt helped her to her feet. They peered out the shattered office window at Axle. Jeff had pinned him to the ground. "I guess someone is still holding a grudge."

Gunner walked out of the office and over to the men. He shooed Jeff aside and kicked Axle hard in the stomach. "If we weren't already men short, I'd kill you myself."

"There's no way we killed Angelo, man. Bitch is lying."

Mandy reached for Gunner's weapon and pointed it at Axle's head. "Call me 'bitch' one more time."

Axle pinched his eyes shut. "We didn't hurt him that bad."

"He's gone, asshole. You and your brother did more than your share."

"Bullshit."

Mandy moved her gaze to Hunt then down to Axle. Hunt took the cue and pulled him to his feet by his shirt.

"Who hired you to do this?"

"No one. He was just due for a pounding. Been getting cocky lately. He needed to be put in his place." Axle spit then added, "Bitch."

Mandy swung her hand back to punch him, but Hunt caught her mid-air with his left hand then followed through with his right fist to Axle's stomach. Axle dropped to his knees and swore. Hunt let go of Mandy and pulled him back to his feet.

"Try again."

Axle looked back and forth between the two of them. "We were just supposed to hold him for a few days. They said someone was going to come get him. They wanted him out of the way."

"For what?"

"What the hell do I know? I don't turn down twenty grand and a go-ahead to beat up on his drunken punk ass."

"Who paid you?"

"I don't know where it came from. Ray delivered it."

"Ray?" Mandy's voice raised a few octaves as she turned back to Gunner.

He raised his hands up. "I swear this didn't come from us, Mandy. I swear it."

"When were you supposed to let him go?"

"We didn't get that info, man. He said we'd get word. We got you instead."

Mandy held the gun to his forehead for a minute then spun it around and gave it back to Gunner. "We're done here. I'll be in touch."

"What about tomorrow's shipment?"

"Handle it as you would. I'm not up to speed on deliveries yet. My priority is to find out what is going on." She motioned to Axle. "Keep a leash on your pets, or I'll cage them myself."

Mandy had the shower on extra hot. She told Hunt she needed to relax her muscles. There was a hot tub out back, but she didn't want to prance around Eddie's men in a bikini. Even though she was pretty much operating on her own, he still had three men at the house at all times.

The shower stall was large with two shower heads. She faced the wall with her shoulders in both streams, trying to relax and not think about anything.

"You okay, baby?"

Mandy jumped at the sound of Hunt's voice. She turned to find him joining her. "Fine. Just tense."

"Well, that's understandable." He rubbed her shoulders.

"Thanks for the save with Gunner. That was fast thinking on your part."

"I know you don't want to hear it, but it was fun. I didn't know I had it in me either. I have to say again that you really turn me on when you're a hard-ass."

She turned around and faced him. "I turn you on when I breathe, Hunt." She motioned her eyes down to his crotch.

"That's true, but not fair. You are naked."

"I was taught to shower this way. Sue me." She took his hand and kissed it. "I wish you would have let me punch Axle. I know that stuff isn't you, Hunt. Don't try so hard to play the part."

"He called you a bitch. I was happy to deck him." He pulled her hand to his lips and gave it a kiss. "I don't want you to hurt these gorgeous hands. Every part of you is hot stuff, woman. And I'm not talking about the temperature in here either. I'm surprised I got this reaction in this heat."

"I'm not." Mandy turned back around. "Get back to the shoulders, Hammer."

He chuckled. "I am so going to pay you back for that name someday."

"I'm sorry. I didn't expect to have to use it again. Ow!"

"Sorry. You have a knot."

"So 'Hammer' it out for me."

He bent down slightly and slid himself between her legs but didn't enter her. When he began to move forward and back, she reached out with one hand to brace herself against the shower wall. She reached with the other and held onto his back.

"Like this?" he asked before he gently bit at her neck and continued to tease her with his strokes. His hands moved from her shoulders, down her back, and then around to cup her breasts. One hand stayed while the other roamed down. Mandy moaned at his touch. She moved her hand from his back to his front and took hold of him. Hunt let out a growl as she guided him in.

Within moments, Mandy leaned back into Hunt, completely satisfied. She wrapped both arms around his back and held him tight, letting out a long moan of contentment.

"Damn, baby. You must really be all kinds of stressed. That was pretty quick, even for you."

She turned and faced him. "Nope. You're just that good. How about you? I was being a little selfish there. I don't think I took you across the finish line."

"I want out of the shower."

"Not doing it for you?"

"No. But you are. Come on."

Hunt took Mandy by the hand. They turned off the faucets and made their way to the bed. Hunt wasted no time continuing where Mandy left off. "I do believe it's a two-for kind of night," he said with a playful growl.

"I think you're right."

Mandy didn't lie. When Hunt finally climaxed, she was right there with him. She could only giggle shamelessly at the noises that had escaped her.

Hunt nibbled at her ear. "Nice one, babe. Should I go for number three?"

"No! You trying to kill me?"

He laughed. "I just like pleasing you."

"Oh, you please me all right. You pleased me right into a puddle. If anyone decided to shoot the place up right now, we'd be toast."

He smiled and gave her lips a kiss then spread a few down her chest and across her breasts.

"I mean it, Hunt."

"I know. But I can't resist the girls."

She ran her fingers through this hair. There wasn't much with it cut so short, but she loved to do it anyway. He rolled to her side and pulled her close.

After a moment of silence Mandy said, "I don't want to spoil the moment."

"So don't." Hunt scooted her up so they were eye level. "I know. I miss her, too."

"Why am I doing this? I don't want to be here. I want to be home with my baby."

"Your baby is a toddler. She's fine with my parents."

"I know she's fine. That doesn't help how much I want her to be with me and not them."

"I miss her, too, but I want to say something, and I don't want you getting pissed at me."

"That means I'll get pissed at you," she said in frustration.

"Not if you hear me out."

Mandy rolled away and stood. She pulled on a robe. "You won't even let me speak?"

"I'm worn out, Hunt. I need food. If you're going to make me mad at you, I want ice cream."

He stood and put a robe on as well. "I'll come with you. I could use sustenance myself."

The house was dark except for the glow of a light above the kitchen sink. Mandy went to the freezer for ice cream. "Can you look for spoons, hon?" Since they had been there, they had yet to do anything for themselves. It was no Hilton, but Mandy enjoyed the break from cooking.

She removed them each a pint of something then walked over to the couch. "You find them?"

He held them up. "In drawer number twenty-two. You need me."

CHAPTER TWELVE

Mandy tried to read the labels, but the lighting was too dim. She gave Hunt a tub of ice cream then dug into hers. She moaned as she took a bite.

"What kind did you get?" Hunt asked.

"Cookie dough, although I don't care what I have right now. If you don't like what you have, we'll switch."

Hunt took a bite and shrugged. "Something chocolate and crunchy. It's okay."

Mandy leaned forward and took a spoonful of his. She swapped tubs. "You never were a fan of nuts in things."

"I didn't really care. You wore me out, babe." After another bite he said, "I'd still like to go back and get number three out of you."

"Not if you piss me off."

He chuckled. "All I was going to say was, I know you miss Hannah, but I can't help but also feel like part of you is enjoying this."

"You're insane." Mandy jabbed her spoon into the tub.

"Babe, I'm not upset. You are an incredible mother and wife. There's something about you when you are in charge and kicking ass. It's like you were made for it."

"You know I don't want to return to this life."

"I think you're trying to convince yourself more than you're trying to convince me."

She finally put her pint down. "Just because I'm good at it doesn't mean I want it, Hunt. You know how much I want another baby."

"One thing has nothing to do with the other."

"Like hell it doesn't. How could I do a job like this and go home to my kids?"

"Same as anyone else in the field. I may have it relatively easy, but don't you think there are thousands of cops and firemen that wonder every day as they kiss their families goodbye if it could be for the last time?"

"Of course. That's exactly why I can't do it."

"But you love it."

Mandy scooted over and straddled Hunt. She rested her head on his shoulder. "I don't want to fight."

"Does it sound like I'm fighting? I'm only stating facts."

"Well, so am I. Maybe I like it to an extent, but I'm done, Hunt. I'm not going to run to the FBI looking for my job back."

"Their loss."

She leaned back and stared deep into his eyes. "You actually want me back in?"

"No. I don't want you back in, but I want you to be happy."

She rested her head back down. "You make me happy."

"Happy enough?"

"More than happy enough."

Hunt leaned forward and placed his ice cream on the coffee table. With one arm he shifted Mandy up while the other opened their robes. He slid her back down slowly, entering her as he did so. "More than happy?" he whispered.

"Third time's a charm."

Mandy almost forgot where they were. She had to be careful to keep the noise down. All she needed was one of the guys wandering out of their room, wondering what the commotion was. Hunt apparently wasted no such fears on being discovered. He kept himself glued to Mandy's breasts, which made it exceptionally harder for her to keep quiet. She did manage to keep her robe over her shoulders in case she needed to cover up in a hurry. Being on round three did nothing for the intensity of her orgasm. Mandy buried her face into Hunt's neck and hoped his body muffled her sounds enough. They both jumped when a hall light clicked on. Mandy hopped off Hunt and closed her robe as fast as she could. He did the same, and they both quickly picked up their ice creams and leaned back. She tried to look as nonchalant as possible.

Milo turned the corner and stopped abruptly. "Munchie attack?"

"Ice cream sounded good." Mandy said. "I hope these weren't yours."

"They're anybody's. You guys hear that racket?"

Mandy fought a laugh, and Hunt spoke. "I think there were a couple of cats outside."

"Damn pests." He opened the freezer and joined them in a few minutes with some ice cream of his own. He sat down and looked over at them, going from one to the other. "Did I interrupt something?"

"Just talking. You're fine, Milo." Hunt reached an arm around Mandy and pulled her closer.

"You getting anywhere?" he asked Mandy.

"I'm getting the word spread that I'm in charge, but that's it for now. I have Willy's team believing it. That's where I expected the most resistance. From here it'll be a matter of getting to the bottom of things."

"So...you're done except for finding out who's doing the killing and being careful not to be killed yourself."

"In a nutshell, I suppose."

"Eddie is crazier than I thought."

"What do you mean?"

"I still don't get why he brought you back."

"My guess still is that he couldn't handle Angelo and hoped I could."

"But you were long gone. This is family business. He might as well have invited the feds in here."

Mandy choked on a nut. "Sorry. Praline."

Hunt patted her back. "It wasn't my choice for her to come back into this either, but I have to respect her decision. I can only hope Eddie will hold true to his word and leave her and Angelo alone when this is all said and done."

"It's not easy getting out. No one has done it. Not that I'm aware of, anyway."

"Maybe no one has ever wanted to," Mandy said. "You remember how I got in. I didn't know what I was marrying into. My husband was killed, and I thought I could leave. I guess Eddie had other plans."

"I know it doesn't seem like it, but Eddie likes you. Maybe you're too valuable a player to let go."

"No way. He thinks he needs me now, so I'm playing along. When this is over, I'm not staying. No way in hell."

"Well, I hope you're right." Milo stood. "Gonna finish this over some B horror mobster movie on TNT. Good night, you two."

"Good night, Milo."

"If you hear that cat again, shoot it would ya?"

Mandy laughed. "I'll get right on that."

"I'll get on that," Hunt said under his breath.

"No, you won't," Mandy said after the hall light was turned off. "I'm ready for bed."

"And I'm ready for a sandwich. This ice cream didn't cut it for me."

"You should have said something. Milo would have made it for you."

"I can handle making a sandwich, baby. He came out to chat, not play my personal man-servant."

"Want me to make you something?"

"You already make me horny. You've done enough."

Mandy opened her robe and flashed him. Hunt growled and tackled her into the couch. He kissed down her chest and past her belly button. "Maybe I don't need a sandwich. Maybe I need some more of you."

"No!" Mandy scooted out from under him and slid to the floor.

"What? Since when do you turn that down?"

"Since we're in the middle of not our living room with four other men in this house. That's not a position I want to be in when someone else decides they want ice cream."

Hunt chuckled then leaned forward and kissed her. "Go to our room. I'll be up in a minute after I make something. If you change your mind, I'll call it dessert."

"If you're more than five minutes, I'll be asleep. You wore me out."

"Ditto, but I'm still starved. I'll be as fast as I can."

"Lay off the onions or you'll be up all night."

"Yes, dear."

As Hunt dug through the refrigerator, Milo came back out. "The cat went back to bed, huh?"

Hunt turned around and smiled. "Sorry about that."

He shrugged. "If I had myself a woman here, I'd've done the same."

"You have someone waiting for you when you're done here?" Hunt asked as he opened a drawer marked "vegetables."

"What are you looking for?"

"Just wanted to make a sandwich."

"Get the hell out of my fridge and let me do my job."

"I'm capable of making a sandwich."

"You'll screw up my kitchen. Go sit." Milo motioned to some bar stools at the island, and Hunt did as he was told. "How hungry are you?"

"I could eat rhino ass. Raw."

"Marathon, huh?"

Hunt grinned. "A good husband doesn't kiss and tell."

Milo closed the drawer Hunt had opened and dug into another. He tossed three different packages of meats on the counter and two packages of cheese. Milo tucked a head of lettuce in his arm, and then held up an onion.

"It was suggested I lay off the onions."

"Won't be as good without 'em."

"You have met my wife, right?"

"Okay. No onions." Milo laughed, reached for a tomato then finally shut the door. "Best hoagie this side of Philly coming up."

"You never answered my question."

"Sorry. No. There's no woman currently."

"Should I ask?"

"Let's say explaining what I do for a living makes the dating game a little hard at my age."

"So, there was someone."

"Lost her ten years ago to cancer."

"I'm sorry."

"Thanks." Milo explained further as he cut the tomato and lettuce. "JoAnn knew what this was. She was one of Vince's men's sisters. We clicked, and back then the whole 'don't date my sister' thing really wasn't in effect. It kind of made life easier when they knew what they were up against right from the get-go. Besides, she was the love of my life. I really think you only get that once."

"I think I know what you mean. I was a devoted bachelor until I met Mandy."

"Don't mind me, but I have to admit that her showing up after all this time is kind of strange."

Hunt wished he could escape before he said something he wasn't supposed to. That sandwich was looking too damn good to abandon the conversation now. "It's just something she has to do."

"Oil?"

"Just mayo is fine."

"Trust me."

"All right."

Milo made some finishing touches then slid the sandwich to Hunt. He picked it up and took a bite. "Holy crap. Your search is over. I'll date you," he said through a full mouth.

Milo laughed and began to clean up. "Told you to trust me. Milk?"

"Just water would be fine."

Milo crossed his arms.

"Milk sounds great."

He reached for the jug after he put away the meats. "I miss the days of a milkman," he said as he poured Hunt a tall glass.

"I imagine you miss a lot of things. I'm sure this city has changed more than most over the years. My hometown..." Hunt stopped. He was probably going to give something away he shouldn't.

Milo came around and sat next to Hunt. "Your accent sounds Vermont to me."

"Yes, it is."

"You've been in Florida for a couple of years, though. Glad you haven't picked up that y'all yet."

Hunt laughed. "Are you that good or am I getting hosed here?"

Milo lowered his voice. "I know more than you think, but we don't need to discuss it. No one else knows quite who Mandy is. I was tighter with Vince than these men know. I'm glad she's back, but I'm even happier it's not for good. Angelo has missed her. I'm glad she's doing what she is to help him."

"It's nice to have someone on our side."

"Eddie's men are on your side, they just don't know the extent of it. They have always done as they were told. Half of them would shoot their mothers if they were told to. No, I take that back. All of them would."

"If they knew what we really were—"

"You'd be toast. Your secret is safe with me. I'm here to fill hungry bellies, nothing more."

"That's enough for you?"

"Eddie promised me a restaurant when this is over. Of course I'll still cater to the same people, and he'll have his take, but it'll be mine. Maybe I'll surround the place with beautiful waitresses and have plenty to choose from."

"I hope you do."

As Hunt finished his sandwich, they shared small talk. When he was done, he stood and picked up his plate. Milo promptly took it from him. "I do clean up, too."

Milo stood, and Hunt extended his hand. "Thanks for the sandwich and the talk."

"My pleasure. Go be with that woman before I steal her from you."

"If you made her that sandwich, I think that's entirely possible. Thanks again."

Hunt entered the room as quietly as he could, not wanting to wake Mandy if she was asleep. She was lying on the bed on her back and hadn't moved. The bathroom light was left on and the door cracked enough for light to come through. He brushed his teeth, turned off the light then slid into bed. Mandy rolled on her side and rested her head on Hunt's chest, draping her arm over him.

"I thought you were asleep. You change your mind about dessert?" he asked softly.

Her only response was a heavy breath and a light stroking of his chest. She was asleep. This is how they usually slept together. Hunt smiled at how the simplest things made him feel at home. No matter what was going on, he was happy to be here with her. He wrapped his arms around her and kissed the top of her head. "Good night, my love."

Chapter Thirteen

Mandy was surprised when she woke up on Hunt's chest. He stroked her arm when she moved. "Good morning, sleepyhead."

"I don't remember you coming in last night."

"You were out cold."

"Well, someone wore me out."

"Really? Should I take him out?"

"Oh. I don't know. He's pretty big and strong. I think he could take you."

Hunt growled and flipped Mandy onto her back. He pressed his chest on her, holding her down.

Mandy laughed. "Uncle."

"Oh, come on. You could get the best of me, and you know it."

"It's too early for a wrestling match, Hunt."

"Is it too early for my dessert?"

"My goodness you have a one-track mind."

"And you don't?" He gave her a kiss and got up. "That Milo makes one hell of a hoagie."

"You had company last night?"

"He came back out when he heard me digging in the fridge. He really protects his kitchen."

"I've always loved him. He's too nice of a man to be doing what he does."

"F—Y—I, he didn't buy the cat story."

Mandy grinned. "I didn't suppose he did."

"You want to shower with me?"

"We'll never get out of here if I do. I'm good from last night."

"I said shower, not sex."

"I know, jackass." She laughed. "That, too. I'm fine. I'm ready for coffee. Meet you downstairs."

Mandy was on her second helping of eggs Benedict when Hunt joined her downstairs. "Good morning, Milo." He poured a cup of coffee before joining Mandy at the table.

"Good morning yourself. You sleep as good as your wife here?"

"Better, I think. You've spoiled me. I think next time I'm craving a late snack, I'm waking your ass up."

"I'd rather that than my kitchen turned upside down."

"Hunt actually isn't bad in the kitchen, Milo. You'd be impressed."

"Doubt it." He placed a plate in front of Hunt. "Should I start another batch?"

"This will do. I'm still good from that bus-sized sandwich last night."

"Lucky for me your wife has an appetite."

"You never have to worry about that."

The light mood left when Eddie walked through the door. Milo stiffened up. "Good morning, Eddie. Coffee?"

"Sure."

"You eat yet?"

"Hell, no. That's half the reason I showed up."

"I'll get right on it."

Eddie took a seat across from the two of them. "No good morning?"

Mandy finally spoke. "Good morning. You're hungry. I'm dying to know the other reason you showed up."

"Why do I look like I just disturbed the party?"

"Because I don't know why you're here. You agreed to let me handle things."

"I did. I'm not doing anything, just following up. I am allowed to do that, right?"

"There's nothing to tell you. I've dealt with Gunner. That was enough for yesterday."

"I heard Axle tried to get at you."

"We handled it."

"It would have also been helpful if you let me know you killed off Angelo. You're lucky I caught on and have a great poker face."

"I told you that was my plan." Mandy didn't let his intrusion affect her appetite. She ignored him as best she could. At least until he dropped two leather wallets onto the table. She picked up the badges and put them in her robe pocket.

"You want to explain those?" Eddie asked.

Mandy lowered her voice, concerned about Milo overhearing. "What the hell are you doing, digging in our car?"

"You can screw yourself senseless all over this house, but you pull any shit like this on me, and I'll have your ass mounted on my wall."

Hunt slid his chair back. "You son of a bitch. You're watching us?"

Mandy took his hand. "Don't, Hunt. We need to pick our battles here. I should have suspected as much." She turned back to Eddie and lowered her voice. "I don't think we should do this here."

"Milo knows," Hunt said.

"He what?" both Mandy and Eddie shouted.

"Doesn't he? I just kind of thought he did."

Mandy gave Hunt's hand a squeeze, and he shut up. Something was wrong. Time to deflect. "I'll ask again. What were you doing searching our car?"

Eddie lowered his voice. "More importantly, why do you have them?"

Mandy leaned back. "You knew I went to talk to an old friend at the agency. I didn't think I had any friends left, but I had to try."

"And?"

"And I was right. They are staying out of it. They don't care if you guys shoot each other to hell."

"So why the badges?"

"Change of heart, I guess. I'm not working for them, Eddie. I'm working for Angelo. As soon as this is done, I'm through with all of you. Again."

"He explained it as a sort of 'get out of jail free' card," Hunt added. "They aren't helping, won't claim any interference one way or another."

"I didn't want the badge, Eddie. You know that. You have anything better to do than watch us? Can't you get someone on the street yourself and use your time more wisely? You're the big, bad fucking mob, and you needed—" She stopped talking as Milo walked over with a plate for Eddie.

"Thanks, Milo," Eddie said.

Milo asked Hunt. "Anything more for you?"

"I'm good. Thanks."

He nodded and went back to the stove. Two more men wandered out of their bedrooms.

"Oh good, Beavis and Butthead are up," Hunt mumbled.

"You two, eat fast and go relieve John and Greg."

"Of course, boss."

"Give us a few minutes alone, would you?"

"Sure, boss."

After they left, Mandy continued. "You forced me here, Eddie. I told you to let me do this my way."

"If your way has any funny ideas about putting me behind bars, you best think it all the way through."

Mandy stood. "Don't flatter yourself. The jail is probably rat-infested. I wouldn't want to put such poor company with them." She walked away, but Hunt stayed back.

"She's not lying. I was there. She didn't ask for the badge, Eddie," Hunt said. "We've talked this to death. She swears up and down she doesn't want that life again."

"And we both know she's full of shit."

Hunt let out a heavy sigh. "I'm afraid so. That's my problem to deal with later. You have nothing to worry about as far as her here. None of this is about you unless you make it that way."

"You're no one to be telling me anything."

"You're right. Don't listen to a thing I have to say. Mandy is dead set on getting to the bottom of this because she wants to go home and leave you guys behind her forever. First and foremost, she wants to help Angelo. As far as the FBI goes, she's not involved with you in any way. But if she finds out you have something to do with the killings..." Hunt stood. He didn't need to finish his sentence.

"Are you threatening me?"

"I'm not. This isn't my business. I'm nobody, remember? I'm playing along for my wife. I don't trust any of you as far as I can throw you. The sooner we're out of here, the better. I'd appreciate a little discretion on your part when we are alone."

"No one watches you here except when you come and go. It was just a good hunch." Eddie grinned in a way that made Hunt want to slap it off him.

"I have to go get dressed. People to maim today and all." He took a step to walk away then paused. "Thanks for the meal again, Milo."

"My pleasure."

"So, Milo, exactly how much were you paying attention over there?"

Milo approached him, placed a plate on the table, and hollered for the men to come eat. "You know me, Eddie. I keep my nose out of what ain't my business. I haven't been the cook around here for thirty-some years by sticking my nose where it doesn't belong." He lowered his voice. "That Mandy can scream like a cat in heat when she wants, though."

Eddie laughed. "That's what Gerard used to say." He took a sip of coffee. "This is kind of fun watching her dig her own grave."

"Yeah. I don't know what's keeping her here. You think she'd take Angelo and split."

"She was always a strange breed. I never did see what Vince saw in her. I'm tired of putting up with her shit already. If I wasn't so curious to see what she thinks she's going to do, I'd get rid of her now."

"Now where's the sport in that, Eddie? You always did enjoy a good show."

"There is that."

The other two guards joined them at the table, and Milo returned to the stove.

"Oh, Milo?"

"Yeah, boss?"

"How do you like the looks of the place next to the suit shop on 9th?"

"Been there a few times. Great atmosphere. Why?"

"All yours when this gig is up."

"Really?"

"Really. It's recently come available. We're prettying the place up for you."

"Hot waitresses on order?"

"Of course."

"About time."

Eddie chuckled.

Hunt joined Mandy in the bedroom. She was getting dressed for the day with an extra slam to everything and a stomp in her step.

"Don't let him get to you, baby."

"How can I not? I have half a mind to blow him away myself and say screw it to everything."

"Who's stopping you?"

Frustrated, she dropped her arms at her side. "You know that's not how I work, Hunt. You'd no sooner do it, either."

"Don't tempt me. I just had a charming five minutes with him."

"What did he say?"

"Nothing new." He closed the gap between them and took her hands in his. "You sure you want to keep this up? We have Angelo safe, let's split. We'll move again and be sure they can't find us this time."

"I don't want to move, Hunt. I like being close to your parents. I'm not having Eddie chase us from our home. I don't want to have this conversation with you every ten minutes."

"I'm sorry, but things are really going down funny. Have you stopped long enough to wonder what your part in all of this is? I mean really, Mandy. Bring in an outsider? This is the mob, not some office bringing in an F—N—G to play manager."

"F—N—G?"

"The new guy."

Mandy pulled herself free. "Enough with your jokes. Don't you think I've tried to make sense of that?" She started to walk away but turned back to Hunt. "What did you mean when you said Milo knew?"

Hunt glanced back to the door as if he were afraid someone was listening. He walked up to Mandy again and explained what transpired the night before. "I sort of let the comment roll away. I thought maybe he was a part of things back when you were in, and he knew you were a fed."

"If he knew, I never knew it. By the sounds of things, Eddie doesn't know he knows, either. Now I don't know what the hell to think about Milo." Her voice was at a whisper. "Do you think he could be an agent?"

"I don't think that's likely. He sounded pretty 'in' with the bunch, babe. He said he's getting a restaurant out of the deal soon."

"He's said that for years. I think Vince was jerking his chain to keep him to himself."

"Then what? How could he know about me if Eddie didn't tell him?"

"I don't know. Just add one more thing into the mix that I don't like about this situation."

"You could try talking to him."

"Not with Eddie here. I want to get going. We'll have to do it later."

"Whose fingers are on today's agenda?"

"We're going to see an old friend."

Hunt thought about it for a second. "An old friend behind bars?"

Mandy stroked his chest. "Not only big and strong but brains, too. That's why I married you."

Pulling her toward him by the waist, Hunt planted a hard kiss on her lips. "I gave you no choice."

"I didn't want another choice."

Chapter Fourteen

When Mandy had been in protective custody, she had moved to Rockville, Maryland. The FBI had wanted her someplace like Montana or Oregon, but she'd insisted she needed city life, and they'd finally given in. The town was big enough that she could blend in and not be noticed. She'd wanted to dye her hair blonde to change her looks but had been advised against it while she was pregnant. Not really worried that she would be hunted, she'd left it. She wasn't bold enough for a dramatic cut. A lot of hats and large sunglasses had helped her feel safe when she was out.

She'd enjoyed the location of her new, temporary home. There were just a few blocks for her to walk to the train station. From there it was less than an hour to get to D.C. The museums never got old. Mandy had wandered them weekly for months.

By the time the initial trial was over and she was moved there, her pregnancy had been showing. Even if she'd wanted to take a menial job, she probably wouldn't have been hired. She hadn't needed the money, but she'd often grown bored.

Mandy positioned herself on the ground at the Washington Monument with her butt flush up to it and her legs flat against the white bricks. Her hands were wrapped around her six-month pregnant belly, and her mind went to where it always did when she was trying to lose herself in thought. Hunt.

As she rubbed her stomach, a tear ran from her eye. She harshly wiped it away and sat up with her back against the monument. She loved to stare up Washington's most famous phallic symbol while on her back, but her belly no longer allowed her to do so. She dried her eyes on her maternity shirt. She couldn't take the loneliness and removed her cell phone from her purse. Even though it was against the rules, Mandy called her college roommate, Shelley. Thirty minutes later, she turned at the sound of her name.

"Amanda?"

By the time Mandy got to her feet, Shelley was at her side. A crying gasp escaped her, and she held her friend tight.

"Honey, what's wrong?"

The friends held hands as they walked. Shelley stopped and placed her hand on Mandy's stomach. "I still can't believe you're knocked up."

Mandy playfully pushed her hand away with a laugh. "Knock it off already. I promise I'm not concealing a basketball."

"Why are you here alone? Where's the father?"

Mandy continued to walk. "That's a long story."

"So. I'm starved. Let's talk over lunch."

After paying for hot dogs, Shelley offered Mandy one then grasped her free hand. "We going to do the memorial walk?" Shelley asked.

"You mind?"

"Of course not."

Mandy briefly rested her head on Shelley's shoulder. "I miss them so much."

"I know. I miss you more, though." Shelley gave Mandy's hand a squeeze. "I haven't been back here since we spread their ashes. That was hard."

"It's what they would have wanted. They loved this place."

Shelley let a slight laugh escape. "Your dad would have tanned our asses if he saw us as stumbling drunk as we were while scattering them everywhere."

Mandy managed a smile. "It's more fun than two urns of ashes ever had."

Her parents had met in DC and visited every year. The one year they chose to go to Hawaii instead, they died in a helicopter tour crash on Kauai. Mandy was devastated but couldn't bring herself to return for the funeral. She was an only child, just like her parents. There was no one she longed to see. No one that could comfort her. The ashes and settlement notification from their lawyers were delivered the following week. Mandy did the only thing she thought they would have wanted.

After walking in silence for a few minutes, Shelley finally asked the question Mandy had been waiting for.

"So...are you going to tell me why you dropped off the face of the earth on me?"

"I want to explain it all, Shelley. I just don't know where to start. Technically I shouldn't even be here with you now."

"Well, why the fuck not? You're my best friend, dammit."

"I'm in witness relocation."

"You're what?"

"I was hired out of college for the FBI. A case they threw me on went sour. It's hard to explain. I was set up to fail and didn't...sort of."

"Holy shit, Mand. You're FBI? Holy shit."

"Ex-FBI, and it was short-lived. It's going to take more time to explain than I want to waste. I just needed someone. I picked this town, hoping to get brave enough to call you someday."

Hot dogs now finished, they strolled over to the closest vendor to get a pretzel. Mandy was a bottomless pit lately, but this was their routine anyway.

Mandy's hands were once again on her belly when Shelley asked, "So where does the father come into all of this?"

"When things went sour, I was told to back off the case—"

"Only you didn't."

Mandy grinned. "Was I always this way?"

Shelley spoke through a mouthful of pretzel. "Hell, yeah. Please continue."

"I went after someone on my own and got caught in a small town by the local sheriff."

"Caught with your pants down, huh?"

Mandy choked on her pretzel.

Shelley patted her back. "Sorry."

"Brat. Anyway...one thing led to another and he ended up helping me. Of course, I had been lying to him about my reasons. Things were intense. I guess we just turned to each other. It was stupid for me to let any of it happen. What little there was between us is over. He doesn't even know I'm pregnant."

"Why is it over?"

"Screwing because we were under stress doesn't mean anything. It's nothing to build a relationship on. And don't even start with me about how he deserves to be told about the baby. It's best if he never finds out."

"How do you know? It sounds to me like you're not even giving him a chance."

"Shelley, I love you, but come on. Be serious for a minute. He was set in his ways. He's the town hottie and not about to throw it away because we were stuck together for a few nights without a condom. I'm too old to be this irresponsible. I have enough money stashed aside. We'll be okay."

Shelley took her hand. "Okay. I trust you. You were just always the one with her head on her shoulders. You were my rock, Mand. It killed me seeing you cry."

"I was just excited to see you. I've missed you." Mandy's head lowered to her chest. "I don't know when I can see you again."

"But you're so close to me now after all this time. Can't we agree to meet up sometime? We'll switch it up. Never meet at the same place twice. I can do this cloak and dagger stuff. No one has to know. You're going to need someone when the baby comes, and I want to be there for you."

"I want to...I'll just have to see." Mandy gave her friend a strong hug and again fought tears. "I love and miss you so much."

"So, talk to someone. Let's fix this."

Mandy wiped away her tears. "I'll try. Thanks for coming."

"Like you could keep me away. Please, Mand. Let's do this again soon."

"I'll try. I promise."

When she got back to her house, two agents were supervising a team of movers.

"What the fuck is this shit?" she hollered as she threw her purse across the room.

"You broke protocol."

"For calling Shelley? What the hell is this? You're bugging my phone now?"

"What do you mean 'now?'"

She wanted to slap the grin off the agent's face. "You son of a bitch."

"A son of a bitch that needs you alive at the hearing for William Roberts. You don't know that the mob isn't watching you. You just put your friend's life at risk."

"I haven't been in touch with her in over a year. No one is watching her."

"We are. Why wouldn't they be?"

"You can't be serious."

"Do I look like I'm kidding?"

Mandy stormed into her room. "Prick." She took a suitcase from under the bed and proceeded to stuff her clothes in it. Bastards weren't packing her underwear.

The agent joined her after a minute. "I would get the notion of getting in touch with that sheriff out of your head while you're at it."

"I never thought about calling him."

He looked down at her belly. "Yes, you have. If you value his life at all, stay away, Agent Smith."

"Fuck you. I'm not an agent anymore."

Before heading to the prison to see Willy, Mandy called James to assure they would be allowed in.

"He's on a short leash," James explained. "But I can get you in. After he flapped his gums about you, Ray and Gunner were cut off, but there are still exceptions made. It won't be a problem. Show your badge and give them my name. I'll call ahead and set it up."

Hunt and Mandy were led into the private meeting room. Willy was handcuffed and a guard stood by.

"You?" Willy said with disgust. "You took me out of yard time for the likes of her?"

"You can un-cuff him and go," Mandy said to the guard. "We'll be all right."

"I have my orders to stay with him."

"Well, consider this another one." Hunt's tone was intimidating, but Mandy didn't think the guard would listen.

The guard hesitated for just a minute. "I'll give you ten minutes alone, but the cuffs stay on."

Mandy was grateful he gave in. She nodded. "Thank you."

After he left, Willy spoke. "What the hell are you doing back? Thought we'd seen the last of you."

"I had hoped so, too. Eddie brought me back."

"What on earth for? You were nothing but a pawn."

"Maybe, but I'm a pawn that Eddie seems to need."

He laughed hard. "You were a joke. Eddie doesn't need anything from you."

"Apparently he does now. I don't have to justify any of this to you nor am I going to waste my breath explaining it. I'm sure no matter what kind of hold they think they have on you, you know everything, anyway."

"They told me Angelo was dead."

"That didn't take long at all," Hunt said. "I think we came to the right guy for information, babe."

Willy ignored Hunt. "I don't have anything for you."

"Sure you do, Face." Mandy turned a chair around and sat down with the back of it facing him. "You played undercover so well, you had me sticking up for you when I thought I was the only rat. You still have a good bunch of them convinced you shouldn't be in here."

"Your point?"

"I know you still have ties at the agency. I need to find out just what side they're on."

"Seriously? You think the feds want anything to do with me?" He stood and leaned toward Mandy. Hunt moved closer and stood at the table between them. Willy looked up at Hunt, frowned, and then sat back down.

Mandy continued. "I'm not back in with them, so I can't say. I did go to speak to someone briefly about this—"

"Asking for help?"

"No. I was trying to get a feel for who knew what. I know someone knows what's going on. I'm sure nothing has changed. They know, and they aren't doing a damn thing about it."

"Hell, Mandy. You were no different. You were working for them but screwing Gerard every chance you could."

"Watch it," Hunt warned.

Willy laughed. "What? Like she's not blowing you on stakeouts, too, Mister Big Time Sheriff."

Hunt grasped the back of Willy's head and smashed it into the table in one quick jolt. Willy picked his head up and brought his hands to his bleeding nose. "You son of a bitch! You broke my nose."

"It's not broken, you big baby. You watch how you talk to my wife."

"Mandy, would you get a leash on your dog? Fuck!" He held his nose again and dropped his head between his knees.

Mandy kept her face expressionless. "Sorry. I must have missed a feeding."

Willy raised his head. "You mean a—" He looked at Hunt and stopped. "What do you want from me? Ask and get the fuck out."

"Who was your contact at the office?"

"Doesn't matter."

"That's for me to decide."

"He's not there anymore, anyway."

"I'm in a great position to take out one of your kneecaps."

"Jesus, Mandy! You know I dealt with Dan. He's kind of out of the question now, isn't he?"

"Who else?"

"There was no one else. The only one I've been in contact with since that day at the cabin is that Agent Stoner."

"James?"

"Yeah. James. You asked, I answered. Is that it? Because I have a few questions myself."

"James? Six feet, brown kind of curly hair? Used to run the training course?"

"I didn't do no training there. You know they took me off the street and bribed me into cooperating, but yeah, sounds like him."

Hunt and Mandy shared a quick glance.

Willy grinned. "He's screwing you, isn't he?"

Hunt glared, and he backed up a bit. "I mean, screwing you over, ass wipe, not you know, screwing her."

"Just quit while you're ahead," Hunt said as he crossed his arms.

"Who are you talking to from the gang? Besides Gunner?"

"Don't even get to talk to Gunner anymore."

"Who is feeding you info, then? How did you hear about Angelo?"

"You know how news travels in here. How does anyone hear anything? Now it's my turn. Is it bullshit about Angelo?"

"Why would you think that?"

"He just seemed...you know, untouchable."

"Vince was murdered, Face. No one is untouchable."

"Yeah, but Eddie brought you in to get him out then he's dead? That sounds fishy, even to me."

"Don't put that on me. If Eddie got off his ass sooner, maybe I could have helped."

Willy nervously searched out the door for the guard. "You don't think that's fishy? Why would Eddie need your help?"

"I'm not an idiot. I'm not doing anything he couldn't be doing on his own. I am curious as hell as to what the big picture is. He doesn't want me dead, or he would have done it when he found us."

"You get me out and I'll help."

It was Mandy's turn to laugh. "I'm in no position to offer you any deals. Even if I was, I wouldn't team with you, Face. How dumb do I look?"

"No comment."

"You can't teach a dumb dog new tricks," Hunt said as he took a step closer.

Willy scooted his chair back a bit. "Enough. Look. Get me out, Mandy. I'll get my boys on this thing. We'll find whoever this is. I know you think I was a sell-out, but I liked Angelo. There's no way someone from my team had anything to do with any of this. You know Axle and Kermit don't have the brains to pull that off on their own."

"So, you do know more than you're sharing."

"Get me some smokes."

Mandy motioned her head from Hunt to the guard. Clearly taking the cue, he walked out and spoke to them.

CHAPTER FIFTEEN

Hunt came back with a pack of cigarettes and a handkerchief. He tossed them both on the table. Willy reached out with his cuffed hands and removed a cigarette from the pack.

"No light?"

Hunt leaned forward with a lighter, and Willy put the cigarette in his mouth. Hunt lit it for him then stepped back. "You were saying?"

Willy let out a long exhale and shuddered as if he were on the border of an orgasm. "Damn." He finally picked up the handkerchief and wiped the blood from his nose.

"They cut you off from smoking?"

"I've been a bad boy," he said with a wink.

"Any particular reason?"

"I'm never gettin' out. What's the point in behaving?"

"You were an asshole and playing both sides. You think the feds would do something for you in here?"

"Yeah. Send me assholes to break my nose." He held his hands up, blocking another blow that didn't come. He took another drag.

"They didn't send me. I'm here on my own. Now tell me something I don't know, Face."

"I don't know what you expect me to know from in here."

"Why the song and dance then?"

"I really wanted a smoke."

Hunt took a step forward, but Mandy stopped him. She stood and kicked her foot hard into Willy's chest. The force sent him backward. She sat on his chest and held his arm still. He hadn't dropped the cigarette, so she removed it and flicked it into the corner.

Willy cried out. "Goddammit! Guards!"

One guard turned toward the door, but the other grabbed his arm, stopping him. They both turned back around with their backs against the door.

"No one's going to help a low-life like you. I'm not screwing around, Willy. Talk. Who told Kermit and Axle to grab Angelo? I know they didn't act alone."

"I don't know anything."

"What's the word on Eddie?"

"Eddie? He's as straight as my grandpa's dick. He worshiped the ground Vince walked on. He wouldn't have anything to do with Angelo getting hurt. Why? You hear otherwise?"

"I'm covering all angles. No one is beyond questioning at this point."

"What's the word with this daughter of Vince's?"

"You heard about that?"

"Of course I did."

"From who?"

"Same people. Everyone, dammit. Let me up!"

Mandy pushed herself off him, and Hunt helped get him upright.

"Can I get my smoke back?"

Mandy hesitated then placed another one in his mouth. Hunt lit it.

"Thanks."

Hunt barked at him, "Speak, or I turn her loose again."

Again, Willy hesitated with a long draw. "I'd kill for a beer." Mandy slammed her hands on the table, and Willy jumped. "Okay, okay. I heard you were passing yourself as Vince's daughter."

"What did you say?"

"Nothing. I was curious to see what you were doing."

"You haven't told anyone otherwise?"

"Nope. I kind of went along with it."

"How?"

"Said I suspected it all along."

"Why would you do that?"

"Like I said, I wanted to see what would happen."

"Gunner told me you tried to convince him I was a fed."

"And he hasn't been allowed back, has he?"

"But you still get messages to him."

Willy took another long drag and shrugged. He winced as Hunt took a step closer again. "All right! It ain't news that there's a grapevine around here. I let it drop, though. Wasn't worth solitary again."

"So, you're getting news about the killings."

"Of course."

"And you have no theory?"

"Eddie ain't involved."

"That's all you can say?"

"It ain't the dick feds. They don't have the balls."

"Then who is it?"

"No fucking clue, bitch. Now get the hell out!"

Hunt slammed Willy's head into the table again. "Now it's broken, asshole. I told you not to talk to her like that."

The guard walked in and examined Willy. He turned to Mandy, shaking his head. "Your time is more than up."

"I'll say. You won't get in trouble for this, right?"

"For the likes of him?" He scoffed. "Nope. Ain't the first time his nose has been busted in here. Wanted to do it myself on a few occasions. If shit rolls, I'm rolling it to you, though."

"I'd expect it. Thanks for your help."

The guard took Willy out. As soon as the door closed, Mandy slapped Hunt hard in the arm.

"What?"

"What did we talk about, Hunter Blaine?"

"Blair."

"This isn't funny! I talked to you in detail about hitting people over me, and this is twice now."

"I thought it would help loosen him up."

"Dammit, Hunt. You're a mobster for a few days and already you're beating people up."

"You gave me the name Hammer."

She smirked. "Stop it. Don't make me laugh, I'm pissed at you."

"I'm sorry. It's not like you went easy on him, Miss Chair Tackle."

"That's different."

"Why is it different when you do it?"

"Because I won't break something unless I mean to."

"I didn't break his nose until I meant to, either."

Mandy sighed. "Come on. Let's get out of here."

"This was a complete waste of a trip, huh?"

"I'm not so sure we're done with him. I didn't expect to get anything out of him. Although I don't like one thing he told us."

"James?"

"Yeah, James. I don't like the fact Willy says he's been talking to him."

"That kinda threw me for a loop, too. You think James is crooked like Abbey?"

"I don't know what I'm thinking right now, Hunt. Someone is issuing orders for killings, and that included us. The only hunch I have to play right now is Willy. Ray was ordered to kill us and him being Willy's guy just leads me to that conclusion. The fact that Face is in jail doesn't mean it's not him. I don't like being lied to about him still having a connection with someone at the Agency. This reeks. I need to go talk to James. And by talk, I think I mean rip his fucking face off. What are my chances of you waiting in the car?"

"Nil to none."

"Shit."

Hunt and Mandy drove back to the Federal building. When the guard tried to stop Mandy, she flashed her badge, and he took a step back.

"I didn't realize you were back with us, Agent Smith."

"That makes two of us, John."

John's attention went to Hunt. "You want me to whip mine out, too?" Hunt asked, pointing at his crotch.

Mandy elbowed him.

"What? It was an honest question." The guard waved them through.

"What is with you, Hunt?"

"Whatever do you mean, oh, love of my life?"

"Come on. Whip mine out? I have never known for your sarcasm meter to be on such full force. Ever. You haven't been yourself the past few days."

"This situation hardly calls for me being me. You'd rather me flip out with every slug we've had to deal with? It goes against everything I've wanted to do my whole life. We're not putting the bad guys away, Mandy. We're eating meals with them. You'd rather I turn up the sarcasm or have a heart attack?"

She stopped her hurried pace and took his hand. "I'm sorry. I knew you being here was a bad idea."

"And so did I, but it doesn't change anything. Just let me deal with this my own way." After glancing down the hall both ways, he took Mandy by the hips. He eased her back the few paces to the wall and placed his lips over hers. She submitted easily to the kiss and kept it going even after Hunt tried to stop. He stared at her lovingly when they finally broke apart. "That's how I really like to deal with stress."

"Happy to oblige you, kind sir."

Mandy was a little less uptight after the kiss, but not much. She'd thought she had an ally in James. Now she had to wonder about his intentions.

"He's down on the training floor with a couple of new recruits, Ms. Smith," a different secretary told them. Mandy frowned. "Sorry. Mrs...."

"Blair."

A look of slight recognition was in the secretary's eyes. "I thought it was Blaine?"

"You have to keep up with this one."

That comment got Hunt another jab in the ribs. They walked out of the office and back down the hall to the elevator. Hunt whispered to Mandy, "You know, if you'd let me take you in a closet somewhere, I could probably turn off the sarcasm altogether."

"Nice try."

They rode down to a lower level, and Mandy headed down another long corridor.

"How did you ever learn the ins and outs of this place? It's massive."

"There are still lots of floors I've never investigated. I only went where I needed to."

They entered a door that looked like all the others. Instead of it opening into an office, it opened into a large room with chairs on different levels like a movie theater. They faced a huge window that overlooked something similar to a gym floor you'd see at a school. Most of the floor was covered with padded mats. There were balance beams, pommel horses, and other equipment.

"Impressive," Hunt said. "This is a little different from where you kicked his ass before."

"There are a few training rooms. They kind of cover everything."

"All this equipment makes basic training look like a snap."

Mandy spun and faced him. "Basic training? You were never in the service."

"I went through basic then was out before I could be sent off."

"What happened?"

"Hardship. My grandfather took ill, and I had to help with the farm. I got out before I was ever stationed. I never went back. When the farm was moving good again, a spot had opened on the force. I was a shoo-in for it with the military training."

"Why have I never heard this?"

Hunt shrugged. "Haven't thought about it in a long time. It was just a few weeks of hell in my life I don't particularly care to reminisce about."

"Let me guess. Marine?"

He grinned. "You're good."

"You're built like a brick shit-house, Hunt. What else would you be?"

"Your amazing lover is enough for me." He growled and pulled her close by her hips.

"Do federal buildings make you horny or something?"

"You make me horny." He leaned down for a kiss, but this time she pushed him away. She pointed down to the gym floor. "There's James."

"Let him get his own girl."

"I'm serious, Hunt. Let me go talk with him. Will you please stay up here?"

"Why?"

"Please?" She walked over and flipped a switch. The room was suddenly filled with sounds from below through speakers in each of the corners. "You can hear everything. I want to deal with him alone, though."

Hunt took a seat. "Help yourself."

"Thank you." She leaned down and gave him a kiss. "I promise we'll look for a closet later."

"Maybe I don't want to now."

She placed her hand on his head and gave it a gentle push. "I love you, you oaf."

He motioned to the glass. "Is it two-way?"

"Nope. It's a normal window."

"Damn."

"Why?"

"He'll know I'm here."

"The point isn't so he doesn't know you're here, Hunt. I just want to handle this myself."

He peered through the glass again. "You going to take out six rookies to get to him?"

"Stop it."

She walked out the door, wishing it could slam behind her. No such luck, the door closure gently eased the heavy metal door shut. No one paid any attention as she descended the stairs. New faces must be commonplace around here. James had his back to her. He was wearing chest padding while a young man practiced torso kicks on him. James turned, and Mandy greeted him with her forearm and clotheslined him. He went down hard. She leaned down and said, "You son of a bitch."

The young man that had been kicking him hurried behind her and wrapped an arm around her waist.

James shouted for him to let her go, but Mandy wasted no time in flipping him to the floor.

She held his arm straight and kept him pinned until James said. "Enough! Jason, break for lunch." Everyone's attention had fallen on them. "All of you take your breaks now."

Without so much as a peep, they filed out of the gym. Mandy was torn between helping James to his feet and jumping on his chest to pound him senseless. While she stood there fuming, he sat up.

"You mind telling me what that was for?"

"In a minute. I'm still debating bashing your fucking face in."

"What the hell now, Amanda? Jesus. You always were a fireball. I'm not so sure I like it addressed at me, though."

"We went to see Face today."

"Yeah, so. I approved it."

"That's funny. You think you'd worry about him ratting you out."

"Ratting me out? You're insane." He reached his hand up. "Help me up." When she took his hand, he raised his foot to her chest and pushed her onto her back. He stood and held her arm straight. "You're slipping, Smith."

She wrapped her legs around his, and he went down. Hurrying to his chest, she dropped down hard then held her forearm over his neck. "Are we done with the foreplay, or do I need to really kick your ass?"

He coughed. "What the hell is up with you?"

She removed her arm then slid off his chest. "You fucking rat."

Chapter Sixteen

As James coughed some more and sat up, Mandy glanced up to the booth. To her amazement, Hunt was still sitting there. He blew her a kiss. She waved back with just one finger.

"You mind explaining to me what you're talking about, Mandy?"

"You know damn well what I'm talking about. Face said the only person he talked to other than Dan was you."

"So?"

"So? He was a rat, James. Where do you think I'm going with this?"

"That's what this is about?"

"What did you think it was about? I wanted your wife's mac-n-cheese recipe?"

"Come on, dammit. You killed everyone the guy had a connection with. Someone had to be his liaison. For a short time, he was technically working for us. Whether it was legit or not is beside the point. I have my reports to do like everyone else. I was just the lucky one to be assigned to him, no thanks to my association with you. Every now and then we cut him a little slack, and he feeds us a little something. Sometimes we feed him some shit just to see how fast word gets back on the street."

"Why does this stink like there's more? You could have told me."

"I thought it would be pretty obvious. You were here long enough to know procedures, Smith. You think if I had something to hide, I would have let you in there?"

"I didn't know he was yours when I went there, asshole."

"Well, you should have asked me about it instead of trying to kick my ass. What exactly do you think I'm a rat about?"

"Lying to me about being in touch with him was a good enough start to set my temper going."

James went over to the wall and removed two swords from a holder. He threw one to Mandy.

"You're kidding."

"I'm getting even with you for that clothesline. What's the matter? You getting rusty in your old age?"

She took a firm stance, holding the sword straight up at her body, accepting the challenge.

He stepped at her first, and the fencing had begun. Several blows were made before Mandy spoke. "What else don't I know, James?" she said with a solid crack of her sword to his.

He took a step back and came at her, grinning. "Damn, girl. You are rusty."

She rewarded him with a few more blows, causing him to lose his balance just long enough to give a swipe at his shirt. He put his sword down. "You still pull the same shit."

"Learned from you. Pussy."

He lunged at her again and swung hard. She was able to block his swings, but he was right. She was out of shape. She landed a few more solid strikes, sending him back a few paces. Mandy was ready for another blow but stopped. Hunt was suddenly standing between them.

"He's had enough, babe. This is fencing, not pirate training. You look like you're about to take his head off."

She threw her sword down and turned to walk away. She stopped long enough to remove the badge from her pocket. "I don't want your fucking badge." Her aim was perfect, hitting James square in the chest.

He picked it off the ground and went after her. "Mandy, wait."

"Screw you." She turned around when a hand was placed on her arm. She expected to be face to face with James, but it was Hunt. "Let me go."

"Hear him out."

"Why? How can I trust anything out of his mouth? Anything out of anyone's mouth in this hellhole for that matter?"

"Hear him out anyway."

James caught up to them. "Let's go talk over some coffee."

Mandy crossed her arms and glared at Hunt. "I don't see that I have a choice in the matter."

"Go to my office. I need to grab another shirt. I'll be right there."

After he walked away, Hunt brought Mandy to his chest. "I'll give you three guesses what I am after watching that, and the first two don't count."

"Gee. I'll take horny for five hundred, Bob."

He picked her up, and she wrapped her legs around his waist. "You could have stopped me sooner."

"I thought you'd make a shish kebob out of me as it was. You're really good with a sword, babe."

"Comes in handy on the streets of New York."

"See how good this is for us? We still learn something new about each other every day."

Mandy's hands went around his neck, and she leaned into him for a kiss.

"Even if you do get pissed at me and flip me off."

"Sorry." She got down and took his hand. "Come on. We have an ass to fry."

"I'll just have the coffee, thanks."

As they entered the office, James was buttoning up his shirt. "You get lost?"

"Just not in a particular hurry to listen to your bullshit."

He groaned. "Sit down." He hit the speakerphone. "Sherry? Bring in three coffees please."

"Right away, sir."

He sat down hard on his chair and rocked side to side for a moment. "First of all, I'm not full of shit. I'm not saying it again." He tossed Mandy her badge back. "You need to keep that, trust me on this."

"Nothing good ever comes out of me holding that. You guys continually pile one lie on after another."

"Stop it, Mandy. You can trust me. Yes, I am the one Face talks to now. That doesn't mean I was in cahoots with him when he was playing both sides. You want transcriptions of everything that has been said since he's been in jail?"

"As a matter of fact, yes."

"Fine."

His secretary walked in with a tray of coffee. "Thanks, Sherry," James said as he accepted it. "Will you please get Ms. Smith—"

"Mrs. Blaine." Mandy corrected.

"Blair," Sherry said.

"Thank you," Mandy said with a smile as she accepted her coffee.

"You're welcome. Now what is it you want?"

"Any transcripts we have on visits with William Roberts. Here and from his jail visits. Anything you can dig up that will help her."

"It will take a few moments. Flash Drive okay?" she asked Mandy.

"That will be great. Thanks."

Sherry gave Hunt his coffee then left the office.

"Now I need a laptop," Mandy said.

James could only chuckle. "You don't ask for much, do you?"

"I'm sorry. We were kind of taken from our home in a hurry. I'm not about to use the desktop at Lonny's with Eddie's goons looking over my shoulders."

"Fair enough. I'll get you one. Would you please start to trust me now?"

"Hate to butt in here," Hunt said, "but I have to side with my wife. Not just because I'm afraid of her, either. She's been nothing but screwed from both sides since day one of joining up with you. I can't really say I blame her."

"I'm aware of that. I was here with her from day one, and personally I haven't done anything to not have earned her trust."

"Aside from leaving this little tidbit out."

"I honestly didn't think it mattered. I'm pretty much the only one around here that even gives a crap about this old case."

Mandy spoke again. "Do you have any idea who feeds him his info?"

"It's a prison, Amanda. Word spreads faster than STDs. It doesn't even have to be true."

"Any chance he's getting word out the same way?"

"I understand where you're going, but this is Willy we're talking about. He's not masterminding anything. I'll bet my life he's not calling any shots. I'm sorry. I know you want to get out of here, and I'd do exactly what you are by trying to eliminate the obvious ones first, but Face is out of the picture. I can all but promise you that. Even Gunner was only there a half a dozen times. No one gives a crap about him anymore. The only other visitor besides his girlfriend—"

"Is that still Heidi?"

"Same one. Know her?"

"She was who he was with when I was in. I didn't expect it to stick. She came off as a junkie just sticking around for the goods. I expected him to move on."

"Her visits were as often as they allowed, but there was never any pillow talk that we caught. Anyway, the only other besides Gunner was Ray, and we stopped hearing from him."

Mandy bit at her lip. "You won't be hearing from Ray again, that's for sure."

He raised an eyebrow at her. "What aren't you telling me?"

"I sort of forgot to mention I killed him."

"You what? Jesus, Mandy." James picked up the phone but then placed it back down. "I'll want details."

"There's not many to tell."

"Tell me anyway."

Mandy shared the story as James took notes. He promised to look into what he could. He wanted to get the body for evidence when this was over.

"I don't want Eddie to be able to try to pin that on you for any reason. I understand it was self-defense. You'll get full support from our end."

"That's fine. We'll deal with that when we have to. I don't know exactly where they left the body, but when you have to know, I'll tell you who knows where it is. For now, I'd like to look all of your files over."

James sighed. "Understandable."

"I want Willy's sign-in sheets of visitors."

"Of course. Those will be on the flash drive as well. You can match the tapes to the lists. I have nothing to hide."

"I guess we'll see, won't we?"

James stood. "You're a pain in my ass, but a thorough pain in my ass. I still wish you were back with us. Maybe my word isn't worth what it used to be to you but dammit, I'll earn your trust again if I have to die doing it."

"I almost wish you were the rat. This would make things that much simpler if I could just kill you and get this over with."

James grinned. "I guess I can't blame you after what you've been through with being lied to by Abbey. I'm not going to hold anything back again, Mandy. If he gets a bad case of diarrhea, I'll be sure to let you know."

"I'll settle for what's on the laptop, thanks."

Rush-hour traffic was the worst Mandy ever remembered. She called Milo and said they were stopping somewhere for dinner.

"Your loss."

"I know, Milo. We skipped lunch, and I'm starved. I'd rather wait out this crap over a pizza and a beer."

"I made—"

"Don't even tell me what you made. I'll only get more pissed."

"Bad day?"

"I don't even know where to begin."

"The freezer is stocked with ice cream. Fat husband, screaming monkey, sweaty nuts...whatever those silly names are."

Mandy laughed. "Thanks, Milo. I owe you one."

Hunt grinned at Mandy when she hung up. "You sure like the old coot. It sounded like you were checking in with your dad. Letting him know you'll be late for supper."

"Just common courtesy."

"I know." Hunt smiled and brought her hand to his lips. "Where to?"

"There's a great place in a few more blocks. Hopefully it won't take an hour to get to."

After fifteen more minutes, they had only gone half a block. There was a parking garage on the left. Hunt put on his turn signal.

"What are you doing?"

"If it's only a few blocks, we should walk. We'll get there faster."

"Good idea."

After parking, they walked together hand in hand. They took their time, stopping at several windows and checking out the various gift shops and specialty stores. Hunt was especially intrigued with an expensive lingerie shop that held nothing back when it came to the goods displayed on their very lifelike mannequins.

"Keep walking, lover."

Hunt growled. "Can I bring back a souvenir from the trip?"

"Yes, you can. Yourself in one piece." She dragged him along for another two blocks. "Sorry. Maybe it's farther than I thought."

"There's a place right there."

"Marvin's? Hardly an Italian sounding name."

"It's New York. It's pizza. It's bound to be good."

"Like sex?"

"I wasn't even going to use that old line. Come on. The best places are always the out of the way dives."

"I'm so tired, I don't care. Let's go."

The atmosphere left a lot to be desired, but it was clean. Glass cases held every type of pizza and pasta you could imagine. The slices were a quarter of a pizza, and the calzones were almost as big as an entire large pizza rolled up.

"You okay with this?" Mandy asked. "It looks like a clogged artery waiting to happen."

"I like pizza now and then."

"And I suffer for it later."

"I'll go easy on the peppers."

She chuckled. "Get what you want. I'll sleep through anything tonight. Even your cheese-coma induced snoring."

They sat with their selections and a tall draft beer in a quiet corner.

"Don't kill me for saying so, but you sure can fight, babe."

"It was training, Hunt. You did it all, too."

"Yeah, but I mean—"

"For a girl?"

"No. For someone your size. You really kick some ass."

"Should I be flattered?"

"Just an observation. I guess I became so used to you around the house, I forgot what a tough nut you were."

"Nuts aren't tough, hon. If I wanted James out, that's where I would have hit him."

"I'm wincing just thinking about it."

"Can we talk about something else? You know I only do what I have to. Trust me. I'd rather be making cookies for you and Hannah than taking James to the mattresses."

"How fitting. A Godfather quote."

"Well, I did literally take him to the mattresses."

"Touché. Are you buying that he's not holding anything back about Willy?"

"I don't know. I'll dig into the transcriptions when we get back. If he is hiding something, it won't be in there, but maybe I'll find another lead or clue."

"Another day down and not much to go on again."

"Fun, isn't it? We really ought to check on the kids."

"Angelo and company?"

"Shhh, Hunt."

"We're in the middle of nowhere, babe."

"Never underestimate the ears—" A woman walking by the window, dressed like a hooker, caught Mandy's attention.

"Who is she?" Hunt asked.

"Willy's girlfriend."

"That Heidi you were just talking about?"

Mandy flew out of her chair and ran for the front door. She cut the woman off.

Startled, the woman shouted, "What the hell are you doing, you crazy bitch?"

"Heidi, it's me. Mandy."

There was finally a spark of recognition in her eyes. "Hey, girl!" They shared a quick hug. "What are you doing back? I heard you were doing time."

"Did. I'm out. I'm back for real and calling the shots now."

"You? Wait a minute." Mandy could almost see her drug-induced haze lift. "Face said you were a fed."

"Face told a lot of people that. I think he was trying to cut a deal. Funny to run into you. I saw him today as a matter of fact."

"Well, whoopee for you. I haven't seen him in over six months."

"You okay with that?"

"Nothing I can do. He ain't ever getting out. Can't get conjugal visits with all the trouble he gets into lately. What's the point? They kept making my visits shorter and farther apart. Wasn't ever much allowed in the first place."

"You miss him?"

"Of course I miss him. Call me a fool, but I loved him."

"Will you come sit with me for a bit? I'd love to catch up."

"Sure. I'm not going anywhere in particular."

Mandy brought her into the restaurant and offered to buy her dinner. She declined. Heidi was barely skin on bones and most certainly did drugs more often than she ate. Mandy explained about Angelo and was surprised at the uncontrollable sobbing that erupted. Hunt passed her some napkins and excused himself to refill their beers.

"I'm so sorry. I didn't realize you were so close to him," Mandy said when Heidi finally accepted her comforting hugs.

"He was a great guy. Just too young to go, you know?"

"Trust me. I know."

CHAPTER SEVENTEEN

When Heidi stopped crying, Mandy explained about being his sister.

"No way."

"I'm serious. I didn't even go into it with Willy. Things didn't really go too well."

"What do you mean?"

"He wasn't cooperative," Hunt said.

"Did you hurt him?"

Hunt ignored the question by taking a sip of beer.

"I need to know what's going on here, Heidi. Too many people are dying."

She fidgeted. "I know."

"What do you know about this?"

She shifted her chair then reached for Mandy's beer and drank half of it in one shot.

"Heidi? Come on. Help a gal out. My neck is on the line now."

Heidi's drugged up gaze darted between Hunt and Mandy. "I didn't know Angelo was dead. I swear I didn't." She paused and wiped her nose. "But I do know they didn't mean to kill him."

"So, you do know what's going on." Mandy had to lower her voice. "You had to know once they took out Vince they were going to go after Angelo."

She fidgeted with her napkin and kept her gaze fixed on her lap. "No. It's not like that. They didn't mean to."

"Who?"

Heidi stood. "I need to pee."

Hunt scooted over to Mandy's side while Heidi walked to the bathroom. "Boy, can I pick a pizza place or what?"

"She's scared, Hunt."

"And high as a kite. You sure you're going to believe anything she says? She sure as shit wouldn't count as a witness if anything became of it."

"You're mistaking what we're doing again for anything that could possibly have any kind of legal ramifications."

"True enough." Hunt was silent for a moment before continuing. "You really think it's going to be this simple? We accidentally stumble across this woman, and she knows who's behind things?"

"It's a step in the right direction, anyway. She knows something. With Willy in jail, she's getting her drugs from someone. There's bound to be pillow talk."

"Must have been true love with Willy."

"He's in jail for life with hardly any visitation, Hunt. What do you think she'd do? If we can't get her to talk, maybe we can get her in there with Willy," Mandy said.

"They won't be dumb enough to talk in there. You show that kind of pull, and he will know something is up."

"She was easy enough to convince I'm Angelo's sister. I'd have to sell it to her so she spread the—" Mandy paused, realizing too much time had passed. She stood and hustled to the bathroom, shoving the door open. It was a single stall, and it was empty. "Fuck!" She pushed through a back exit and went running into the alley. Hunt was right behind her. "You go that way!" she yelled as she ran in the opposite direction.

Mandy refused to give up and ran frantically through a couple of blocks and alleys before coming back to the restaurant. "Nothing?" she asked Hunt.

"No sign. We should have thought about her splitting, babe."

"Hindsight, Hunt. Not helping."

"What now?"

"We'll have to give it a day or two before she resurfaces. She will. I guess in the meantime, we could go for a drive."

"You want to go to the cabin?"

"I think we should check in. There was too much going on, and he was in a lot of pain when I sent him up there. Maybe his mind has had some time to clear."

"And we can't do this over the phone?"

"Angelo never was one for conversation over the phone. If we get him relaxed and talking, his expressions will tell me what his voice won't. We never could lie to each other."

"Except for the part about you being in the FBI."

Mandy grinned. "Except for that. Hopefully I can get some answers about Heidi from him. She took off because she's scared. She knows something. He's bound to know who she's been with lately. That will give us something else to go on."

"Someone else to track down and beat the piss out of?"

"Whatever it takes, Blaine. I want this over and to get home to my daughter."

"We'll head out first thing in the morning. Just do me a favor and don't freak out on Angelo over the answer to your question about who's doing Heidi."

"Why would I?"

"I have a feeling he was sleeping with her, too."

"Because of how she reacted?"

"That and because of the position he is in. It seems natural to me to screw the significant other of someone you don't particularly care for."

"He and Willy got along."

"All the more reason."

"So basically, liking or hating someone has nothing to do with it. You service their girlfriend when it's convenient, and they are indisposed?"

"Pretty much."

"Men are pigs."

"I don't write the rulebook."

"You just keep the scorecard?"

"It's not like it's my way. I'm just saying, Mandy. You're trying to help Angelo, I don't want you getting pissed off at him. She wasn't much to look at, but that isn't going to stop a drunk and horny man."

"Heidi is gorgeous. What are you talking about?"

"You think? Guess I couldn't get passed the stoned look." He held the back of her neck and pulled her close to him for a kiss. "That and I only have eyes for you."

"Quick thinking, Blaine. I know. Blair."

"Come on. Let's get back and dig through the files. Hopefully no one has stolen the laptop from the car."

They arrived back at the house at eight, receiving only a grunt from the man on watch outside. With big-screen TV's in every room, there was no need for anyone to hang out in a common area. They had no idea if anyone else was home or not. Mandy and Hunt went to their room undisturbed. After three hours of going over the log sheets and conversations, they were still at square one.

"If these aren't altered, James was telling us the truth," Mandy said.

"The key word there being 'if.'"

"Unless they keep a fake second set on hand, she produced these too quickly for them to be altered."

"Enough for tonight, babe. Let's put this aside and take a long shower."

"You weren't fond of shower action yesterday."

"That was yesterday. Now I'm thinking about you mopping the floor with James, and there's all kinds of swelling going on." He grinned. "Hey. Think you could flip me?"

"Like a pancake."

"Put your money where your mouth is."

"I don't want to hurt you."

"Like you could. Come on."

"I don't want to, Hunt."

"Pussy."

That's all it took.

Hunt leaned against the side shower wall with both shower heads on full blast as hot as he could stand it, pounding at his back.

"I said I'm sorry," Mandy said as she gave the center of his back a kiss. "You asked for it."

"Yeah. I know. Kiss lower and I may forgive you."

"You would have landed on the bed if you let yourself relax and fall right."

"I'll never hear the end of it from my favorite guard, Ricardo Montalban, out there."

"That's who he looks like!" Mandy squealed. "That was driving me crazy. He's your favorite?"

"Sarcasm, babe. Who can have a favorite goon in this bunch?"

"You'd go running if you heard a thud like that in this house, too. No worries, my love. If he picks on you again, I can take him." She kissed his back again.

"Lower. And more toward the front."

After a slightly less rigorous workout than the night before, they crawled into bed and shared one last goodnight kiss. After a couple of hours, Mandy found herself digging through the kitchen drawers in search of a spoon. The hall light flicked on, and she about jumped out of her skin. Spinning around, she was happy to find it was Milo and not one of the guards.

"Doesn't anyone ever sleep in this house?" he said before yawning.

"Sorry to wake you."

"My kitchen calls to me when there are people in it that shouldn't be." He walked to the island and opened a drawer. "Big spoon or little spoon?"

"Little." He bumped the drawer closed with his hip and handed it to her. "None for you tonight?" she asked, accepting it.

"Can't. I'm watching your figure."

Mandy laughed at his word play.

"Bad day?"

"The usual, I suppose. It's just that Hunt is up there snoring like a buzz saw from the cheese he ate tonight."

"I forced milk on him last night. Is that an issue?"

"Milk doesn't bother him as much as cheese. And not even that so much. Mostly only when we have pizza. You want to sit with me? I'd kind of like to ask you something."

Milo motioned toward the couch, and they sat together. "Fire away," he said.

"You know where I'm going."

"Yes, I'm afraid I do."

"Then kindly spill the beans. How do you know about me?"

"Like I told your man, Vince and I were close. A man will tell two people things he doesn't tell others."

"His barber and bartender?"

"Oh...those are good too. In Vince's case it was his chef and his tailor."

"Do I need to worry about the tailor?"

"Died four months ago at eighty-six."

"Then I guess he's okay. How doesn't Eddie know that you were told about me? He went everywhere with Vince."

"I guess there are some things Vince kept from Eddie. I'm sure Eddie thought someone like me didn't need to know details like that."

"Did he catch Hunt's slip? I'd hate for you to be in any kind of trouble."

"If he did, he didn't say anything. He probably doesn't care one way or another."

Mandy enjoyed a few bites then talked with a mouth full of ice cream. "Is there anything else you may know that'll help me?"

"If I could help you, I would. There are some things I am not at liberty to share, even with Vince in the ground. Trust me, if something pertained to helping you, I would. You want to share a game plan with your favorite chef?"

Mandy wasn't sure why this made her uneasy. "Nothing to share. We ran into a friend of Willy's, but that was a dead end. I do want to go check on Angelo tomorrow. I'm getting nowhere fast, and I need to be sure he's doing okay."

He placed a hand on her leg. "You sure care for that boy. He's in good hands. You were smart to pull a switcheroo on the cabin. You never know who you can trust. Mind if I go up with you? I'm sure they could use a good home-cooked meal."

"I really wanted to get an early start, but I'll let you know how the morning goes."

"I'm usually up with the birds, anyway. Think on it."

"I will. Thanks, Milo. I'm sure they'd appreciate it."

He kissed her on the head and said good night.

"Can't leave you two alone for a second."

Mandy smiled at Hunt, standing there in his boxer-briefs. "Sorry. Was I snoring again?"

"Like a buzz saw."

He sat next to Mandy and took her ice cream. "It's your fault. You let me order the calzone."

"You're the one that ate the whole thing."

Milo laughed. "Two of the best anti-criminal minds in New York and they're arguing over cheap Italian food. I'll make a note to keep the cheese dishes on a downlow. I'm going back to bed. Just leave the spoon in the sink. The dishwasher is full of clean dishes."

"Thanks, Milo."

After his door clicked shut, Mandy stood. "Fuck me."

"I thought you'd be good till morning but okay." Hunt stood, pulled her up, and took her by the waist.

She stepped back. "I think I'm going to cry."

"What?" He pulled her close again. "I'll give you three again. Promise."

"I'm not kidding around, Hunt." She slapped his hand away then pulled him onto the couch and lowered her voice.

"Milo knows more than he's telling me. If I thought I could trust anyone, it was him."

"What happened?"

"He knows I didn't send Angelo to the same cabin."

"You didn't?"

"I didn't tell anyone except the driver right before they left. I spoke with Angelo, too. Darin, Angie, and the guards won't know any different. None of them have been there before."

"You didn't even tell me. What the hell is up with that?"

"Like I need to worry about you, asshole. You would have found out tomorrow when we headed up. Anyway, Milo just said it was a good call that I did that."

"Only he shouldn't have known."

"Exactly. He wants to go tomorrow. I can't let him. We have to leave now. I can't make a good enough excuse in the morning for him not to go."

"Are you sure he's a worry?"

"No. But I can't be sure he's not. Why else would he know? Who went looking and told him this info?"

"Don't know, babe." Hunt stood and pulled Mandy to her feet. He picked her up, and she wrapped her legs around him. "I'll drive us up there. You sleep," he said as he carried her to the bedroom.

"We can stop and get a room when we get closer. I'd just feel better bugging out now."

"What are we going to do about Guido outside?"

Mandy smiled. "Do you have names for all of them?"

He grinned.

"What do you call Edwin?"

"Pinky dick."

Mandy laughed hard then covered her mouth. "I don't even want to know." She dropped two small carry-on bags on the bed. "We're not prisoners. We'll tell him we decided to get a head start since we couldn't sleep, anyway. I don't think Milo would be suspicious. I didn't react in any way to what he said."

"You think he'll catch his slip up?"

"Doubtful. If he's playing two sides to this, I'm sure it's hard to keep straight. Eddie must have something on him if he's taken to lying to me."

"Don't tell me you're really surprised, babe."

Mandy put her hands on her hips. "No, but would you let me live in my own little world for a minute? It was nice to think I had one person to talk to and trust."

Again, he closed the gap between them. "That's why I'm here."

Her hand went to his chest. "Don't take this the wrong way, but you aren't enough."

Not long after they left the house, Mandy fell asleep with her head on Hunt's lap. Even though he promised to pull over to a motel when he was tired, he didn't stop. He had a few hours of sleep before joining Mandy downstairs and was plenty rested for the five-hour drive. Traffic was great this time of night, and he made good time with no hassles. The route he took was so close to their old house, he couldn't resist swinging in for a quick break.

They both hated having to leave their first home. Instead of selling it, his parents assumed the mortgage, using it as their summer get-away. Hunt and Mandy were still very attached to it in an odd "Oh, honey. It's the house we ended up at after I almost killed you" kind of way.

When he turned into a gravel driveway, she stirred. "Where are we?"

"Home."

"Home-home?" She sat up and smiled wide. "I never thought it would feel so good seeing this place. Are you sure we're okay stopping here?"

"Anyone we didn't want to find us already has. I think we're okay."

Leaning into him, she gave him a kiss. "Why didn't you stop somewhere?"

"I wasn't tired." He opened his door and motioned for her to follow him out.

Hunt picked up their bags then they went in through the garage, which wasn't locked. He found the key for the house stashed where they had always kept it.

"You want to rest?" Mandy asked.

"I'm still fine. I only stopped to stretch a bit and grab coffee. As soon as you're ready, we can go."

"As long as you think you're fine, that sounds good to me." Amanda took down the coffee and filters. Her phone rang. After retrieving it from her purse she mumbled, "Shit. It's Eddie." She answered the phone with a harsh, "What?" and walked to the living room.

"Tiny said you guys took off for Vermont."

"I didn't lie. I need to check on Angelo and the kids."

"Didn't you send guards and a doctor with him so he'd be covered?"

"Yes, but I have some questions for him, and I didn't want to do it over the phone."

"Why didn't you let Milo go with you?"

"We couldn't sleep, and we wanted to leave right away. Heaven forbid I'm here long enough to have to do this again, but if I am, I'll bring him then."

There was only silence from Eddie.

"We're not here for tea and cakes. I need some answers from him. I am here on a job, am I not?"

"Your job was to fix things here."

"That's what I'm doing. I sort of found a lead, and I needed to ask Angelo a few things. I really don't have the time to hang around while Milo cooks for them. I want to get this job done and get the hell away from you. How many ways do I need to say this?"

"What about the deal going down today?"

"I'll do my best to be back for that. If I'm not, it'll be okay. I'll talk to Gunner. I'm not new here, Eddie. I'll get your shit divided and on the streets. It's against everything I am, but I'm not risking our deal. You just let me work, and

you keep to your side of the fence. I do have it covered."
When he didn't reply, Mandy's voice softened. Something
else was wrong. "Is everything okay?"

"Someone else was nailed last night."

"Who?"

"One of Gunner's boys. One of the newer kids. I don't
think you knew him."

"Dammit."

"He was nobody. We think they were aiming for
Gunner and just got sloppy." Eddie paused. "Just do what
you have to do and get back here. I want you on the streets.
This shit has to stop."

"I'm doing what I can. Trust me. This is going to point
somewhere. I'm not up here for a road trip. If it was for
pleasure, I would have waited for Milo."

"Then keep me in the loop like I keep telling you. You
make me think you've run off and—"

"You even think about threatening my daughter or
Hunt's parents, and I *will* show up and kill you with my
bare hands, Eddie." Hunt entered the room, Mandy held
her hand up and shook her head. "We left at two in the
morning and only slowed down enough to take a short
break. I would have called you in another hour. Just stop
this playground bully routine and let me do my job!"
Mandy ended the call.

"He threatening my family?"

"No. I felt like he was going to, and I beat him to the
punch." Mandy dropped onto the couch. "No matter how I
look at this from the outside, it doesn't make sense. The
mob bringing in an outsider to find the bad guy? How crazy
is this, Hunt?"

He sat down next to her. "As crazy as it gets, but we
both know that's not all this is about." He took her hands
in his. "I know I'm coming off like a smart-ass here, but I
have been trying to figure this out myself. No offense, but

him throwing you into this is like a principal using a first grader to stop the freshmen from fighting." He placed his hand over her mouth when she opened it. "I said no offense. I know you know your shit, but you know where I'm going with this." He dropped his hand.

"Yes, I understand, Hunt. I'm not insulted. We're on the same page here."

"I hope that part of his plan is not to harm you in some way. I think there's more to this than him being worried about getting killed or taking the throne, so to speak."

Mandy rested her head on Hunt's shoulder. "I know. I guess I can only keep up the game and hope we get out of it in one piece." She leaned up and gave him a quick kiss then stood. "You sure you don't want a quick nap?"

"I'm sure. Let's get going, so we'll make it back for the deal tonight. I'll leave you with Gunner and then find a place to scope things out. Maybe our guy will get stupid, and we'll get lucky."

"Damn."

"What?"

"We're home, and there's not even time for a quickie." She curled her bottom lip.

He stood. "If you're going to pout about it, we can always take time for a shower, babe." He kissed her forehead then brought her to his chest and rocked with her.

"I do need a little freshening up after the long drive."

"Good thinking."

Mandy was toweling off after their shower and extracurricular activities. "What is wrong with us?"

"How much time do you have?"

Mandy laughed. "I mean it, hon. With everything that's going on, we still have to sneak in sex everywhere we can."

"Does this surprise you? I mean, come on. Considering how we met and the first time we did it, you'd think our libidos lived for this kind of excitement."

"Gangsters don't make me horny, Hunt."

"No, I do."

"True enough. I guess when it comes to stress relief, there is no better way, right?"

"I'd have to agree with that."

"Did you ever finish making coffee?"

"I didn't. I was too busy eavesdropping on your conversation. Let's head out. I'll grab a crappy gas station cup then we'll go pop in on Mom's coffee shop when we're closer to the cabin."

Mandy brightened up. "I'd love to stop in and see if she's still there!"

"I'll never forget how pissed you were when she asked when you were due." Mandy placed her hands on her stomach. Hunt closed the gap between them and held her tight. "It'll happen soon, babe."

CHAPTER EIGHTEEN

"I wonder if Mom will remember us," Mandy said as Hunt opened the door to the coffee shop. Mom, the owner at the coffee shop, rushed right over, answering Mandy's question. "Where's the little one?"

"She's with her grandparents," Mandy explained. "You know, I didn't even realize I was pregnant when we were here. How did you know?"

Mom smiled. "I told you. Lots of grandbabies. It's not just a saying about that glow. There's nothing like it." She placed her hand on Mandy's cheek. "Just tea again, dear?"

Mandy tilted her head at the question. She had tea last time and couldn't believe the woman remembered. She wanted caffeine but didn't want to insult the woman. "Sure. That'll be fine." She ordered a tall coffee with a shot of espresso for Hunt. He said he wasn't tired, but he was bound to start dragging soon.

"Afraid you wore me out?" Hunt said with a grin.

"Just keeping you on your toes." They ordered some egg and bagel sandwiches then sat at a table by a window, enjoying the last few minutes of peace before going to the cabin. Hunt was somber as he stared out at a small park. "You miss it up here?" Mandy asked.

"A little. I grew up here, babe. It's nice to come home now and then, but home is where you and Hannah are now. I don't care if we have to run to Timbuktu to get away from these goons. I'll go wherever you are and with a smile on my face."

"It's prettier than I remember."

"You love the beaches in Florida, too. I don't want to play this game. I'm happy, babe."

She gave him half a smile then her attention went to the counter. There was a young girl trying to order something, and Mom was having a hard time understanding her. Mandy made the connection at the girl's motions; she was deaf. "I'll be right back," she said and walked over.

Mandy tapped the girl on the shoulder. When she turned around, Mandy greeted her with sign language. The girl brightened up and eagerly signed back. After a brief exchange, Mandy turned to Mom. "She wants a vanilla latte but wants to know if you have rice or almond milk. It's not on your board."

"Oh, heavens. I am so glad you were here. I have soy milk. Will that work?"

Mandy signed some more, and the girl responded. Again, Mandy turned to Mom. "She said that'll be fine."

"I'll get that on the board. Silly of me. I'll get something written up in case this ever happens again."

The girl signed to Mandy, and she laughed. "A pen and pad on your counter would do wonders. She's great at reading lips."

Mom laughed. "I'll get right on it. Ask her if she lives around here. I'd stock one of those milks if she wants it on a regular basis. I've honestly never been asked before."

Mandy asked her, and the girl shook her head as she signed again.

"She's passing through, but thanks."

They signed more light conversation while her drink was made, then Mandy said her goodbyes. She joined Hunt again who was grinning wide. "What?"

"I didn't know you could sign."

"Took it in college. I guess I haven't had the chance to use it lately. I'm glad I haven't lost it."

"Have I said how much I love you?"

Running her foot up Hunt's thigh, Mandy smiled. "Not in about eighteen minutes."

"Damn, girl. We need to get this shit over with and get home."

"Home-home?"

"Yes. Home-home. Wherever that is going to be when this is over." He stood. "Come on. Let's get going before I take you here on the table."

They waved goodbye to Mom as they walked out hand in hand. "You two come back and see me again soon. And bring those babies with you."

Hunt gave her hand a squeeze when they got outside. Mandy gave him a slight smile. "She's too sweet. I'm not about to go on about not being able to get pregnant."

"Maybe when we come back this way, you will be, babe."

"Maybe."

Hunt switched subjects. "Is the new place hard to find?"

"It's not that far away. I'm sure Mom could give us a history on it, but I wanted to stay incognito about any involvement. Hopefully the crew we sent isn't dumb enough to come out in public and make a scene about being there."

"I'm sure we would have heard something."

They climbed in the car, and Mandy had to roll down her window. Mom was rushing out to catch them. "Here's some cookies for you, straight from the oven. Thanks again for your help with that deaf gal." Mom patted Mandy's arm. "A gal in your condition has to keep your strength up. Take care." She ran back in before Mandy could even say thank you.

"Why does that woman always assume I'm preg—" A smile spread over Mandy's face. "You have got to be kidding me."

Hunt took her hand and gave it a kiss. "Don't get yourself excited over it yet. Okay? I can't take your let down if you find out you're not. She's just a nice, little old lady."

"A nice lady who happened to nail it last time I didn't know, either."

"We were at the doctor a week ago, babe."

"That was testing you this time, not me, and we've had a lot of sex since then."

"I know. I was there." He waggled his eyebrows up and down.

"I told you I knew I was ovulating when we left."

"If it was recently, it'd be too soon for even wonder-preggo-detecto-woman to see you glow."

"It was only days last time, too."

"Babe..."

As Mandy's chin dropped, he picked it up. "I don't want this to destroy your focus. Okay?"

"It won't."

Hunt put the car in gear. "Please. I am married to you. Give me some credit."

The cabin was as Mandy expected it, with one of the guards outside not trying hard enough to hide the fact that he was standing guard.

"You should have called and let us know you were coming," he said.

"Why? You have a party going on?" Mandy asked as she brushed by.

"I was instructed to shoot first and ask questions later."

"I'm the one who assigned you here, and I didn't give that order, so I suggest you lighten up. No one knows you're here unless one of you bozos blow it."

He mumbled something under his breath. Mandy ignored it and continued inside. They were greeted by the doctor.

"How's Angelo?" Mandy asked.

"He's actually recovering well. I expected more of a fight from him."

"Has he been drinking?"

"There's nothing here, and he hasn't even asked."

"That's something, I guess."

"Where are Darin and Angie?" Hunt asked.

"At the lake. They're actually enjoying this little vacation. I can only say I thought log walls were a little more soundproof."

Hunt grinned. Mandy was not amused. "Is he up?"

"He was when I was in there a few minutes ago. See if you're able to convince him to come out on the back porch for a while. The fresh air will do him some good."

"Are you coming with me?" she asked Hunt.

"I'll hang here with Doc. Angelo may open up more with you if you're in there alone."

Mandy knocked before opening the door. "You decent?" she asked, poking her head in.

Angelo smiled at the sight of her. "Too late now if I wasn't. How's my favorite sweetheart?"

She walked over and gave him a tight hug. "Fine. Better now that I see you're looking so good."

"Pffft. I'm always looking good."

She joined him on the bed then placed her hand on his cheek. "Not when you left you weren't."

He placed his hand over hers and held it there. He closed his eyes and sighed. "I'm okay." He lowered her hand but still held onto it. "So, why are you here? Don't tell me you've cleaned up the streets and obliterated the bad guys already."

"Not quite, but I do have a few interesting leads."

"What do you have going on?"

"Before I start." She turned and made sure no one was at the door before meeting his gaze. "I need you to know something."

"What?"

"You know I love you, right?"

He blushed.

"I know you know how I mean that."

"I know. It's still funny. I've missed you, Mandy. I didn't think I'd ever see you again."

"I know." Her second hand joined her first, and he followed suit. She smiled. "If Hunt walks in, he'll kick our asses."

"I can take him."

She gave a soft chuckle. "I need you to know you can tell me anything. I really need some answers here, Angelo."

"I promise I have nothing to hide from you. Fire away."

"Were you sleeping with Face's girlfriend?"

"Ouch."

"Is that a yes?"

"Yeah."

"Since he's been in prison or before?"

"Just since he's been in prison. I ain't that stupid. She was always showing up where I was. Complained constantly about being so horny with him in jail. What's a guy to do?" He shrugged, trying to look as innocent as possible.

"Were you giving her drugs in return?"

"Sometimes. Sometimes she showed up already high."

"Did any of Face's men know about this?"

"I didn't tell any of them, and I didn't think so, but when Axle and Kermit were pounding on me, they said a few of the blows were from Face for doing his girl."

"Why didn't you tell me this earlier?"

"I don't know. I didn't think it was relevant. A beating is a beating. I wasn't taking notes. I really didn't think I was leaving the place alive, Mandy, but I thought that was the least of why they were doing it. Why is this coming up now? Face taking responsibility or something? Did you get in to see him?"

"I did get in to see him, but that's not where this is coming from. We ran into Heidi."

"Where?"

"It was totally by chance. I asked her a few things, and she was able to give me the slip. I didn't expect it. I don't know how I was so stupid to let her do that to me."

"Don't be hard on yourself. You don't belong here in the first place. I still don't like that you're sticking your neck out for me."

"It's my neck. I'll do what I want with it, dammit." She stood and walked to the window. "It's a gorgeous day. Think I can get you to sit on the back porch for a while? Doc thinks you could use some fresh air."

"My ribs are hurtin' pretty bad today."

"I'll get Hunt to come help you."

He rested his head back for a bit with his eyes closed then finally turned to her.

"Fine. Get him."

"Thanks. We'll finish this talk over some lunch."

"You bring food in? No one here cooks for shit."

"I'll send someone to go get something."

"Bless you."

Hunt helped Mandy get Angelo settled on the back porch. As they eased him into a chair, Mandy asked Hunt, "Do you know of a place you can go around here to grab something quick to eat? I don't trust sending any of these goons. They are bound to create a scene."

"I know a great burger place. I'll call in for a variety, I'm not taking special orders."

"That'll be fine."

He kissed Mandy goodbye and nodded to Angelo as he pulled out his cell phone.

The drive took Hunt twenty minutes, which was perfect. The person who took the order said it would be ready in twenty-five. Quick in, quick out. No hassles. Immediately after stepping inside the restaurant, a man called out to Hunt.

"Hunter Blaine?"

Shit.

Hunt spun around and faced a man in a sheriff's uniform. "Eric?" The two men shared a hearty handshake.

"How the hell have you been, you old dog?" he asked Hunt.

"Doing good. Married now, have a daughter. Just came back home for a quick visit."

"You? Married? If that don't beat all. Congrats, man." They shook hands again. "I haven't heard anything from you since the night all hell broke loose."

Eric was one of the men on the scene when Mandy and Hunt had the final shoot-out at the cabin that left Craig Abbey and a few of Vince's men dead, and Vince and Hunt shot.

"Nothing near that exciting has gone on since. Sure beat the piss out of a stolen bike here or there, not that I want to see that kind of carnage again anytime soon." He stared at Hunt, making him suddenly uneasy. "You kind of fell off the grid. I talked to Roy a while back, trying to check up on you. He said you moved to Europe or something."

"Yeah. We're kind of here and there lately. Wife has some family money and likes to do the traveling thing."

Eric pulled him aside and lowered his voice. "You're a lying sack of shit."

Hunt grinned. "Yeah, I guess I am."

"Relocation?"

"You could call it that."

"Then showing up back here isn't for pleasure or the smartest thing, is it?"

"No, but it had to be done. Just pretend you never saw me, okay?"

"Anything I need to know?"

"Not at all. If there was anything to worry about, I'd contact your department. I didn't even bother Roy with this."

"You're not making me feel better."

"I swear you're fine. I wouldn't—"

"Shit in my backyard. Yeah, I still don't feel better. Care to stop by and fill me in, anyway?"

"We're leaving in an hour or so. Nothing to tell. You have to trust me on this. Please."

Eric sighed heavily. "I'll trust you, but the minute anything changes, I want to know."

"You have my word."

Hunt was grateful Eric drove away in the opposite direction. But he would have to take extra care in getting back to the cabin just in case he was being tailed. So much for it being a good idea to send him. The hostess called his name, and he walked over to get his order.

After getting everyone set up with their food, Hunt and Mandy went down to the lake to eat alone.

"Any trouble in town?" Mandy asked. "You've seemed a little distracted since you got back."

He explained about running into Eric.

"Are you sure you weren't followed?"

"I'm sure. I took a round-about way here and doubled back a few times."

"I'm sorry I had you go. I should have done it."

"We're okay. Did you get much out of Angelo?"

"He was sleeping with Heidi, but you already figured that."

"You go easy on him?"

"Of course, Hunt. I'm here for information, not to play mother."

"Anything he tell you lead to any bright ideas?"

"Not really. We talked for a bit about Face, Gunner, and the rest of the gang. Things seemed like they changed a bit, but I can't really put my finger on it."

"What's changed? Think of what bothers you the most."

"I can't say. When I worked with Angelo, we were more like bosses to Face and his guys. The way Angelo talks, it's more like they're a team."

"Is that not good?"

"I'm not sure. I don't know why it sits so funny with me."

"Did it affect a chain of command?"

"Didn't seem to. Essentially, they answered to Angelo, but they ran a number of deals on their own and reported back to him. Angelo said he was really beginning to slide into not caring what they did on their own. He received crap from Eddie about it, but as long as Face gave Angelo his share of everything, Eddie cut him some slack."

"Is this when he was drinking himself into a stupor? Maybe Gunner felt someone needed to take over. Maybe he's pushier than Face was."

"That's probably it."

"And while Gunner was taking charge, Angelo was sleeping with Face's girlfriend, who was probably getting anything she could out of him to help Gunner with his undermining."

Mandy closed her eyes. "Dammit. I'm an asshole."

"But you're my asshole, babe. You just needed to talk it through. You're too close to the situation, and so is Angelo. He was probably too loaded to think anything he was saying was of any importance. He no longer gave a shit and just wants out. He's not purposely hiding anything, he just doesn't care. This whole Heidi mess didn't get us any specifics."

"Yeah, but it helps. We know she was getting something, just not what. We need to figure out if Gunner was getting info to Face and how involved he is from behind bars. We don't know if he's behind the killings and if Angelo was unknowingly helping him."

"Still a stretch. I wouldn't put too much blame on the boy's pecker for the killings. If any of the mob is going to get capped, they don't need a specific location given away. It can happen anywhere."

"True enough, I guess. Obviously Gunner still has a certain amount of loyalty to Face, even if he thinks he may never get out of prison. We didn't catch anything in the transcripts, but it doesn't mean it wasn't happening somehow."

Hunt gave her a kiss. "We could have called and gotten this much, you know. We didn't have to take a five-hour drive for this and a burger."

She grinned. "I know. I just really needed to check on him. I did pick up something else coming here, though. We got talking once he got comfortable. I don't think he would have thought to just spill it, and I wouldn't have known to ask."

"What was that?"

"From what Angelo has told me, things have changed since I've been out of this mess."

"Continue."

"This deal tonight is going down with a group we didn't deal a lot with before. Angelo made it sound like they've more or less joined forces and work as a team now. This is the biggest deal they've ever done together. I really should be there."

"Unless there's unforeseen traffic again, we'll make it in time, babe."

"Can I start warning you now to keep your cool tonight?"

"Why? Someone in particular I won't like?"

"The head honcho, Sully, and I didn't really click."

"I won't ask you to define that."

"Thanks."

"One more little thing about the drive."

"And that is?" he asked with a raised eyebrow.

"I'm not going to lie and say I didn't secretly want you to stop at the house. I never would have asked for that."

"I know that, too." He picked up her hand and gave it a kiss. "I'm not new here."

"We need to hustle back now if we're going to hit that deal tonight."

Hunt stood and offered her his hand. "Let's go get him tucked back in and get going."

Once they reached the cabin, Mandy turned to Hunt. "I'm going to take a minute and say goodbye to Angelo. I'll meet you at the car."

"No problem, babe." He waved to Angelo as he walked around the corner.

"You okay out here, or do you want help back in?"

"I'm actually enjoying the fresh air. I'll stay for a bit. I'll holler for help when I'm ready. You're leaving already? That was a short visit."

"It's all the time I can afford. Eddie had a fit as it was that I was coming here."

"He didn't want you seeing me?"

"That's not it. He's just being Eddie and trying to be in control of everything. I don't really care. I needed to know you were okay."

"And find out where I've been sticking it."

"It was relevant."

"I know. Sorry to sound like a dick about it. I'm beginning to understand what the phrase 'cabin fever' means."

"It's only been a few days."

"Yeah, but those two are driving me crazy."

Mandy crossed her arms. "You should be having fun, catching up with your sister."

He shrugged. "A little, I guess, when they aren't banging their brains out."

"Stop being a grump." Mandy gave him a kiss on his forehead. "I'll come back again next chance I get. You heal up."

"Just get this wrapped up before the morning sickness sets it. Sex sounds are one thing. If I have to listen to her yacking, I'll puke myself."

Mandy stopped dead in her tracks. "What?"

CHAPTER NINETEEN

"**D**idn't she tell you?" Angelo asked. "Angie's pregnant."

"Un-fucking-believable." Mandy stormed into the house and shrieked, "Angie!"

Angie slid off the couch and came over to her. Hunt ran into the house, eyes wide.

"What's wrong?" Angie asked.

"You're pregnant?"

Hunt shook his head then went back outside.

"Yeah. So?"

"So? What are you thinking?"

"I'm thinking I love Darin, and I'm having his baby." She crossed her arms. "What's it to you? You don't want this life. Good for you. The man I love is here, and that's where I'm staying."

Darin appeared and wrapped his arm around her. "We'll get married as soon as we get back."

"Does your father know?"

"I'll tell him when we get home. You said to keep the calls to emergencies only. Don't you tell him, either. I want to do it."

Mandy ran her fingers through her hair. "You're all idiots." She stormed out of the house and joined Hunt. "Just leave. For God's sake, just go."

"Yes, ma'am."

Mandy was silent for a long time. Hunt knew her well enough to give her space. Anything he would say could bite him in the ass bad.

"I'm not only upset about her being pregnant," Mandy finally blurted out.

"I know, babe."

"She's too young for starters and an idiot about her choice of a father."

"I agree."

"She needs to get away from these people, not play house with them."

"Absolutely. You are completely right."

"Don't patronize me, Hunt."

"I'm agreeing with you. How is that patronizing you?"

"You're just agreeing to shut me up."

"No, I agree because I agree. That's no life for her or for a baby."

Mandy rested her head on the window. "It's not fair."

"I know." Hunt placed his hand on her thigh. "Babe...you can't live their lives. They'll do what they're going to do no matter what. Don't let it upset you."

She sat up straight. "Watch your speed. There's a cop car up there."

Hunt tapped his brakes for a minute, but when he got a better look at the car, he floored the gas pedal.

"What are you doing? Hunt! You'll get us pulled over!"

"That's the point."

"Are you insane?"

They flew past the police car at seventy-five miles an hour. The cruiser's lights came on and hurried after them. Hunt chuckled as he pulled over.

"I'm glad you're happy with yourself." Mandy crossed her arms and leaned back in the seat. "I can't imagine how a two-hundred-dollar ticket will help things."

"Babe, I'd know that fat head anywhere." Hunt stepped out of the car and walked toward Roy with his hands behind his neck. "Don't arrest me, officer. My foot was stuck on the gas pedal."

Roy laughed hard. "Blaine, you son of a bitch." The two men exchanged a hug and a back pat before they broke apart. "What the hell are you doing around here?"

"Between you and me? Family business."

Mandy approached them, and Roy gave her a warmer welcome than Hunt expected. "I have to say it's actually good to see you, Mandy. I see you're keeping our boy in shape here and not letting married life get the better of him."

"He's an okay guy to have around."

"How's Hannah?"

"She's an absolute doll. Thanks for asking."

Roy turned back to Hunt. "Should I be worried about why you're here?"

"If you need to worry, you'll be the first to know."

"I'll bet."

"Whoops. You're right. You'll be the second to know. I'll call you right after I'm done with Eric."

"Eric? You involved Hamburger Harry and not me?"

Hunt laughed. "You lose one eating contest to the man and you hold it against him for life. And no, I happened to run into him at Hamburger Heaven."

"See. Bastard was practicing." Roy grinned then winked at Mandy.

"Look...I really need this on the down low. I don't want you up there. There will be no problems, and you're out of your jurisdiction, anyway. I couldn't ask for your help if I wanted it."

"You have someone up at the cabin?"

"The general area. There won't be any problems. I honestly thought about calling you when we sent them up there, but it's really not an issue. Especially not for you. Just trust me on this."

"I would have been out a boss and friend if I'd trusted you last time."

Hunt sighed. "This is different. Look, I saw you and wanted to say hello. If I thought you'd give me grief, I'd've outrun your ass."

"Like you could if you wanted to. Who's up there?"

Mandy interrupted. "Roy, please. We needed a quiet place for Angelo."

"The kingpin's son? What the hell for?"

"We're putting him into custody. I needed to handle a few things first."

"You're back with the feds?"

"Not exactly."

"Oh, do define 'not exactly.'"

"She can't," Hunt said. "I won't have you arresting my wife."

"You're doing stuff with Menusco's gang again?"

"And I'm helping."

"What?" Roy screamed.

"Chill, dude. It's all good. I promise I'll be in touch if we need you in any way."

"I don't like this, but I'll trust you. Call me."

"Only if I have to." They shared a quick hug. "Great seeing you again, man."

"That's sheriff-man to you." Roy turned to Mandy and hugged her. "Take care of this oaf, would you?"

"I will. I actually love that job."

Hunt and Mandy were at the warehouse with Gunner when a large, white van with a laundry logo backed into the bay.

"I'm going to get on the top of that building and get a bird's-eye view," Hunt said. "See if I can catch anything out of the ordinary."

"Like anything would be ordinary for you, watching a few hundred-thousand dollars of cocaine exchange hands."

"You know what I mean, baby."

"I know. I don't like to be separated from you."

"I'll be fine." He kissed her before he took off for an alley across the street. From there he entered a building through an unlocked side door, climbed a few flights, and found a door with roof access.

As Hunt watched from above, the access door boomed closed. He ducked down behind a roof vent. The gravel crunched under the newcomer's feet as he headed toward Hunt. Wanting to be the one on the side of surprise, Hunt stood and aimed his gun. "Freeze!"

The black man stood calmly with his hands at his side. "Freeze? Sounds like a cop thing to me."

"Maybe I watch too much TV. You are?"

"Hammer. And you?"

Hunt lowered his gun. "Well, shit. Must be the name they were handing out too freely."

"You Amanda's boy?"

"That's me."

"I guess great names think alike. See anything unusual?"

"Nothing moving down there other than our boys."

"Whoever the chicken shit is, who's causing the trouble, hasn't had the balls to come around a big deal like this. I don't think they have the insight to really know what's going on. They seem to pick our guys off out of the blue when they're doing nothin'."

"You'd think if they wanted to hurt anyone, it would be in the wallet."

"In this case, it seems to be about thinning out the crowd, not about taking our product."

"That doesn't seem right no matter how you look at it. Who exactly are you covering? You're not one of Gunner's men, right?"

"We're a little west of Gunner. This town is a lot of territory to cover."

"Who's your guy?"

"Sully. You writing a book?"

"I need to know the faces, same as you. I may be the new kid on the block, but I don't plan on keeping it that way."

"I've been waiting for Amanda to show up at our place and give us the scoop. I hear she's Vince's kid."

"You heard right. She's glad to finally get the chance to get that out there. Vince held her back. She has plans to really kick some ass. Things have been pretty crazy since she's been back, and we had some business to take care of today."

They were both silent for a while, as they watched what was going on below.

"Sorry about Angelo. He was a good dude."

"Yeah. Mandy took it pretty hard. Just makes her more serious about everything, you know?"

Hammer grunted. They stood together and watched as a tall, thin black man approached Mandy. She talked to him with exaggerated hand expressions. Hunt wasn't sure what to think. The man took her by the waist and dipped her down. They were far away, but Hunt could tell he was kissing her. He took a step closer to the edge, and Hammer held his arm.

"Give it a second."

Mandy was released and stood straight back up then leaned toward the man and slapped him hard.

"Bingo," Hammer said. "That would be my boss, Sully. You think he'd learn by now."

"He's kissed her before?"

"If you want to call that a kiss. She has one hell of a follow through."

"Maybe I know why we haven't been to see you yet."

"Nah. Amanda's tough. She don't take his shit. I guess it's been a while, and he needed a reminder. You doin' her or what?"

"She's my boss."

"So?"

"I don't mix business and pleasure."

"Too bad for you. Always wanted me a piece of that."

"I'll be sure to pass it on."

Hammer took a small, brown vial out of his coat pocket. He knocked out a pile of powder on his knuckle and sniffed it up with his left nostril. After doing the other side, he offered the bottle to Hunt.

"Thanks, but again, I don't mix business and pleasure."

"It's really good. It was the sample off this shipment."

"Still good. Thanks."

"Well, I'm heading down. You staying for a while?"

"A little. I want to watch as the van leaves. See if anything goes on in the aftermath."

"Good plan. I'll catch your act later."

"I'm sure you will. See you."

"Later, Big H."

Hunt laughed. He had to remember to rag on Mandy about that name again.

After watching for another fifteen minutes, the truck drove away. The delivery bay cleared out, and everyone that should have left did. Mandy went back inside with Gunner. Hunt decided everything was clear and went back down. Hammer had been right. No one was out to mess with the drug haul.

Hunt walked into the warehouse and assumed his best stance outside the office where Mandy talked to Gunner. After spotting him, Mandy said her goodbyes. He strode quietly beside her until they were outside. Once they were in the car, Hunt spoke.

"So, 'didn't really click' means he always tried to probe your tonsils with his tongue?"

"I figured by your silence you were pissed. I was hoping you didn't catch that, and no. He didn't slip me any tongue, oh jealous oaf of mine. He likes to make a big production of everything. Sully knows I can't stand him. That's the whole point of it."

"I'm not pissed. Just playing the strong, silent type, sweetness. I'll let him live for now. Did you learn anything new out of him?"

"No. He confirmed what Angelo told me. They have this whole new understanding. I take it you didn't see anything, or you would have spoken up."

"Nothing out there to see, but I made a new friend."

She turned her head to face him. "Who?"

"My namesake."

"Hammer? How did you meet him?"

"Showed up on the roof I was on. It was so romantic."

Mandy slapped his leg. "Stop it. I'm really sorry about the name. I honestly forgot about him. I told you, we weren't the friendliest. I don't know why it popped in my head."

"That's all right. It's not like I have to live with it for long. But just so you know, next time I play gangster, I get to pick my own name."

She chuckled. "Deal. We'll have to do some rounds again tomorrow. There is a whole new territory divide, and everyone seems effing peachy. I'm not sure what to think at all. If someone is trying to shoot their way into Vince's spot, it's not Sully."

"'Effing,' babe?"

"I'm tired. Too much driving today. I want to crawl in bed and not move for a day." She rested her head in Hunt's lap. "I'm sorry. You've been up a lot longer than I have. How are you holding up?"

"I'm fine. I didn't even need a blast of coke from Hammer."

She let out a heavy sigh. "I'm really sorry I brought this into our lives."

"It's not like we didn't foresee excitement, babe. When you meet with a bang like ours, I guess it should be expected."

"I suppose it should, but it isn't. Life has been so pleasant until now."

"It'll get back to normal soon." Hunt stroked her hair while he drove until she fell asleep. She hardly stirred when he carried her into the house.

The next morning, Hunt and Mandy wandered down the stairs to the kitchen. Milo put his paper down. "You two have looked better."

"Long day yesterday," Hunt said, running his hand over his face, still trying to wake up.

"Sit. I'll bring you coffee." As he approached with the pot and cups he said, "Sorry you couldn't wait for me to go with you."

"They were, too. Trust me. Angelo made more than one complaint about the food," Mandy said. "We'll take you next time if there is a next time. I'll give you warning to pack some provisions for them. They'd appreciate it. We were awake and wanted an early start. We had to be back for something last night, so it just wouldn't have been worth it for you to come all that way." Mandy quit talking. Even to herself, she sounded like she was rambling.

"Do I expect you for dinner tonight?"

"Hard to say, Milo. I'd like to think so."

"I'll plan on it. It doesn't hurt anything if you're not." He lowered his voice. "The oafs eat well, anyway."

Mandy smiled at him. Inside, her mind was racing. She wanted to trust Milo and hated that she now had doubts about him.

Mandy made Eddie her first stop that day. She had gotten grief for not filling him in as often as he'd like, so she wanted to get it out of the way. After being announced, they walked into his office and sat in the loveseat against the wall rather than in the two chairs across from his desk. It was less intimidating that way.

"I'm humbled you took the time to stop in."

"Can the shit, Eddie. I'm here. There's nothing to tell you, but I'm here. Angelo is fine, and the deal went down without a hitch. I'm going to follow up with Sully today. I learned things are a little different between the groups, and I want to be seen and let them know who's in charge."

"Just so you don't forget who's really in charge here. Me."

"You have me. You figured it out. I wanted you to kidnap me in my own home and disrupt my life, so I could come and pretend to be Vince's daughter and take over the Menusco fortune."

"I'm glad you mentioned that. Angelo would have gotten everything if he was here, but I can tell you...we're not a Fortune 500 company. I won't be sending him a monthly allowance if he bails out. He'll be given a nice sum then he's on his own."

"I'm sure he doesn't expect any more than that. His mind is made up, Eddie. Word is spreading like wildfire that he's gone. Do whatever you need to as far as what your plans are for Vince's money."

Eddie leaned back in his chair. "Honestly, I expected more of a fight."

"It's not about the money. I would have thought that was clear."

"What did you learn at the cabin?"

"I had to follow up on a lead. I needed to find out what Angelo knew."

"Who is this 'lead?'"

"Someone I'm tying in with Face. I'll let you know if it pans out. If there was something I needed you to do, I'd ask."

"Would you?"

Mandy stood. "Yes, Eddie, I would. I want out of here, remember? If I thought you could speed things up for me, I would ask for your help."

"Nice to hear. To think, all this time, I thought maybe you didn't trust me."

"Don't get me wrong, I still don't know what to think of you."

Eddie grinned. "Same old Amanda."

"Yeah. Fancy that. Same old me."

"You want to meet with the man who replaced your husband?"

"Do I? You think it's of importance?"

"That's your call. I know he's not involved. To quote Kevin Costner, 'the man couldn't hit water if he fell out of a boat.' He's not our shooter, but he does have the insights on everyone in the immediate family."

"Does he have the will?"

"I have a copy of it here," he said as he opened a bottom desk drawer. "I keep going through it, looking for something I may have missed."

Mandy stood and walked over to take a look at it.

"There's nothing in it out of the ordinary. Angelo inherited everything except, of course, there were provisions in it for Angie."

Mandy flipped through it. "And you have final say in case of accidental deaths."

"And you planning his death puts me in charge. I know how this looks. If I was after money, I could have killed him anytime. It also wasn't my idea to kill off Angelo. That was you."

Mandy tossed the will back on the desk. "If you don't mind, I'd like to get a head start on my day."

"I'll follow you out. I have a few things to do today myself." He stood and removed his coat from the back of his chair. "This job ain't all glamor."

Mandy motioned for Hunt to get up and join her. "You're doing the strong, silent thing well, hon," Mandy said when he reached her. She wrapped an arm around his waist, mostly because she wanted to piss off Eddie. He had always frowned at public displays of affection. Mandy had never seen him with a woman. She had no idea if he was married and never cared to know. She'd only feel sorry for the poor woman.

They rode the elevator in silence. When they exited into the lobby, Eddie spoke up again. "I know you and Sully don't get along very well, but please don't be burning any bridges. All these killings really come as a surprise. They would have been at the top of my list before, but lately things have been going too well." He held the door open for her to step outside. "I know how you feel, Mandy, but I'm not—"

Shots were fired by Eddie's head, and everyone scrambled to the ground. Eddie touched his head and inspected his hand. There was no blood.

Hunt crawled toward him and checked his head. "You're not hit."

Another shot hit the wall. They lay there with their hands over their heads. Hunt was the first to stand. After hearing a car squeal away, Mandy shot to her feet and caught sight of Hunt already running after the car. Mandy removed her gun and took off after it as well. Seeing it turning at the corner and taking the alley, she changed her mind and went back for the car. It was being held at the front in a reserved parking spot.

Speeding away from the curb, Mandy almost took out a cab. She was given a heavy dose of car horn and a one-fingered salute but kept her focus and floored the gas, sliding around the first corner. Catching up to Hunt in another block, she slowed enough for him to open the door and jump in.

Traffic was thick but not at a standstill, and she was able to keep the car in sight. She had to run a yellow light to keep up, barely avoiding an accident.

"You think this new twist has Eddie off your list of bad guys?"

"I don't know. Maybe."

The car took a ramp down, and Mandy had to cut off another car to keep up.

"Careful, babe."

"No shit. Can you catch anything of the plates?"

"Still too far away."

Mandy managed to get closer by another two car lengths, but they were still too far. The car ran a red light and took a left turn. Cars were sliding everywhere, but Mandy managed to dodge through them without hitting anyone. After another block, a police car pulled out behind them.

"Shit!"

"Keep going, babe. Don't lose them. Let the cops follow."

"I wasn't planning on stopping." Flooring it to make her point, she managed to get another car length closer. The car pulled into an alley. Within seconds Mandy pulled in behind it, but the car had already been abandoned.

Mandy slammed her hands on the steering wheel. "Goddammit!" She took her gun off the seat and hurried out of the car. The police car screeched behind them. Two officers got out with their guns drawn.

"Drop the weapon!"

CHAPTER TWENTY

Hunt knew whoever they were after was long gone. He played the only card he thought would keep them from getting arrested. Getting out with his hands high, he held up his badge.

"Put your guns down. We're FBI. Call in the plates on this thing and see what you come up with."

The officer from the passenger side came running over and went to the car. He called in the plates while the one who drove walked over to Hunt. "What's the problem?"

"Shots were fired over at Vince Menusco's building."

The police officer laughed. "And I give a shit why?"

"Because they went over my head, that's why."

Mandy had tucked her gun back in its place and joined them. "Word is you boys in blue aren't doing anything about the killings. I guess I hoped for a little backup if needed."

The officer pointed to his partner. "We're calling in your plates. Don't get huffy with me, lady. We've been dealing with this shit for far too long around here. If some Dudley Do-Right is going to thin out the thugs, I'm not going to stop him."

"Even if one of you gets caught in the crossfire?"

"I'll worry if and when it gets to that. For now, there's no investigation from our end. I don't know you, and I don't know where you're from." He reached his hand out for Hunt's ID. "I wasn't aware the Feds were involved in this."

"I'm sure my partner meant no offense," Hunt said to the officer. "But I guess with everyone's attitude about it on the local level, someone bigger wanted us to take a look before innocent people get hurt."

He gave the ID back, apparently satisfied with it and Hunt's answer. "This is our territory. If you're up to something, you should have stopped in and spoken to our chief at the station."

"My apologies. Truth be told, this was our first stop. We're starting off with routine questions and trying to get some idea of a place to start. Once we heard Vince was killed, the bureau no longer wanted to sit on this."

"Long overdue housecleaning if you ask me."

Hunt knew that was going to send Mandy over the edge.

She stepped forward. "And Angelo being killed? That was more deserved housecleaning?" She poked at the officer's chest, and Hunt cringed.

He shoved her hand away then his head tilted. "Angelo's dead?"

"Think we need to get involved now?" Her hands went on her hips.

The other officer interrupted them.

"The car was reported stolen about an hour ago. I can dust it for prints, but I doubt that'll do much good."

"Do it anyway," Hunt demanded, grateful for the change of subject. If the officer dared bad mouth Angelo, he was sure to be wearing his police cruiser on his back, courtesy of his wife.

"Are we taking orders from Feds now?" he asked his partner.

"Just do it."

The officer mumbled as he walked back to the patrol car.

Hunt stood by Mandy, hoping she took the cue to let him take it from here. Amazingly, she did. He read the officer's name and precinct number off his uniform and said it out loud. "I'll give a call there in a few hours and see if you lifted anything for prints. We'll stay out of your way. If I hear anything that will be of use to you, we'll be in touch. We didn't expect trouble this early in the game, or we would have had back up."

"You think you were the target?"

"I believe Eddie was. We just happened to be there."

"With Vince and Angelo gone, I guess he should watch his back then, huh?"

"It would appear so. Sorry for the bother, gentlemen." Hunt took Mandy by the arm and put her in the passenger seat then went around to the driver's side. "You mind moving that thing so we can get out?" he shouted to the second officer still digging the fingerprint kit from the trunk. He slammed it closed and looked to his partner.

"They're free to go."

He shook his head, slid behind the wheel, and backed it up.

Once they were on their way, Hunt spoke up. "Thanks for letting the subject of Angelo drop. We needed to get out in a hurry. I'm lucky he didn't try to get a card or something from me."

"He didn't give a shit. No one gives a shit. This is why I never wanted back in. No one does anything about the situation. They just piss and moan. If someone's child was caught in the crossfire, would they care then?"

Hunt pulled the car over to the curb and hit his flashers. A few cars honked, but he ignored them. "Come here," he said as he motioned for Mandy to slide over to him. She did, and he held her tight. "It's okay."

"No, it's not," she said into his chest.

"Yes, it is. And holy shit, you sure know how to drive, babe."

She smiled and sat up. "Woody worthy?"

"I could pound a twelve-inch spike with it."

She laughed. "I love you."

"Prove how much later. We need to get back to Eddie."

Eddie was in his limo when Mandy and Hunt returned. Hunt stayed in the car while Mandy went to give him a quick update.

"Any luck?" Eddie asked.

"Lost him. Did pick up a couple of cops, though."

He scoffed. "They're mine or they don't care, am I right?"

"Thanks for caring how we managed to get ourselves out of it. This is where those badges came in handy. They're dusting it, but I don't expect anything to come of it. The car was stolen of course. We're off to Sully's. Just keep your head low and watch your back, Eddie."

"You still think I'm behind it?"

"I don't know what to think about anything anymore. I'm chasing my tail here."

"That bullet could have been for you, too. Keep that in mind. You're creating quite a stir with your 'Vince's daughter' act. I never expected it to fly."

"Well, then, call me the queen of crap." She climbed out of the car and closed the door with no other words of wisdom.

Hunt asked, "Sully's?"

"We'll get there eventually. We need to try to find Heidi first."

"You have any clues where to look?"

"A few. She won't stay away for long. She'll want her fix."

"Gunner's?"

"You catch on fast, my love."

Hunt and Mandy pulled up to the warehouse and had no problem getting to the office. The man at the door immediately opened it and stepped back as they approached. Mandy held back her grin. She hated to admit she liked the small level of fear she instilled on the peons. She gave him a slight nod as she walked in and nothing more.

Gunner's office door was open. He stood at the sight of her. "I didn't expect to see you so soon. Something wrong with the way last night went down? Sully crying over his cut?"

"I haven't been to see him yet. Is that going to be an issue?"

"Shouldn't be. I was just wondering what you were doing here."

"I'll pop in any time I want, Gunner. You treat Angelo this way?"

"No...I...I just didn't expect you. That's all." He turned to Hunt with a raised eyebrow, but Mandy snapped at him again.

"Don't give him that 'the bitch is crazy' look. He does as he's told. You'd best learn from him if you know what's good for you. We're not here about the deal. I need to find

Heidi. What do you know about where she hangs out lately?"

"Heidi? Why do you need to find Heidi?"

Mandy motioned for him to come closer with her forefinger. When he moved in, she whispered, "None of your fucking business."

"Geez, Mand. Who pissed in your cornflakes this morning?" She took out her gun and pointed it as his head. His hands went up. "Shit! Knock off the crap!"

"Who pissed in my cornflakes? Let me see. Maybe the guys that shot at me when we were talking to Eddie? Now tell me what you know about Heidi."

"Put the gun down first for crying out loud," Gunner pleaded.

Mandy was surprised to see Hunt by her side. Her attitude must have been scaring him. She flipped the gun down and gave it to him. She turned back to Gunner but left her attitude on high. "Better? Now what do you know?"

"Damn, woman. Come sit down and take a chill. You should lay off the goods. Looks like last night's haul was a little too pure for you." She wasn't about to correct him and took a seat.

"I don't see Heidi around these parts much since Face has been locked up. She comes by now and then, looking for a fix, but that's it."

"But of course, out of respect to Face, you give it to her."

"Of course."

"And when she wants sex."

His expression went blank.

"Like I'm an idiot. You're not going to give it away. Face isn't getting out, so you figure 'what the hell,' right?"

"It's not like that. And I still don't see what you need with her."

"She was sleeping with my brother, and I want to ask her a few questions."

"You knew about that?"

"We were closer than you think. Yes, he told me about her. It would have been helpful if you mentioned you knew about it."

"Why would I? I don't see what she could possibly have to do with anything."

"Just do me a favor and tell me everything from now on. Just because you don't think it's important doesn't mean that's the case. I may need to take the streets back over, but what is going on is top priority. This morning's shooting put it back up at the top of my list where it belongs. Sorry if I was edgy. Now please, will you tell me where I can find her?"

He leaned back in his chair and held his hands at the back of his head as if he was contemplating his answer. "You gonna hurt her?"

"Of course not. I just want to ask her a few questions."

"Can I be there?"

"No. I don't think she'll talk with you there. You do know where she is though, don't you?"

He sat forward again. "She's at my place. Been hiding for two days and won't say why. I gotta take care of her, you know."

"And that includes servicing her." Mandy put her hand up before he could protest. "I just need to talk to her."

"I'll take you there, but you have to go easy on her. No gun crap like you pulled on me."

"I don't think she'll need that much motivation." Mandy opened her hand. "Gimme an eight."

"An eight-ball? Damn, girl. You want info bad. You must really think she knows something."

"Anything will help at this point."

Gunner stood and went to the tall cabinet behind him. He removed a sealed bag of cocaine and tossed it to Hunt. "It ain't the good stuff. She don't need that."

"Don't care," Hunt replied before he put it in his breast pocket.

Once they arrived at Gunner's, Mandy told them she was going up alone.

"I don't like it," Hunt said.

"I don't want to freak her out. You know I can handle her. You two watch both exits in case she tries to leave."

It was obvious Hunt wanted to say more, but he nodded and headed toward the front while Gunner went to the back.

Mandy gave two quick raps on the door before opening it. Heidi was stuffing clothes into a small carry-on bag. She spun around then cursed at the sight of Mandy.

"What are you doing here?"

"I think that's obvious. Please don't try to split. I need to ask you a few questions, that's all."

"I don't know anything."

"Then answering a few questions isn't going to hurt. Look, I don't want to hurt you. You're a friend. Who you see and what you do aren't my concerns. I have a position here now, and I worry about my people. You made a comment about them not having been supposed to hurt Angelo, and I'm begging you to tell me who *they* are."

"You know he was with Kermit and Axle."

"Yes, but I also know those two don't have the brains to scratch their own asses without Gunner or someone else telling them to do so."

"They were just going to hold him for a while."

"Hold him for who?"

"I don't know! They drank with him like they were buddies and took him to the crib when he was really loaded. The more Angelo drank, the more he would lip them, especially after they asked him about me. They got crazy with the pounding on him. I tried to get them to let him go."

"You were with him when they took him?"

"No. They came and got me. They said he wanted to see me and brought me to the warehouse where he was tied up. Kermit said they got word from someone that I had been doin' him, and Willy was pissed. They wanted me to watch to teach me a lesson. I wasn't there for long. Just seeing him spit blood made me puke. They let me leave."

"I know you're also sleeping with Gunner. Do they?"

Heidi looked up, afraid again.

"Face did order this, didn't he? He wanted to stop you from sleeping with Angelo."

"I wouldn't know the answer to that. I told you I haven't even seen him in a while. I never would have allowed this. Don't you think I would have warned Angelo if I could? I'm sorry for what happened to him, but none of this is fair to me at all. Willy isn't ever getting out. I should be able to have someone. I want to break it off with Willy, but Gunner is afraid."

Mandy stood silently, waiting for her to talk it out.

"Look, I really like Angelo, but he doesn't want anything past sex. We were sort of done. Gunner wants to be together, but right now, we need to keep it from the guys because of Willy."

"And what happened to Angelo proved why it should be kept a secret." Mandy rubbed her forehead. "So, the boys didn't mean to hurt Angelo as bad as they did is the bottom line. They took him, but you don't know why." Heidi nodded and buried her face in her legs. "There is no connection to what's going on and all the other killings."

Heidi's eyes filled with tears. "I don't know anything about that. I swear. They said they were supposed to take him and hold onto him. His attitude about me is what got him so beat up, though."

"Why didn't you tell me this at the pizza place?"

"I don't know. I've always been afraid of you. I was high, too." She shrugged. "Just afraid, Mandy. If he was beat up because of me, I killed him."

"I'm in no mood to comfort you on your logic there. If you want to call it off with Willy, do it before someone else gets hurt. Please. I need you to think for me. You have no idea who told them to grab him?"

"I already said no."

"Well, fuck." Mandy stormed out of the room and went downstairs to find Gunner.

"Gunner! Get in here!" Mandy yelled out to the backyard.

She had a blade on Gunner's neck when Hunt caught up to the shouting in the kitchen. He pulled her off him and held her at his hip while she fought to get free.

"What the hell is going on now?" Hunt asked.

"Did you think she'd keep her mouth shut, Gunner?"

"I don't know what you're bitching about."

"Who told Face about Angelo and Heidi? You, so she could be all yours?"

He turned away from her and punched a hole through his kitchen wall. "I didn't do that!"

"Then enlighten me on who did!"

He removed the knife from her hand and slammed it into the table. "Face is pissed off. He heard about Angelo and Heidi. He wanted those two meatheads to shake him up a little."

"How did he get word to them?"

"Somebody was recently released from prison. Said he was doing time with Face, and he was madder than hell when he heard about Angelo. And don't ask me who. It's prison, Amanda. Figure it out. Word just spreads. Half of the guards will do anything for a buck, and the other half will do it for a blow job. I knew they were going to shake him up a little. I'm sorry I couldn't do anything to stop it. I didn't know details. You know I would have helped him if I could have."

"Bullshit. You figured he'd leave her alone, and she'd be yours now?"

"No. Dammit." He spun around and ran his fingers through his hair. "Be pissed off, but this wasn't my fault. Those two would have let him go when they had their fun. Hell. You're blaming me, but I'm still waiting for my turn at being found out and beaten."

Mandy shook free of Hunt's hold and took a few paces closer to him. "If I wasn't so pissed about being back at square-fucking-one with the big picture, I'd kill you myself."

"You need me. This is a waste of time. What happened to him wasn't about the killings or business—"

"It was about pussy. Goddammit, Gunner. Grow a set and tell the world you're doing Face's girl. Get the word to him while you're at it, and deal with the consequences before it starts another shit storm. I don't need this crap on my streets. I have real issues to deal with." She slammed the coke on the table. "Didn't need it. Go have a party with your whore." Mandy stormed out of the house with Hunt close at her heels. "Find your own way back to the warehouse."

Again, Hunt was at a loss for words as they drove away. Maybe Mandy was starting to buy her own con. She almost did it too well.

"Babe?"

"I know. Angelo's alive. Stop getting so upset."

"That's not what I was going to say. I need to know where to go to get to Sully's."

"I'll tell you when to turn and where."

"Okay, boss."

"I'm sorry. I really thought we were going to get somewhere with Heidi. Gunner doesn't think so, but we know Angelo was taken for something other than Heidi, and we don't have the foggiest idea why. This shit is really pissing me off."

"I'm glad you told me because I haven't noticed."

"Don't give me crap. You know I have to act the way I do. I don't exactly like it, either."

"I'm just glad you're on my side." He let her sit quiet for a while longer. "You have a game plan for Sully's?"

"Basically, I need to show my face. Let anyone new see me and let them know I've taken Angelo's place. I have to stand up to Sully, especially after last night. I can't stay away after he pulls that crap. I'll look like I'm afraid to be around him."

"Hammer said he tried it before."

"It's also how he acquired a broken arm."

Hunt whipped his head around. "You?"

"No."

Her look said enough. He didn't need to ask. It had to have been Gerard's doing. Mandy stared out the window in a daze. Hunt hoped she snapped out of it in time to give him directions.

"You did what?" Mandy screamed at Gerard.

"Had his arm broken. Should have had his dick ripped off. He should consider himself lucky."

"You can't go maiming everyone who looks at me cross. Who exactly do you think I'm dealing with on a daily basis?"

"I know who you're dealing with. Don't think I like it. I'm tired of the same damn fight all the time. I wish you'd just stop already."

"You know I can't do that."

"Well, dammit, quit playing so tough. You're with Angelo, for crying out loud. Why isn't he watching you better?"

"Because it's my job to watch him, not the other way around. You know what things will be like the next time I have to go there?"

"Yeah. He'll keep his lips to himself."

"Dammit, Gerard." Mandy walked over to the bar, poured herself a healthy serving of vodka, and downed it in one shot.

"Why do you even care what I did to Sully?"

"Because you're screwing with my turf. You just screamed 'Mandy can't handle herself. You'd better watch your backs, boys, or her big bad husband will have your asses in a sling.'"

"You say that like it's a bad thing."

She tried to storm past him, but he caught her by the arm. "Where are you going?"

"Anywhere you're not." She shook herself free, but he seized her again. Before she realized she had slapped him, a stinging burned her palm. "Let go of me," she said through bared teeth.

Mandy went to one of Angelo's regular hangouts that night. She'd found him on the first try. The two of them told personal stories they had never shared before. Mandy got so drunk, she was finding it hard to remember what was real and what was her cover. Trying to keep them straight sober was hard enough.

She cried for her parents for the first time in months. Angelo had lost his mother when he was young and expressed his happiness at finally being on the comforting end of things for a change.

Mandy wiped away a tear. She had been undercover for almost eight months. Her daily activities were starting to wear on her. She hated what she was doing. Finally releasing the feelings she had bottled up felt good. "My parents would hate what I've become."

He picked her chin up and held her gaze. "You're a good person. Don't ever let anyone make you feel otherwise."

"I work for the friggin' mob. What part of that should I be proud of?"

"Hey." He pulled her head to his chest and kept an arm around her. "You're a tough nut and a caring person. I've seen you with Darci. You'll be a great mom someday."

"Sure. I'll carry a diaper bag around with us and a teething ring made of bullets."

Angelo gently shook her shoulder and pointed up. Her eyes froze at the sight of Gerard.

"You even think about touching him with a pinky, and I'll kill you," she slurred.

"Wouldn't dream of it. Let's go home, baby."

She made her way out from behind the booth and poked at Gerard's chest. "In fact, you even think about touching anyone again because of me, and I'll kill you."

"We're not doing this here."

"Yes, we are."

He took her by the arm and started to walk her out. Angelo slid out from behind the table and blocked him.

"She's drunk."

"No shit."

"Just go easy on her, okay?"

"I think I can handle my wife. Thanks, Angelo. You should go home yourself. Even for you, you look pretty damn drunk."

A woman slinked up beside Angelo as Gerard spoke. "Sounds like a great idea to me. I've been waiting for that woman to leave all night."

Angelo took the stranger's hand and headed for the door.

"You were keeping him from his adoring public by crying on him, Mandy."

"Too bad for you, that's not your fate tonight." She straightened and ran toward the bathroom to throw up.

It was then that she knew she had to close this job quickly. She was now playing wounded wife. The fact she just helped spill close to a million dollars of cocaine onto the streets of New York should have been what bothered her most, not her marriage. Marriage? Fake marriage? Did it really count if she got married under cover and with an assumed name? Her head was spinning. She needed to sober up, get her priorities back on track, and get the info to Craig Abbey the next day. This had to help the case against Vince. This needed to be over. Soon.

CHAPTER TWENTY-ONE

"Babe?"

"Huh? Oh, sorry. Take the next exit." Mandy was lost in memories. She hated Gerard for interfering in her work, but Hunt was doing the same thing. Of course, they wanted to protect her, but she always had to play the hard-ass anyway. Even when she was little, she'd prided herself on being the protector among her friends. Maybe that's what had made her take the defense classes. All the weapons training. She may have ended up working for the FBI on a total bogus visit from Craig Abbey, but she did like the work, and dammit, she was good at it.

Maybe if they had to relocate again, she'd consider James's offer to teach others what she knew. She wasn't sure how Hunt would take this news, but she'd jump off that bridge when she had to.

"Take a left after two more blocks. The warehouse looks a lot like Gunner's." When they reached it, Mandy directed Hunt where to park. Before they got out, she placed her hand on his arm. "I know why you do what you do, but could you please keep your cool in here?"

"I won't make promises I can't keep, but I promise to try. You have to admit I've done pretty good so far."

"For the most part you have, and I love you for it. Please, though, watch yourself around these guys. Remember, they're relatively new territory. We have to play this just right."

"Understood."

The two of them entered the office where Sully and Hammer were talking. Sully stopped mid-sentence and approached Mandy.

"I notice you still wear your wedding ring."

Mandy fiddled with it. "He was killed while we were married. It doesn't seem right to take it off yet."

"So, you are on the market." He stepped closer to her. "What was with the slap last night? Come on, sugar. Gimme a shot."

Mandy held her stance firm. "Just because I'm available, that doesn't mean I'm on the market. Come on, Sully. Cut the crap. You wouldn't treat Angelo this way."

"He doesn't have your ass." Hunt stepped forward. Sully put his hands up and took a step back. "Hey...you can't blame a guy for trying."

"Yes, I can. It's unprofessional as hell. The lady asked you to back off, now back the fuck off."

Mandy gave Hunt a brief nod of approval for Sully to see. Hunt wasn't wrong in what he did. Any of the bodyguards would have reacted that way. She turned to Sully. "I understand things have been a little different between our two groups. If you want to keep it this way, I suggest you respect my boundaries. If you're going to continue to act this way, we'll go to the east side and let you find your goods elsewhere."

"You really want to start that war, lady?"

"I'm not starting anything. You are. I demand respect. If you aren't going to give it, I'm no longer going to associate with you. That's as plain as I'm going to spell it."

"Is there an alternative?"

"Sure. Hammer here can break your other arm."

Sully laughed hard. "I knew you ordered that."

"As a matter of fact, I didn't. I like to fight my own battles. But I won't discuss my personal life with you. I'm especially not going to stand here and let you speak ill of the dead. What's done is done."

"Then by all means," he said as he pointed to a chair, "have a seat. We have some talking to do."

Dropping into the chair, she said, "So talk. That's what I'm here for. I want to see what kinds of rules have been established if, of course, we are going to continue this relationship civilly."

"You sure that's what you want?" He cupped his crotch. "Them Italians don't have anything on us homeboys. You know that, right?" She went to stand up, and he laughed. "I give up. You're off limits. Un-bunch your panties."

"Business, Sully. That's my only request."

"Okay. First, I have some questions for you."

"By all means, fire away."

"I heard some things through the grapevine about you. I honestly didn't expect to see you again, Amanda."

"Lemme guess. I'm a fed. You caught me. I give up. I think you should know that Hammer here is a cop, but he grew tired of fighting crime and decided to turn to drugs instead. Is that all, snookums?"

"Yeah. That's what I heard. I figured Face was full of shit as usual and has it out for you for one thing or another. He's looking at life. What could a little bullshit hurt?"

"I'm really getting tired of it. You and your boys need to consider me Angelo. Better yet, consider me Vince himself. I'm in charge now. You can play this the way we used to or the new way. That is totally your call. I'm game to continue what my brother started, as long as you don't screw around and cross lines you shouldn't. That includes messing with me and the territories we've established. Capiche?"

"Got it."

"Now I have a few questions."

"I can't tell you anything about the shit that's been going down, Mandy."

"Can't or won't?"

"Can't. I don't know anything."

"That puts you in a bad position." She paused and glared at him. "And not a word about 'position.'"

He chuckled and held his hands up in defeat.

"I know none of your people have been axed. Things have changed, and now our people are disappearing, but yours aren't. Would that strike you as strange?"

"I suppose if I was looking at it from your angle, you could think that. But let me also ask you this. If things are going so well with us after all these years, why would my men start to kill yours off now? You'd think if that was my goal, I'd've started that years ago."

"I guess you have a point."

"Look. All kidding about hooking up with you aside, I like the way things are now. Angelo was starting to make good headway between the different...organizations. People liked him. I can't say how sorry I am that he's gone. I want to keep things the way they are. I have no problem answering to a skirt. If there is any way I can help in getting this jackass or group of jackasses caught, count me in. We're already on the lookout and careful. That's how our boys met last night."

"I heard that." Mandy turned to Hunt. "We'll have to do something about the two of you having the same name."

Hunt grinned. "I don't think he'd be too crazy about going by Black Hammer."

Hammer spoke up. "Maybe we should call you Cracker Hammer."

Hunt shook his head. "Sounds like cheese. What'd you call me last night?"

"Big H."

"Works for me."

Mandy couldn't suppress her laughter. "Big H it is."

"Don't worry, babe. I won't make you call me 'Big H' in bed," Hunt said to Mandy as they drove away.

She burst out laughing. "I never would have thought you could be so much fun on a drug deal, hon."

"I'm a man of many secrets."

Although they were in a shadier part of town when conversing with Sully, it wasn't long before they found themselves in a richer area. The layout of New York's neighborhoods never ceased to amaze Hunt. As they drove by a hotel fitting of a Lifestyles of the Rich and Famous episode, Mandy screamed for Hunt to stop.

He hit the brakes and luckily wasn't rear-ended. A few cars honked as they passed. Mandy ran out of the car and into the lobby. Hunt was about to get out, but a doorman stopped him. "Keep it moving, buddy."

"Sorry. No can do." He tossed his keys at a valet. "I'll give you twenty to keep it handy."

"Make it fast, mister."

Hunt caught up to Mandy as she held one elevator open while staring at the other.

"Babe? Who did you see?"

"I have to be imagining things."

"Who?"

The elevator dinged on the fifth floor, and Mandy lunged into the open one and hit five. Several times. "There's no way..."

"Who, dammit?"

The elevator was faster than most. Mandy flew out without answering Hunt. She stood still, quickly looking both ways. A door closed, and she ran in its direction. She knocked on a door. An elderly man opened it.

"Can I help you?"

"Sorry. Wrong room."

"No problem, young lady."

Mandy turned and knocked on the opposite side. Hollering, "Room service," she stepped back.

"Why are you—"

Mandy covered Hunt's mouth.

The door opened, and a woman's voice spoke. "I didn't order any—" Mandy stepped out in front of her. The woman's eyes widened at first then her lip trembled as if she was going to cry. "Oh, Amanda!" She threw her arms around Mandy's neck and choked back a sob.

Mandy held her tight and rocked with her. "What are you doing here, Sue? Why are you back, and what's wrong? Why didn't you call me?"

Sue leaned back and wiped away a lone tear that ran down her cheek. She gave Hunt an obvious once-over. "You're even more handsome than your picture. Very pleased to meet you." She extended her hand, but Hunt pushed it aside.

"That's not how family says hello." Hunt gave her a strong hug.

"Please." Sue motioned toward the room. "Come in for a drink." She walked them over to a small table. "I usually avoid the minibar in these places, but you two are more than worth it. What's your poison?" She dropped ice cubes into glasses, but Mandy stopped her, placing her hand on Sue's.

"I don't want a drink, Sue. I want to know why you're here. I haven't heard from you in over a month. I was about to get worried."

Once Mandy moved her hand, Sue continued mixing a drink for herself. "I know. I'm sorry. Paris became old news, and I just missed home. I've had it with foreigners up to here." She held her hand flat over her head.

"I understand that, but couldn't you have picked one of forty-nine other states? I saw you by chance driving by. Who else is going to spot you? You know it's not safe here, Sue."

Sue dropped on the bed with her drink and took a long swallow. "I missed home, Mandy. Can anyone still be looking for me? Really? Vince is dead. He can't still be after me for his money." Sue stared at her drink and swirled around the ice.

"How did you know Vince was dead?"

There was just a hint of hesitation. "I've been here for almost two weeks. Word travels on the streets. I didn't have to go looking for any information or anything. I'm not that stupid."

"Did you go to the store?"

She didn't answer.

"Sue? Did you?"

"No. Of course not. Well...I did walk by. You would never have recognized me, though. I was a dead-ringer for Jackie O., walking by in my scarf and big sunglasses."

Hunt turned around and ran his fingers through his hair. Mandy simply screamed, "Why?"

Sue stood and moved over to the window. She pushed away the sheer curtain. "This was my home." Again she took a gulp of her drink. "I bet if I stare out this window long enough, I'll witness at least one mugging."

"That's what you came home for? I'm sure you could find a mugger in Paris," Hunt said as he walked over to the bar. "I don't know about you," he said to Mandy, "but I actually do want a drink."

"Fine. Make me something." Mandy joined her by the window, placing her hand on Sue's shoulder. "Why didn't you call me?"

"Because you'd say what you are now. That I shouldn't be here. I needed to come. I promise I was going to leave in a couple more days and call you with my new number. I was actually thinking Colorado. I need a few months of the states."

Mandy gave her a hug. "I'm upset because I'm concerned. You need to be safe. I can't bear the thought of losing you, too."

"You won't. I'm careful, I promise. I just needed to do this."

Mandy leaned back. "You need to leave tomorrow. You don't know what's going on out there." She took a step back. "Do you?"

"Do I what?"

"Know what's going on? Sue...you haven't even asked me why I'm in New York."

Sue let out a loud laugh. "Oh, my goodness! I got so choked up at the sight of you...the familiarity of it all...it felt so nice." She hugged Mandy and rocked with her for a moment then leaned her back again. "Why are you here? Where's that gorgeous niece of mine? I'd love to see more than a cell-phone picture."

"Eddie brought me here to help with Angelo."

"Why on earth would he bring you back into this? What's happened to Angelo?"

"I don't want to get into it with you right now."

"Is he okay?"

Hunt chimed in. "He's dead."

"He's what? No…"

Mandy glanced at Hunt then back at Sue. "We didn't get here soon enough."

"Why is he…why would someone…" As she buried her face in her hands, Mandy rubbed her back. Again, she glared at Hunt.

"Someone is killing off a lot of Vince's gang. We don't have any leads as to who it is or why yet. That's why I want you to leave. If word gets out about you, you could be a target because of who you were associated with."

"I guess that makes sense. If that's what you want, I'll go."

Just then the door opened, and a tall, handsome man walked through. He stopped when he caught sight of Mandy and Hunt. He dropped a duffel bag and went to Sue's side. "Who are your guests, mon amour?" he asked with a heavy French accent.

Sue wrapped an arm around the man and motioned toward Hunt and Mandy with a wide smile. "Sinclair, this is Mandy and her husband Hunt. They happened to see me outside. Isn't it great?"

Hunt was eager to discover who this man was. He approached him with his hand extended. "Nice to meet you."

"Your sister-in-law and her husband? I'd say so." He gave Hunt a hearty handshake. "I kept telling you to get in touch while we were stateside. How lucky they are in New York." When he released Hunt's hand, he hugged Mandy. "What brings you here? Are you free for dinner? I'd love to catch up."

"Sue?" Mandy asked.

"He knows about my past. It's okay, you can talk in front of him."

Mandy faced him. "No, I'm sorry, but I don't really think we can."

"The less you know, the better off you are," Hunt said. "We were just explaining to Sue that it is in your best interest to leave town right away. We'll have to go over the details with you at a later date, but for now, some things are best not said."

"I certainly appreciate that. I come from a law enforcement background myself."

"Nice to hear," Hunt said. "So, you'll have no problem getting Sue on the next available flight out of here?"

"Of course not. Her safety comes first. I really wasn't thrilled with the idea of coming here, but it is very hard to tell her no." He wrapped an arm around her.

"We need to get going," Hunt said. "We don't want to leave Eddie to his own demise and have him question how we use our time again."

Sue stood and gave Mandy another hug. "I'm sorry I stayed quiet and didn't tell you about coming here. When we're settled somewhere, I'll call you. I promise."

"I love you and need you to practice better judgment. I can't lose anyone else."

"I'm so sorry about Angelo. I know it's a front you are putting up, but I'm sure in a sense you felt like a sister to him. I'm so sad he's gone."

"Me too." Mandy released her hug and gave a brief hug to Sinclair. "Take care of her."

Once in the elevator, Mandy let out a swearing tirade.

"You caught that too, did you?" Hunt said after recovering from her newly created cuss words.

"We never told her I was calling myself Angelo's sister. I'm not an idiot, Hunt."

"You going to say sorry for giving me your level-five evil eye for telling her Angelo was dead?"

"I suppose you're going to make me, aren't you?"

"You were too close to the situation to think straight, babe. This was just too much coincidence. I can't believe you saw her."

"I can't either. First Heidi, now her. Who says you can hide in a big city?"

"Now you know why I said no to a vacation here."

"I don't want to play 'I told you so' right now." Mandy leaned hard against the elevator wall. "This smells bad, but I still can't believe she has anything to do with the killings."

"But she knows something she's not telling you. What are you going to do about her?"

"I don't have a choice. I have to call in James to put a tail on them. She's violating her protection rules. They'll want to know about that if nothing else."

"We are agreeing not to tell Eddie about her, right?"

"Absolutely." The elevator opened, and they had to stop the conversation. The lobby was bustling with people. Mandy took Hunt's hand. "Buy me a drink in some upscale, overpriced joint, so we can talk."

"Anything you say, baby."

Once they were outside, Hunt asked the valet to hold on to the car for a while longer. He was happy to with another twenty-dollar tip. They walked two blocks and finally picked a French restaurant named Rendezvous. There was sure to be a few quiet nooks where they could talk with a name like that. They were led into a small room that had two sliding wooden doors for added privacy.

The small room sported an already-set table for two and an oversized chair. As Hunt gave the maître d' their drink order, Mandy took a seat.

"The waiter will close the doors when he returns with your drink," the maître d' said. Hunt tipped him heavily then joined Mandy. He pulled her chair closer and gave her a quick kiss. "I'm going to go broke on this little vacation."

"At least you're calling it a vacation. I'm still calling it a kidnapping." She leaned up. "I want some more of that."

They shared a lingering kiss until the waiter cleared his throat at the doorway. They parted and accepted their drinks.

"This will be it. I'll take the bill now. We'd like not to be interrupted, please."

The waiter gave him the check, and Hunt fought to keep his eyes in their sockets. He paid the waiter and thanked him. The doors were closed with no further words.

Hunt pulled Mandy close. "You wanna do it?"

Mandy laughed. "You're insane."

"The waiter thinks we're going to, anyway. Might as well take advantage of it."

"We're here to talk things out, not have a fling."

"Come on. Where's your sense of adventure?"

"Hound dog."

"It's Big H to you, lady."

She smiled and gave him a quick peck on the cheek. "I'll take care of you tonight." She took a sip of her drink and coughed. "Holy crap. What did you order me?"

"Liquid gold by the price of it. I have no idea. I said whatever the house martini was. I didn't expect it to be blue."

She took another sip. "Jeez. You shouldn't have closed the tab. Two of these and you'd be doing me on the table."

Hunt stood and pretended to rush to the door. Mandy laughed as she pulled him back by the shirt. "Come on. We need to get serious. You have no idea how upset I am about Sue."

"She did seem genuinely upset about Angelo. Were they close?"

"Not necessarily, but Sue did really like him."

"I thought he was kind of a punk back then."

"He sort of was as far as most of the men were concerned, but we liked him. He didn't have to play tough guy for us. Of course, he was a man about town and a playboy, but he was always a gentleman at formal affairs. He danced with us at some of the parties and such. He did have respect for the women in the family, even if he didn't have any for the ones he brought back to his bedroom."

"Any chance he and Sue...you know." Hunt cupped his hand and put his index finger in and out.

"Hunt! That's horrible. No. Of course not."

"You sure?"

"Of course. Angelo had more respect for Lonny than that."

"Guy hormones, babe."

"I know she's gorgeous, but no. There is no way. She was a very dedicated wife and mother. Darci was almost always with her. Any time I popped over at the house, she was there. She didn't go sneaking around."

"Just had to ask. So...she knows about you playing Angelo's sister. She had to know you were only calling him dead."

"I suppose. Now the question is, who is she getting the information from? I don't think she'd contact anyone from Vince's office. Any of the older crew would want the money back."

"And, who is this Sinclair? He knows something. If he's just her French lover, I'll kiss my crazy aunt Nellie on the ass."

"He didn't pull 'happy to see us' off nearly as good as he thought he did."

"Okay. Eddie is on the 'maybe' list since someone tried to pop him."

"Or us."

"Or us. Milo is under question because we know he's lying, too."

"We can almost rule out Gunner, since he pretty much is only after a piece of ass, but we know he holds back info until we directly ask him, so there still could be something missing."

Hunt stood and slammed his drink. "This little chat got us nowhere and cost me fifty bucks, not counting valet or maître d'. I want a payback."

Chapter Twenty-Two

unt was grinning on the drive home.

"I swear, Hunt. You're like a teenager every time we mess around."

He took her hand and gave the back of it a long kiss. "Not every time. I just love the whole sneaky feeling. I'll never say no when you want to come to New York again. I think you get as hot and bothered as I do."

"It's not the town, nut job."

"Reminded me of the day I first met Hannah."

Mandy smiled. "Me too, only this time I wasn't leaking breast milk." As she said the words, Mandy gently pushed at the sides of her breasts and winced slightly.

"Was I too rough, babe?"

"I don't think so. They're just..." She covered her mouth with her hand.

"Just what? You're scaring me. Do I need to pull over?"

"No." She chuckled. "My boobs are sore."

"This is funny why?"

"Mom was right."

"Babe. Would you please not do this?"

"I'm serious, hon. You weren't around for Hannah. This is how I knew I was pregnant."

"By your boobs?"

"I swear! I know this feeling, Hunt."

He reached for her hand again. "Please. We have so much on our plate right now. Don't go sliding back into this."

"I'm not sliding into anything. I have to be pregnant."

"Because a nice old lady thinks you are, and your boobs hurt?"

"Men don't get it." Mandy crossed her arms and peered out the window. "If you were around while I was pregnant with Hannah, you'd understand."

"And whose fault was it that I wasn't? Do you really want to go there? 'Cause I for one don't." Hunt pulled the car over at a bus stop and hit the emergency flashers. "Come here."

"No." She was now into a level-two pout.

"Come here, dammit." He didn't wait for her. He leaned over and pulled her by the waist until she was next to him. Despite her struggling, he held her tight. "I don't want to do this. Please." He kissed the top of her head. "We'll stop at a drug store, and you buy a test kit. Okay?"

"I don't want to now."

Hunt sighed. "Fine. Maybe you shouldn't know. We need to figure this out and get the hell home. I don't need you any more distracted than you already are. Let's wait and find out. You're not due for another week, anyway. Maybe if that doesn't come and go, you'll know."

"I already know. If you don't want to, that's fine."

He threw his head back in frustration. "You really think I don't want to know? Of course I want another baby, dammit. What I don't want is you upset when you're not. Please. You need to stop acting like this, Mandy."

"Acting like what? Someone who wants a baby?"

"No. I don't want you to get your hopes up and freak out if you find out you're not pregnant. I love you more than life, but we need to start living ours and not relying on whether or not you'll get pregnant again. I'll love our life whether we have one baby or ten. I don't care where we are as long as we're together. Please let this go."

"I shouldn't have had that drink."

Again, Hunt sighed. "So, don't drink until you find out." He moved a hand over her stomach. "You know I want to be there from the beginning this time."

She placed both her hands over his. "Maybe you won't love me with a bulging belly."

"Bet you I will. I seem to recall liking the titty fairy."

Mandy finally smiled. "I want another one so bad."

"I know, babe." He kissed her forehead. "Our time will come. Have faith in that doctor I paid a bundle for, okay?"

A few loud blasts of a bus horn made them both jump. Hunt pulled back into traffic and headed to the house.

Milo had dinner waiting for them. Mandy was thankful they were alone. "Where is everyone?" she asked.

"Eddie pulled them away. Said they'd be back before dark. He was really pissing and moaning about wasting time having them here when you weren't."

"He can take them away for good for all I care."

"You play tough all you want. I like at least someone here at night. I didn't get this close to retirement to get blown away."

Hunt couldn't hold back his laugh. "Got a good severance package and 401K, do you?"

Milo smiled. "I guess that does sound funny. It's a nice night. Since it's just the two of you, I set up the table out by the pool. Go sit, I'll bring it out to you."

There was a bottle of chardonnay and a Shiraz on the counter. Hunt reached for the Shiraz and picked up two glasses. Mandy cleared her throat, and Hunt put one of the glasses back. Milo raised an eyebrow to Mandy. "Is there something I should know?"

"No. I want to keep alcohol out of my system while we're trying to do a job."

"You're not doing such a good job of it. You smell like vodka."

"I decided this after a martini lunch."

"Ah, I see. Go sit. I'll be a minute."

Rather than sit at the table right away, Hunt and Mandy sat at the pool's edge with their feet dangling in.

"We should hit the hot tub tonight, babe."

"You're still treating this like a vacation."

"We need to rest up here and there and give our brains a break. We are finding out something new every day, only each something is a different lead. So far we have five suspects and nothing solid to go on."

"Something has to tie together. Since you got your fix this afternoon, we have extra time tonight to work on it."

"You mean you're cutting me off because of a nooner?"

Mandy laughed. "You're hopeless."

Milo walked out with two plates. Hunt stood then helped Mandy up with the hand that wasn't holding the glass of wine.

"I need to speak to you two. If you don't mind, I'd like to sit with you for a few minutes."

"Of course," Mandy said.

Milo put the plates on the table. They never heard the shot, only Hunt's glass shattering then Milo falling to the ground.

Mandy screamed, "Milo!" and dropped to his side. Hunt knocked the table over and pulled it down to give them cover. As Mandy placed her hand on Milo's wound she cried, "Call 9-1-1!"

The wound was close to his heart. He wasn't going to make it, but she couldn't sit there and do nothing. Mandy removed the cloth napkin from the table and tried to keep pressure on the wound. "You're going to be fine, Milo. Hang in there."

Hunt dialed nine-one-one and got up and ran in the direction the bullet came from.

"I've done you a horrible injustice, Amanda."

"Shhh. You haven't done anything. Just rest. You'll be fine."

"Eddie thinks I was on his side, but I wasn't. I never would have given away anything."

"I know, Milo." Mandy stroked his hair. "I trusted you."

"I wouldn't have given up the cabin location. I was just playing along. I'm too fond of the boy."

"Don't try to talk. The ambulance will be here any minute. You'll be fine."

Milo coughed. "I needed to tell you...Sue was here earlier."

"She was? What did she want?"

"The safe..." Milo coughed. "She cleaned out a safe."

"What was in it?"

"Mostly jewelry. Paperwork...I don't know."

"It's okay. We're watching her. Nothing is your fault."

"She was so sad about Angelo."

"She loved him, too."

"I told her he was alive."

Inside Mandy screamed, but she calmly stroked Milo's hair again. He wasn't to blame for anything. "It's okay. No harm done. It'll be okay."

He coughed again. "Be careful, Mandy. Eddie doesn't think you'll last another day..." His eyes closed slowly, and his head lolled to one side. One last breath escaped as Mandy whispered, "No."

When Hunt joined Mandy again, her head was resting on Milo's. "He gone?"

She nodded with tears in her eyes.

"I didn't see anything. Go pack. We're out of here."

Mandy threw together what little they had in a hurry. When she reached the front door, Hunt was backing over the lawn, speeding toward her. She hurried over with her bag while Hunt ran up for his. Sirens from the ambulance were already blaring. Hunt rushed back, tossing the suitcase in back with Mandy's, and hit the gas.

"Where to?" Hunt asked.

"This may sound odd, but Gunner is who I trust most right now. Go to the warehouse."

"I'll trust you on this. What are you going to do about Eddie?"

"Nothing right now. He's not going to give us any answers. It's not like Milo had any great info that he was hiding and about to spill. We don't know if that bullet was for one of us or him. Let Eddie get word about this and see if he tries to contact us."

"I don't think Eddie would have Milo killed. Do you?"

"I wouldn't think so, but why did he happen to pull out his men? If he knew we were going to be hit, why not take Milo too?"

"Maybe it was the vigilante. Maybe Milo knew more than we thought. Did he say anything that seemed important before he died?"

She told him about Sue cleaning out the safe.

"Did he say what she got?"

"Jewelry and paperwork."

"Did he know what the paperwork was?"

"If he did, he didn't get a chance to say." Mandy sniffed then swore. She dropped her head to Hunt's lap and cried.

Once they were in Gunner's office, Mandy filled him in. "Who do you have out right now, and where are they?"

"Everyone is accounted for and home with their families or here."

"So, you really have no idea if someone is out there okaying clean up, do you?"

"This isn't one of my guys. Why the hell would we kill a chef, for fuck's sake?"

"What about us? That bullet was inches from hitting me," Hunt said.

"You haven't pissed anyone off enough. Don't flatter yourself. It's not my guys, Mandy."

"Where are Axle and Kermit?"

"I just did a pickup and left the two dipshits. They're drunk as skunks and playing that stupid Xbox thing. Damn kids."

Mandy sighed heavily. "Where's Heidi?"

"Waiting for me at my place. She visited Face today. Told him it was over."

"She what? Did she tell him about you?"

"Yes. I'm tired of all the hiding. Maybe Angelo would be alive if I could have given Heidi the time she wanted. She wouldn't have needed to go to him. I *was* going to schedule a visit and own up to it and let the consequences fly."

"Why did you say 'was' like that?"

"He hung himself today not long after she left."

"Oh, my God." Mandy sank down hard in a chair.

Hunt ran his fingers gruffly through his hair. "Well, at least our list of suspects is shrinking."

Mandy took out her phone.

"Who you calling?" Hunt asked.

"James." She turned to Gunner. "Hate to kick you out of your own office, but can I have some privacy?"

"Do I know this James? He east-side?"

"No. But he may have more for me about Face. I'm not so convinced it's a suicide. How did you hear so fast?"

"We have another guy in. He called as soon as he heard."

"Why didn't you tell me about someone else in when I was asking you about Face getting information?"

"It didn't seem important. He's nobody. Just some junkie that attached himself to us, so we put him to work. Punk kid. Got himself arrested right away selling to an undercover."

"I thought you had an understanding with the cops around here. How could he get so sloppy?"

"Kid hit up a rookie. Hit him pretty hard for a first offense. No skin off my nose. The kid didn't rat on us."

"You're sure he's not feeding anyone anything he shouldn't?"

"Billy? No. In all honesty, I sort of forgot about him until his call. I was about to call you before you showed up. I thought you'd want to know."

"Thanks, Gunner."

"You want me to set you up with a place to stay?"

"No. Thanks, though. We'll pick something random. The less people who know, the better."

"I gotcha. No offense taken either." He left and closed his office door. Mandy called James.

James answered with, "What took you so long to call?"

"I just heard."

"Where are you?"

"Gunner's warehouse."

"Well, I guess it is his warehouse now with Face gone."

"What do you know, James? Does it really look like a suicide?"

"He was alone in his cell. I'm afraid so."

"Your logs can lie."

"There's no discrepancies, Mandy. I oversee those personally. He was a two-bit loser at best in there. He may have thought he was so special, but he was on nobody's list. He hung himself after his girlfriend left. And don't even start with me about listening in. We gave him a conjugal on this one, and the guards turned a deaf ear to the wailing. I'll play the tapes if you want more detail, but my guess is after she got her ride, she told him goodbye. The guard who took him back said there was nothing that made him want to put him on a special suicide watch or anything."

"I guess we'll have to go with what you say, then."

"Why are you calling from Gunner's? Isn't that risky?"

"Believe it or not, he's all we have right now. We're here because Milo was shot. But we don't know if the bullet was meant for us."

"I received the call on the house shooting. I wanted to call, but I was afraid of who you might be with. You had me worried, kid."

"So, you are watching the house."

"Just a little."

"What else do you know?" Mandy's voice raised.

"Meow."

"You fucking pig. You care enough to eavesdrop on us having sex, but you don't keep an eye enough to stop an innocent chef from being murdered?"

"It's not like that."

"Goddamn you, James."

"Look. Chill out. We have a tail on Sue. We know she was at the house, but we don't know what she did."

"Was anyone else at the house while she was? Other than Milo?"

"The guards were already gone."

"Shit. Only Eddie can call them off. He cleared the way for Sue. Sonofabitch!"

"Where are you going to go?"

"To move Angelo. Milo told Sue about him. If he mentioned the cabin, she now knows where to go."

"Do you want me to send people there?"

"He's not where she thinks, so that will buy me some time. He's too close for comfort, though. What are my chances of getting a plane and getting him out of there?"

"Tomorrow? Pretty damn good. I want you with him, though. You're done there. This thing is going to shoot itself out with or without you. We'll relocate you again. Hunt's parents, too."

"Dammit," Mandy mumbled.

"Sorry, sugar. I'm pulling the plug."

"It was never yours to pull."

"It is now. Call me tomorrow, and I'll give you the name of the airport. Get the hell out of New York tonight."

"I need to find Sue. I need to know what paperwork she has. Where is she?" There was silence. "James?"

"They lost her. She knew she had a tail. That guy she's with is one hell of a driver."

"He said he had law enforcement training."

"You could say that."

"You did a background on him?"

"Of course. He's about the equivalent of one of our Navy Seals. If he's just her boyfriend..."

"You'll kiss Hunt's crazy aunt's ass."

"Pardon?"

"Never mind. I have to go. I'll call you tomorrow morning." Mandy hit end before he could argue.

Chapter Twenty-Three

"**W**e going to the cabin tonight?" Hunt asked.

"Yes. They lost Sue. I can't worry about where she is or what she has anymore. We're getting Angelo out of here."

"Did I understand from what I heard that we're moving again?"

"I'm sorry." She dropped her head low.

Hunt knelt at her side. "I don't care, babe. We'll start fresh and go anywhere you want."

"James wants us to move your parents, too."

"Then we have to be somewhere warm."

"Won't they mind? Shit, Hunt. This is so unfair."

"It would take Eddie and his whole gang to keep them from following us, babe. You think they'd be away from Hannah? You're insane." He kissed her forehead right as Gunner came back in.

"I knew you two were screwing."

Hunt straightened up and turned around. "Had to claim her. Seems everyone else wants in her pants. I figured the easiest way to keep them out was to be there myself."

Mandy stood. "It kind of just happened, Gunner. I'd appreciate a little secrecy until we're able to share it. There's enough going on without throwing this into the mix."

"I don't really care. Everyone seems to have accepted you in charge. They're not going to care who you're screwing. Maybe better if Hammer here has the hot seat. Angelo was a stud for what he did, but if you got that reputation, that would make you a slut."

"Now there's a fair statement."

Gunner shrugged. "It's the truth. So, what did your friend James say?"

Mandy had to lie. "He hadn't heard anything yet."

"Where is his connection again?"

"Just some new territory I'm looking at expanding into. Don't worry. It's not going to step on your toes. I just wanted to see if he heard anything. See if he was willing to be a team player right out of the gate. Word has it he's supposed to have someone at the prison. Paying off a guard or something."

"For whatever that's worth."

"Look, we have to split. Watch yourselves. I have a feeling this is going to come to a head pretty damn fast."

"I have things here covered. You watch your own back. Holler if you need us."

"Thanks."

Once they were in the car, Mandy's cell phone rang. The name on the caller ID read "Asshole". She answered. "What, Eddie?"

"Where are you?"

"None of your damn business."

"Milo is dead, and your shit is gone. What am I supposed to think?"

"There is no way you think I killed that sweet man! Where were your men, Eddie? Where were they when Milo was killed, not to mention when Sue cleaned out a safe no one knew about?"

"Sue? Lonny's Sue? What the hell does she have to do with this?"

"Oh, bullshit. You took your men out of there so she had a clear shot at it."

"Shot at what? I have no idea what you're talking about."

"The hell you don't."

"Amanda, quit your screaming. I had no idea Sue was even alive, let alone that there was a safe. What did she get?"

"I have no clue. Before Milo died, he said it was jewelry and paperwork."

"Paperwork? For what?"

"I don't know, and I don't care. I'm done. You brought me here to get Angelo safe. I did that, and now you want this killing crap solved. I can't do that when every finger points to you no matter where I go."

"I paid someone to shoot at myself? You're making no sense."

"Twice now a bullet barely missed Hunt and me. I don't believe you didn't set that up."

"Why would I have bought a restaurant for Milo if I was going to kill him?"

"You what?"

"It was his as soon as you were gone. I didn't kill him, Amanda."

"Then explain why you pulled the guards away from the house."

"You weren't there, and I needed some muscle today. I didn't see the harm."

"Arranging furniture were you?"

"Funny. You think Earl and I sit around and get manicures all day? You're not the only one in the hot seat, little girl. You have Darin off playing house with that bimbo, and we're men short 'cause I gave you everything you wanted on that damn cabin detail. We have work to do the same as you. If I considered for a second the house needed a man, I would have left one. Come on. Meet me. Let's talk."

"No. I'm done. I no longer care if you or anyone else gets shot. I'm taking Angelo away from here. If you ever try to find me again, I'll kill you." Mandy hit end. "Just go to the cabin, Hunt. I'm done. I'm so sorry this has ruined our lives."

"No, it hasn't. It's the next leg of our adventure together." Again, he took her hand and gave it a long kiss. "As dumb as it sounds, we never would have met if it wasn't for all of this. I don't regret a second of it."

"What would I do without you?"

"Have a lot less great sex?"

Mandy laughed. "I want to get home to Hannah. I don't care where home is anymore."

"Ditto, babe."

Mandy called the cabin to let Doc know they were heading up and going to take Angelo. She didn't care what Darin and Angie were going to do. Let them dig their own grave.

"I'm fine. I need to go for a walk. Can I please have ten minutes alone?" Angelo begged Egan, the one guard he didn't mind being around. Egan had caught up to him as he walked toward the lake.

"Amanda would have my hide if anything happened to you."

"What's going to happen to me here? No one knows where we are, imbecile. Not even you guys."

"I'm supposed to watch over you."

"Fine. Do it from up here. I'm going to the lake for a minute. If I'm not back in ten you can carry me back."

The guard glanced behind him to make sure no one else was watching. "You have ten minutes."

"Thank you."

Angelo carefully descended the stairs to the lake. His ribs still hurt like a sonofabitch. He strolled out into the water, grateful for the peace. He was getting sick of listening to the guards playing cards and even more so, the sounds of Angie and Darin having sex. He was long overdue himself and tempted to sneak away to get some action. He doubted this hole-in-the-wall town had prostitutes, but he could pick someone up if he could just get to a bar. Maybe he could bribe Egan tonight.

Angelo was knee-high in the water when he turned at the sound of his name. He smiled at the sight of Sue by the docks. "Sue? Is that really you?" Sore ribs be damned, he ran to her side and gave her a hug. "What the hell are you doing here?"

"I had to see you, Angelo."

"Did Mandy tell you where to find me?"

"Yes. I hooked up with her in New York. Hunt is a really great guy."

"Yeah. He's okay for a cop."

Sue smiled and placed her hand on his cheek. "I'm really glad you're okay."

"Me—"

Something solid hit him on the back of his head. His world became fuzzy as he fell to the sandy ground.

"What do you mean he's gone?" Mandy screamed. "Why didn't you call me?" It was one a.m., and she was already tired and cranky. Unlike the last trip, she hadn't slept at all. Her nerves were too shot.

"Check your phone. We tried."

Mandy dug it out of her pocket. It was dead. "Dammit!" she screamed, ready to throw it against a wall. Hunt took it from her hand.

"He said he wanted ten minutes alone."

"And you let him go?"

"He didn't really give me much of a choice."

"Really? With three broken ribs, he was that threatening?"

"Don't give me shit, goddammit! Angelo was dying for some alone time. He probably wandered off to get some pussy. Those two have been banging like jackrabbits constantly, driving everyone mad. I don't know why they're even here."

Mandy turned to Darin. "Leave. Take your little girlfriend and go. Tell your father what your plans are. I no longer care about either of you."

"Well, tough shit," Darin replied. "I care about Angelo. I'm not leaving until he's found."

"I'm not going anywhere without Darin." Angie wrapped her arm around Darin's and stood there, feet firmly planted.

With no phone in hand, Mandy picked up a coffee cup and threw it against the wall. Again, her cussing talents caught everyone's full attention. She turned to the two guards. "You two start knocking on doors. Ask around and find out if anyone noticed anything. Try not to look like mobsters, for Christ's sake. The last thing we need are cops coming out, looking for suspicious characters. Better yet, ditch the coats and ties. Put on a T-shirt and take a beer."

"What? Why a beer?"

"Tell them you think your buddy is drunk and wandered off. It'll be easier to explain that way. Stop at the houses with their lights on for now. I really don't want to make a scene. My hopes of finding him nearby aren't very high." Mandy stomped over to Egan and punched him hard in the jaw. "You stupid son of a bitch."

Mandy was in just the right mood for a fight, but Egan glanced toward Hunt. She was sure he was thinking twice about hitting her back. He turned and walked away without another word.

Hunt went over to Mandy after the two men left. "You didn't need to do that."

"No? Wait and see what happens if we find Angelo dead. There will be two funerals that day."

"Babe...he's okay. I'm sure he just got cabin fever and took off."

"He knew we were coming for him. That wouldn't have happened."

"What about us?" Darin asked.

"If I can't get you two to leave, then make yourselves useful and keep an eye out. Call us if he comes back. Do me a favor and try to not screw for two hours."

"Don't put this shit on me."

Mandy now squared off with Darin. "I didn't want you here, remember? You've done nothing but get everyone's hormones out of whack and knock up a girl who could have had a decent shot at life."

"I didn't knock her up here."

Mandy pulled back her fist but stopped herself. "Just keep an eye out and call Hunt's phone if he shows back up, asshole."

"Where to?" Hunt asked Mandy when they reached the car.

"There's another cabin on the next lake."

"Another one? With the two from last time, this makes four. You'd think Eric would know more about what's going on around here being a cop and all."

"No one says he doesn't, Hunt."

"No way. Not Eric. Accusing him would be like accusing me, Mandy."

"I never would have suspected Abbey either."

"No way. I can't even wrap my mind around that right now. Whose cabin is this next one?"

"It's Lonny's. He was into hunting. He and Sue came here to get away from it all. The others were Vince's. Vince entertained some clients at one but kept another private. As far as she knew, Gerard never used Lonny's. She may think I don't know about it."

"Why do you know about it?"

She looked away. "We did use it...once."

He gave her hand a reassuring squeeze. "Never mind that, babe. You still think Sue didn't know what Lonny really was? After all this you think she has no clue he was with the mob?"

"She had to know to some extent. I think she chose to ignore it."

"Is this place far?"

"Twenty minutes."

"I'm still not sure she's dumb enough to go there."

"She doesn't think we're on to her, Hunt."

He started the car. "Let's hope not."

They arrived at the cabin and drove past two more houses. They parked across the street in a wooded area. Carefully, they made their way to the cabin and around the back. Both of them had their guns drawn. Hunt was ahead and motioned for Mandy to stay down. He took the corner and peeked in the screen porch. His eyes went wide then he returned his attention to Mandy.

She mouthed, "What?"

"I think I've just seen more of Sue than you'd care for me to," he whispered back.

Mandy went around him and peeked in. Sue was naked on top of Sinclair. He was sitting on the couch as she ground herself against him. Mandy couldn't watch and hastily turned away.

"Doesn't anyone use a bed anymore?" Mandy whispered.

"It's really hard to screw against log walls."

Mandy wanted to smack him for his comment, but her hand still hurt from punching Egan.

"What do you want to do, babe? Wait for them to finish?"

"I could give a crap if she gets to climax, Hunt. We—" A loud moan from both Sue and Sinclair kept her from finishing her sentence. "Well, there you go." Mandy kicked in the door with her gun drawn. Sinclair jumped so bad, he knocked Sue to the floor. She screamed and reached for an afghan to cover herself.

"Mandy? What the hell are you doing here?"

"An even better question is 'what are you doing here?'"

"I think that's obvious," she said as she motioned up and down her body. "You told me to get out of New York, so I did."

Sinclair tried to stand, but Hunt cocked the hammer on his gun and aimed it at him. "I don't think so. Keep your hands at your sides."

"Can I put my pants on?"

Hunt walked over to the coffee table where they sat. He checked the pockets then tossed them to Sinclair.

"What gives, Mandy?" Sue asked.

"Sit down," Mandy said as she pointed to a chair.

Sue sat down hard and crossed her arms. "Why are you here? Why are you pointing a gun at me?"

"Because, Sue. I love you, but you're lying to me."

"I'm not lying to you!"

"Your little friend here is the French equivalent of a Navy Seal. You know what is going on around here more than you're sharing. Somehow you convinced Eddie to call off his guards and got Milo killed in the process."

"What?"

"After you took whatever it is you wanted out of the safe." Sue's expression went blank. "Yes, I know about that. They killed him when we got home."

Sue's head sank to her chest. She let it hang there for a minute before she stood and slapped Sinclair. "You went back to the house? You didn't have to kill him."

"He was going to talk. I told you he would."

"Well, he did anyway now, didn't he? You stupid asshole. He didn't know enough to say anything."

"Oh, my God. You do know what's going on?" Mandy turned to Sinclair. "You killed Milo?" She stepped forward, but Hunt held her arm.

"Not now, babe." He put the gun to Sinclair's head. "Where's Angelo?"

Sue piped up. "He's in the back. He's probably still out, but he's fine."

Mandy ran to the kitchen and opened the pantry. After knocking a few things to the floor, she returned with a container of zip ties and tossed it to Hunt.

"Legit hunting cabin, huh?"

"These things do have other uses. You got this?"

"Yeah. Go to Angelo."

Mandy found Angelo in the second room she tried. He was tied to a bed and unconscious. She cut him free then sat at his side. Shaking him gently, she called his name. On the third try, his head gently rocked from side to side. He swore then placed his hand to his head. Opening one eye, he looked up at Mandy.

"Hey. We have to stop meeting like this." He forced a half smile then closed his eye again. "Shit hurts."

"Lemme look."

"Don't make me move. I'll puke."

Mandy reached for her phone and swore when it wasn't there. She ran out and took Hunt's then called Doc. She rattled off instructions of how to get to the cabin and begged for him to come alone. After she ended the call, she took Angelo's hand.

"Doc will be here in twenty minutes. I'm going to get you some ice."

He gave a slight nod.

"How are your ribs?"

"Okay, I guess."

She placed her hand on his cheek. "This will be over soon. I have a plane coming for you."

His eyes opened. "Where am I going?"

"That'll be up to you."

"Any chance I'm allowed to recuperate anywhere near you?"

"I don't know, Angelo. Hunt and I are relocating, too."

"Seriously?"

"Seriously. I'm not exactly done here, but we're officially done."

He removed her hand from his cheek and held it tight. "I'm sorry."

"It isn't your fault."

"Yes, it is. You only came to look for me."

"Eddie would have made me come anyway. He had something planned. I never could figure this whole mess out."

"What did Sue want with me?"

"I'm about to figure it out. You okay?"
"Yeah. I want to lie here for a while."
"Holler if you need me."

CHAPTER TWENTY-FOUR

When Mandy returned, Sinclair had his legs and hands bound, but Sue was still sitting in the chair, wrapped in the blanket.

"Why is she free?" Mandy asked, coldly.

"I thought you could take her to get something on first."

Her clothes were in a pile on the floor. "Grab your shit and come to the bathroom." She waved the gun as she spoke.

"You don't need the gun, Amanda," Sue said as she stood.

"Like hell." Mandy took three long paces toward her and held the gun to her forehead. "I ought to pop you right here. What in the hell are you doing? Why did you take Angelo? You could have fucking killed him!"

Hunt shouted "Babe" three times before Mandy lowered the gun with a huff.

She motioned it toward the bathroom. "Get going."

"You'd really choose Angelo over me?" Sue said with her voice cracking.

"Unless I missed something, *he* didn't just almost kill *you*."

Sue lunged headfirst into Mandy. They went flying backward onto the kitchen floor. Sue straddled her and pulled back her arm, but Hunt caught it before she landed a punch. He picked her up by her waist and pulled her off. Mandy swung with all her might and knocked her out cold.

"Great." Hunt made sure the blanket was wrapped on her well, then swung her over his shoulder and walked over for the container of ties. "I'll get her attached to the bed."

"I don't care if you lock her in a closet." Mandy stormed to the refrigerator and took out a beer then sat across from Sinclair. "What happened to her? You fill her mind with delusions of taking down the big bad New York mob?"

"Quite the opposite, actually."

"Do tell." She took a long swig of beer. Mandy stared at it for a moment then placed the beer on the table, suddenly remembering she might be pregnant.

"She came looking for me."

"And I suppose you have an ad in Assassins Monthly?"

"Don't be so cocky. A killer for hire is never hard to find."

"So, you're in it for the money."

"The sex is pretty outstanding, too."

Mandy kicked the coffee table, slamming it into his shins. He cried out as Hunt turned the corner.

"Were your anger issues this bad when you were pregnant the first time? I'm beginning to think there's something to this theory of yours." He took the beer she abandoned. "You're cut off."

"I already cut myself off."

Sinclair shoved the table away. "What a team. You're harassing assassins and mobsters while pregnant? I think I've heard it all."

"What I am is none of your business. Tell me what happened to Sue. She seemed happy to be staying abroad. There was certainly enough money to last a lifetime. I can't imagine she needed the jewelry to sell for more."

"My fees were a little high."

"Even after you began sleeping together?"

"Business is business."

"Why did she turn?"

"She couldn't stay away anymore. Needing answers about her daughter consumed her. She finally got someone to give her answers and heard the whole story. You're not on her favorite people list at the moment."

"Why?"

"She knows you killed her brother."

"And he killed her daughter."

"Which she blames on you."

Mandy stood. "No one misses that child more than I do! Okay, maybe she does, but I was almost killed getting that revenge."

"And how does that taste now?"

"So, what is this then? She was having you kill anyone remotely associated with Darci's death?" Mandy sat back down hard. "How could I be so stupid?" Tears formed in her eyes. "Why kidnap Angelo? Why didn't she kill him?"

"Bait."

"She knew I'd come for him."

Sinclair chuckled. "You run a hell of a theory in your mind. Don't get me wrong. Sue is a great piece of ass, but she doesn't have the brains to pull this off."

"What are you talking about?"

"This is more than revenge. More than money. She wanted you, yes, but there's so much more. Don't you get it yet? All anyone wants is power."

Without a sound, Sinclair's head went flying back. A bullet hit him square in the forehead. Mandy and Hunt dove for cover. No other shots were fired. Hunt's phone vibrated loudly in Mandy's pocket. Her heart stopped. Not wanting to give away her location to the shooter, she hit "answer", but didn't say a word. It was James. He would hear what was going on and trace the call. They had to be close enough to help. She could only hope none of the goons from the cabin shot them in the process.

Another shot flew over Mandy's head. It hit a lamp and sent ceramic flying. She kept low to the ground and tapped Hunt on the arm. She wanted to get down the hall toward Angelo's room before he tried to come out. They crawled to the hall without any more shots fired. Sue had been screaming from her room. Mandy went in after directing Hunt to Angelo's.

"Is that shots?" Sue shrieked.

"It stopped for now. Shut up."

"Whatever he said, he was lying."

"I said shut the fuck up." Mandy opened a bottom drawer and removed a pair of socks. She coldly stuffed it in Sue's mouth. Baring her teeth, Mandy spoke softly.

"I killed your sonofabitch brother for killing your daughter. He would have killed me if I didn't. I loved him, and God knows I wanted a different life. He refused to make a change, and this is how the cards fell. I walked away. You chose to get back in. If you live through this, it will be with no help from me. You come near me, my family, or Angelo again, I will kill you."

Sue screamed through the gag, but Mandy couldn't make anything of it out. She crawled to Angelo's room. Hunt was there waiting.

"What now?" he asked her.

"I don't know. If he was doing the killing, who's out there trying to shut him up? Eddie? Sinclair said it was about power. Maybe what was the most obvious from the start really is what's going on."

"Not to toss out that theory, but if that's all this was, Eddie could have done this by himself. He wouldn't have brought in you, let alone Sue."

"We need to get those papers. Sue has to have them here."

"I'm not searching with gunfire. We need to get out of here."

"And whoever is out there will clean the place out while we're gone. No."

A door was kicked in. Mandy jumped.

"FBI. Freeze!"

"James! We're in here!" Mandy shouted. "There was someone shooting from the lakeside."

James hollered instructions to his men then he called out to her. "Stay the hell where you are!"

James's men came in from outside and told them the coast was clear.

"Why is Sue gagged in the next bedroom?"

"It's a long story."

One of James's men walked in with Doc. He had Doc's arm pinned behind his back. "This one just pulled up. He with you?" he asked Mandy.

"Yes. Please let him go. He's a doctor here to see Angelo. I'm sorry, Doc. I'll explain later. Please do what you can." She motioned to Angelo. Thankfully he had passed out again and slept through the commotion. "He took a hit to the back of his head again, but he seems okay otherwise." Doc shifted his gaze around the room. "They're FBI, but you're okay. Nothing is going to happen to you."

"Can I at least give the boy some privacy while I look him over?"

"Of course." Mandy herded everyone out and closed the door behind her.

They went to the kitchen. Mandy faced James. "You traced that call pretty fast."

He grinned. "We were already on our way. The badges have tracking devices in them."

"You're an ass."

He shrugged. "Now what's with Sue, and more importantly, what's with the stiff? That your French dude?"

Mandy gave him a brief explanation of what they'd learned.

"So, this really isn't over. She's as much of a pawn as Sinclair here."

"I guess so."

"Have you talked to her yet?"

"Other than threaten to kill her? No. I was a little busy dodging bullets."

"We'll take her in and see what we can get out of her."

"Then what? You can't just set her free. Somehow a screw came loose with her. She's not fit to be released into witness protection."

"I'm not new here, Blaine." He hesitated. "I know, Blair. That name isn't going to last much longer either, so I hope you're not attached to it."

Hunt put an arm around Mandy. "We'll make do. It's only a name."

Mandy leaned into Hunt and wrapped her arms around him. "I do love you."

James put his finger in his mouth like he was going to puke.

"What are you? Four?"

He chuckled. "We're prepared to take Angelo now. We'll take this Doc, too." Mandy opened her mouth, but he silenced her. "We're not about to go pressing any charges on their doctor. He doesn't have a choice about coming. And neither do you for that matter."

"I can't go with you now."

Hunt and James both said, "What?"

"We can't go, Hunt. We're so close."

"Oh, no, you don't," James protested. "I told you this is over."

"And I told you that's not your call. I don't work for you, remember?"

"Look, dammit. I'm sticking my neck out for you. I don't do field work anymore, if you recall. You'll do as I say."

Hunt took a step back, waiting for Mandy to explode.

Mandy crossed her arms. "Oh, no, I won't." Mandy's hand suddenly covered her mouth. She darted to the sink and threw up. Hunt rushed to her side.

"What gives, babe?"

James handed her a towel. She mumbled a thanks. Resting her head on the sink, she groaned. "Guess I saved fifteen bucks on a pregnancy test."

James screeched, "What?"

"Apparently morning sickness." She stood and smiled at Hunt. A smile spread wide over his face as he picked her up. She wrapped her legs around him and cried happy tears into his shoulder.

"You sure it's not the excitement?" Hunt asked.

"I'm sure. Your kid doesn't seem to like beer."

"Then I think someone else knocked you up." He grinned.

"You two can't be serious." James said.

Mandy stayed in Hunt's arms, but she turned to face James. "Yup. I'm pregnant."

"You picked a fine time."

"We've been trying for a long time. It's not like I planned on getting kidnapped by the Menusco mob."

"Well, this settles it. I won't be responsible for another innocent life. You're done."

"No! I think I have this figured out. Just give me another day."

"You going to enlighten me?"

"What do you care? You guys wanted nothing to do with this."

"We became involved when you got involved. Like it or not. Let me know where your train of thought is going. Eddie?"

"That's too easy." Mandy walked out of the kitchen and went back into the room where Sue was. Hunt and James followed. Someone had already removed her gag and dressed her. She glared at Mandy with hatred in her eyes but didn't speak. "Where are the papers you took from the safe, Sue?"

"Go to hell."

"We can do this the easy way, or we can do this my way."

"What do I have to lose? You people have already taken everything away from me."

"That wasn't my fault. You could be living the life of a queen if you hadn't decided to take an undeserved revenge trip. I handled things the only way I could a couple years back. You were to never see Gerard again, anyway. I know that's not the same as him being dead, and I'm sorry you can't see it that way. But if Gerard had to, he would have killed you himself."

"You're a liar."

"He was trying to kill me, Sue. I do feel responsible for Darci in a way. He was aiming for me when he killed her. I didn't want to give you the gory details when I learned them. It wasn't going to change anything."

"Quit your lying. He worshiped you."

"He knew who I was from the day we were married. He was waiting for the chance to kill me. Waiting for me to outlive my usefulness to them. Unfortunately, I was too involved in loving him and didn't see it. I was a stupid kid. If I'd left earlier, maybe Darci would be alive right now. Don't think for a second I don't punish myself every day." Mandy rubbed her locket as she spoke.

Tears ran down Sue's cheeks. "They had to pay for what they did."

"We know there's more to this. You don't have to deal with this alone."

"I'm not telling you anything."

"Suit yourself." Mandy turned to James's men. "Search the house. There's a pile of jewelry and some paperwork to be found. I'll go search the car."

"Wait!" Sue screamed. "Where's Sinclair?"

Mandy wasn't much in a coddling mood. She pulled her index finger across her throat.

Sue screamed, "No!"

"And it wasn't even me."

Hunt walked out with her to the car. "You were a little hard on her, weren't you, babe?"

"I'm pissed off."

"No shit."

Mandy stopped and spun around. "We just found out what we've wanted to happen forever has finally happened, and we can't even take two seconds and enjoy it."

Without hesitation, Hunt pulled Mandy to him and held her tight. He leaned down and whispered, "So take two seconds." He rocked with her. She wrapped her arms around him.

"How can you do that?"

"Do what?"

"Snap me from Queen Bitch-la back to human so fast?"

"Years of practice."

She laughed. "I really love you."

"I know. I really, really love you, too. Even for a bitchy broad." He hopped back and took his best stance, preparing to be flipped again.

She laughed harder. "You're in the clear. I have to start taking it easy soon." She placed her hands on her stomach and smiled. "Are you really happy?"

"Are you kidding? Of course I am." He covered her hands with his. "And not just because you'll stop stressing over it, either. I'm thrilled, babe. Don't ever doubt that. I can't wait to tell Hannah."

"Me, too." Mandy turned back to the car. "Crap."

"What is it?"

"I think I have to pee."

"I think it's a little soon to be having those complaints."

"You failed the first test. Never deny me anything even remotely strange from this moment on."

"I'll indulge your every whim, my queen." Hunt caught up to her and took her arm. "Wait. I do recall you saying something about horny months."

"Oh, hell yeah."

"Hot damn!"

"You still going to want me with blue-cheese breath?"

"That was your craving with Hannah?"

"Oh yeah. There wasn't anything I didn't dip in it. And shut up."

Hunt chuckled.

Chapter Twenty-Five

Mandy searched under the seats while Hunt rummaged through the trunk. He found what they were looking for stored with the spare tire and called Mandy over.

She quickly flipped through the paperwork. "Let's get this to James."

Once inside, they went through what Hunt had found.

"Why would Sue have the deeds to the main building and what appears to be everyone's houses?" James asked Mandy.

"It was in a safe no one knew about. Maybe there was more to Lonny leaving than I realized. Maybe he was looking for more security when he left."

"What about the money you gave Sue?"

"That was money for a deal I botched. As far as I know, Lonny had no intentions of taking that money."

"Wouldn't Vince be concerned about missing titles to everything?"

"If it was an issue, I was never around for it, remember? If it's the deeds he was after, Vince would have found a way around it. He'd have a lawyer draft up some good fakes or replacements. That's not such a big deal. You can lose your deed in a fire and get them redone."

James held up a hardcover notebook that was at the bottom of the stack. Everyone watched as he looked through the sheets. "That's a little harder to do when you come across the properties by sordid means."

Mandy snatched the book from his hand and paged through it. "Holy shit."

Hunt took it from her hands and went through a few pages himself. "Gotta love a mob who keeps books."

Mandy grabbed it back. "Why would they even record this stuff? For crying out loud." She opened it and read through a few more entries. "Political payoffs?" She slammed it down hard on the table. "I suppose if we keep going, it'll give us latitude and longitude of a dozen missing bodies."

James picked the book off the table and tucked it under his arm. "We'll figure out what to do about this later. If Eddie knows this is what Sue was after, she's in for a world of hurt."

Mandy leaned against the counter and crossed her arms. "I still can't make heads or tails out of what he knows or what part he took in her getting those."

"It only makes sense if Eddie knew about what it held, he would want it. It's not the most flattering piece of evidence against any of them. I can't see him just letting it out there."

"Apparently killing everyone wasn't enough for Sue," Hunt said.

"She wanted to be sure anyone she may have missed went down in flames, anyway. It's odd," Mandy added. Shoving away from the counter. She went into the room where they held Sue and stood with her arms crossed. "If the book is what you were after, why didn't you turn that in to somebody? Why try to be a mastermind behind killing everyone? It seems to me jail would have been a way to drag out the suffering of those who caused you harm."

"I couldn't be sure anything would happen at all. Have you read any of it? What was I supposed to do? Read the whole thing and try to find who wasn't corrupt? Look what happened to you."

"What happened to me?"

"You played both sides. Who's to say if you were really on the side of the law?"

"Sue—"

"You're why Darci is dead. You also murdered my brother and walked."

Mandy asked the guard to give her a few minutes alone with Sue. She pulled up a chair and sat by the bed. "All your views on everything are so damn distorted. I wish you would have come to me."

"You wouldn't have helped."

"All I've been is there for you. Don't you know all I wanted was to try to make everything up to you? I loved you. You and Darci were all I had for a year. Would I have helped you kill everyone? No. But something like this in the right hands may be what it takes to do some good around here. I would have been behind you one hundred percent. I could have picked up where I left off. I hated spending a year with these people to essentially get nowhere."

"You weren't in anymore. Why would you have started up again?"

"I would have if you asked me to."

"There was no point. If we'd stopped them, some other gang would just take over."

"James give you his coyote speech?"

"His what?"

"Never mind. What the hell were you doing if you knew that was the case? If you can lie there and know it was for nothing, why did you risk it?"

"Same reason you killed my brother."

Mandy considered this for a long moment before she replied. "Touché. Now tell me what else you know, Sue."

"I don't know anything more than the list of people I wanted dead."

"So, share the list."

"What's the point? I'm done." She choked back tears. "You killed Sinclair, and I'm off to jail."

"Because now I'm involved, and I want the time away from my daughter to have meant something. Help me, and you can help your daughter's death mean something."

Sue wouldn't look at her.

"I took the blame for everything, but what you pulled out of that safe tells me Lonny may not have been as innocent as I thought. Or you for that matter. Look at me."

Reluctantly Sue turned her focus to Mandy.

"How much do you know, and what can I do?"

Sue stared hard at Mandy for a long time before she spoke. "You can go to hell."

Mandy stood and left the room. James was coming down the hall as Mandy walked out. "Just get her out of here. We're getting nowhere."

"I was just coming to get you. We're moving Angelo. Go say your goodbyes. I'll get Sue and take her back to headquarters until we decide what to do with her."

Mandy sighed. "Sadly, I don't even care right now."

"You loved her."

"I loved a lot of the wrong people."

Mandy wanted nothing more than to collapse on a bed with her husband, but she wasn't about to do it here. She followed James's men outside. Hunt was helping support Angelo.

"I'll get to you when I can," Mandy said. "I'm not throwing you out there alone until you're ready. Any idea where you want to go?"

"I'm thinking a nice beach in California for starters."

Mandy smiled. "I think that shouldn't be a problem." She hugged him goodbye. "Take care of yourself." Tears were hard to fight. She didn't even try.

She turned around to find James and another guard walking Sue out of the cabin, with her hands cuffed in front of her. Within seconds, Sue shoved the man on the right into the doorjamb and reached into his coat. She came out with his gun in her hands and fired. Someone by Angelo returned the fire. There was a clean shot to her chest. Mandy screamed and started to run to her, but Hunt shouted her name, and she stopped. She whipped her head in Angelo's direction. He had been hit.

Three days later, Mandy stood at a cemetery between Eddie and Hunt. A Catholic priest gave his final blessings over three caskets. As the crowd dispersed, Eddie turned to Mandy.

"I'm glad Vince could finally be at peace; laid to rest the way he would have wanted. I don't think he ever expected to be laid with Angelo so soon, though."

"I don't really believe he's thinking much of anything, Eddie." Mandy didn't want to deal with him anymore, but she wasn't ready to go home. There were too many questions left unanswered.

"It's nice to not worry about a damn sniper," Eddie said.

"Don't stop completely watching your back, Eddie. There are still a lot of questions out there, not to mention I'm sure a copycat or two will pop up. We still don't know who nailed Sinclair or why. You're not entirely in the clear."

"Come and see me tomorrow. I want to talk."

Mandy's eyes welled with tears. She was filled with more disgust and hate than ever. "I call the shots. I'll tell you where we're meeting."

"That's more than fair."

They walked away from Eddie and the crowd. Hunt helped Mandy into the black limousine waiting for them. Once they were on their way, she nodded at the figure on the seat behind the driver.

"Pleased with the turnout?" Mandy asked.

"That was good, wasn't it? Damn Catholics. We always did funerals with as much pizazz as weddings."

"Will you go now?"

Angelo adjusted his arm in his sling. "I would have liked one last drink with my dad, but sure, I suppose I can go now."

"How were you going to have one more drink with him?"

Hunt answered for him. "Pour it on his grave."

Angelo nodded. "You know the difference between a mob wedding and a mob funeral?"

Hunt chuckled. "One less drunk."

Mandy elbowed him. "You two are horrible."

While the arrangements were being made for the funerals, Hunt and Mandy had visited with his parents and Hannah at their home in Florida. James said they would be safe, and he wasn't worried about having to relocate them right away, but he did post two men on the house to be safe.

Hunt rocked with his daughter sound asleep on his shoulder. Although spoiled in their absence, it was obvious

Hannah missed them both dearly. She had gone constantly between the two of them, sharing her stories until she wore herself out.

"I'm ready to rent her out as a personal GPS for Disney World," Hunt's mother laughed.

"Blame her mother on that one," Hunt said, winking at Mandy.

Mandy had remained glued to his side. She didn't want to leave her daughter for a second over the short visit home. "I accept that with pride." She picked up her baby's hand and kissed it. "She loves it there. I'd hate to move away."

Hunt turned to her. "I know you've made it darn near her second home, but a lot of families only go once a year, every few years, or never for that matter. She'll be fine, babe. Don't you have other things to worry about?"

Hunt's mother's ears perked up. "Something to worry about? I don't like the sound of that."

"This is a good worry, Mom. Tell them, babe."

Mandy stood in front of them. Placing her hands over her belly was all it took. Hunt's mother clapped her hands together then quickly stood for a hug. They were soon sandwiched by Hunt's father with a hearty, "Congratulations!"

The peaceful visit wasn't long enough, but Mandy was refreshed and ready to go that following Sunday for the funeral. What to do from there was going to be tricky.

They met Eddie at the pizza place where they'd run into Heidi. It was inconvenient enough for Eddie that Mandy liked the sound of it. It was neutral territory with enough foot traffic that she didn't have to worry about him trying anything funny. She never would have risked a civilian getting hurt. Having to deal with Hunt's cheese-induced snoring was the only downfall.

Eddie was good at blending in with a crowd when he had to. He looked like any other overweight, slightly balding Italian man out for the pizza his wife no longer allowed him to have at home. He topped it with a heavy helping of Parmesan cheese and crushed peppers, added a draft dark beer, and then joined Hunt and Mandy at a table.

"You came alone?" Mandy asked. "That's surprising."

"Earl is in the car." He put down his plate and glared at Hunt. "You could have given me the same courtesy."

"I'm staying," Hunt said.

He took a large bite of pizza then spoke with his mouth full. "So, what now? I didn't expect you to come back after the funeral. I figured you'd stay away."

"I'm not back for you this time. I'm back for me."

"You have nothing left here. You never really did. I can't believe the likes of Angelo was enough to draw you back."

"Of course I'd come for Angelo. And it's not like it was up to me. You were threatening me and my family, if you recall. I believe the word is kidnapping."

Eddie took a sip of beer before he answered. "The way I see it, you got him into that mess."

"How so?"

"The boy going soft was your fault."

"My fault? I knew he wasn't cut out for this the day I met him. You remember how the story goes. Two guys were beating up on him, and I jumped in and helped. I didn't know who he was."

"I know the story. As I recall, it was Kermit and Axle then, too. Funny how things tend to repeat themselves."

"Then those two idiots actually served a purpose. Twice. Don't get me wrong here. I'm grateful things turned out the way they did, and Angelo's free now, but I can't believe your goal was to get me to take him away from all this."

"You're right. He was just the excuse I needed. Not that I don't care about the boy but mainly I just don't like you. Never have. In all my years of running these streets with Vince, you were the sorriest excuse to come along. A few palms get greased; a few get killed. We've never needed an undercover with the FBI to have our backs covered."

"Yet you brought me back when the going got tough."

"I never thought you'd see day two."

"Is that a fact?" Mandy leaned back and crossed her arms.

"Vince died wanting his revenge on you. I followed through with a promise I made to him."

"I guess it was dumb of me to think he'd ever stop looking for me."

"You got him shot and changed his son. It wasn't something he was going to forget. I'm surprised he didn't have someone go after you sooner. I think him trying to keep it from Angelo was your only saving grace. That and the fact he must have wanted to do it himself when he was out of jail."

"And he told you this on his death bed? Or sidewalk?" Hunt asked.

"Never judge a dying man's wish, cop."

"Most men want to make peace with their maker at that moment. His last thought was of killing my wife? I'm touched."

"Keep it up. It sure as hell won't take nothing more to convince me to lay you out right here, crowd or not."

Mandy placed her hand over Hunt's mouth.

"Can we just get back to the facts and quit the pissing match? What this boils down to Eddie, is you using me like a pawn like Abbey was all those years ago, hoping I'd fail.

Sorry to disappoint you, but we found your shooter and something you didn't even expect."

He leaned back in his chair. "I knew about the book."

"Why didn't you take care of it?"

"I knew about it, I didn't know where it was."

"So, you were going to let Sue run away with it?"

"She didn't, now did she?"

Mandy's eyes widened. "You killed Sinclair?"

He took another bite. "Wish I could say I did. That frog of hers was disposable. I never would have killed her, though, out of respect to Lonny, no matter how much of a pain in the ass she'd been."

"You do realize where the book is now, don't you? You aren't the least bit worried?"

"Do I look like I'm shaking in my boots? None of that is ever admissible in court. The only thing you've given anyone is something else for their files. One more piece to a puzzle no one bothers to put together. All the info in that ledger is about Vince. He's dead. I don't see that there is a lot that can be done about anything now."

"You're connected to Vince, Eddie."

"And I'll be connected to the next boss. Oh wait, that'll be me." He took another bite. "I know you're not green enough to think any of this ever goes away."

"No, I'm not. It just gets passed on to those more young and stupid."

Eddie regarded her for a second before taking a sip of his beer. "Your point?"

"Sue wasn't behind this. It wasn't by chance she found Sinclair. I don't know how you found her, or how you convinced them to go through with this, but it was a pretty ingenious plan."

"What are you talking about?"

"Come on. You knew about Angie. You and Earl are as close as you and Vince ever were. He wants his son in the hot seat, and knocking up Angie was the way to secure his ass on the throne."

"The little bitch is pregnant?"

Mandy and Hunt exchanged glances. "Didn't Earl tell you? Darin and Angie were on their way to get married after leaving the cabin."

"They never came back as far as I know. Did you see them at the funeral?"

Again, Mandy turned to Hunt. He shrugged. "I never saw them."

"My mind wasn't on those two," Mandy said.

Eddie took out his cell phone. "Get in here."

Earl came flying in the door within seconds, expecting trouble. When Eddie pointed to a chair, he took it without question.

"You seen Darin?"

"Not since you shipped him off with Angelo. I expected to hear from him after this went down." He turned to Mandy. "Is there a reason you're still keeping him up there?"

"He left the night Angelo was shot. He said he was coming back to you." She glanced between him and Eddie, trying to read them. Their expression made her believe they were honestly in the dark. "He did say he was going to make one stop, though."

"What kind of stop is keeping him for two days?"

Mandy leaned back, reluctant to tell him.

Hunt jumped in. "They were going to get married."

Earl screamed. "What?"

Hunt continued. "Angie is...in the family way. They wanted to get married."

"That stupid sonofabitch."

"You really didn't know?" Mandy asked.

"You think I'd let him do a darn fool thing like that? He's twenty, for crying out loud."

Eddie faced Earl. "Amanda thinks it was our doing to set him up to take Angelo's place; seeing as how she's the new *queen* and all."

Earl laughed hard. "Right. Because this is England, and she's the boss now because Vince couldn't keep his dick in his pants, and she's the last heir. What are you two smoking?"

"You have to admit it's a plausible thought, Earl," Mandy said. "It only makes sense if Angelo was in line after Vince, another child would take that spot if Angelo were out of the picture."

"But an eighteen-year-old girl who knows nothing about any of this?"

"She doesn't have to. Darin has practically had a gun for a teething ring. He's bound to have dreams of being Mr. Big. He thinks the world of you and Eddie. Of course he wants to be like you."

Earl shook his head. "He can't be that stupid."

"Then where is he? Let's figure this out. I need to find the connection between him and Sue."

"If there is one."

"There has to be."

Mandy's phone rang. She took the call; it was Gunner. "What's up?"

"Are you nearby?"

"Sort of."

"Get here as soon as you can."

"I can be there in a few minutes. I'm with Eddie. What's up?"

"Earl with him?"

"Yes."

"Good. Bring them, too."

"Everything okay?"

"Just get everyone over here. Pronto."

"Give us twenty."

Gunner hung up.

"Who was that, babe?"

She stood. "Gunner. He wants us there now. Both of you, too," she said to Eddie and Earl.

"He say why?"

"You heard my part of the conversation. I don't have a clue."

Eddie took another large bite of pizza. "Damn good stuff. I'll have to remember this joint." Earl took care of Eddie's beer.

They arrived at Gunner's warehouse in just over twenty minutes. The man at the door waved them through, directing them straight to Gunner's office. He was sitting alone at his desk. He stood and motioned for them to sit. Mandy was the only one to take him up on it.

When he resumed his position behind his desk, Mandy asked him, "So what's up?"

"You're not Vince's daughter, are you?"

"Why question me now?"

"Just answer my question." His tone wasn't angry. It intrigued Mandy more than anything. She looked back at Eddie. He shrugged as if to say "go ahead."

"We've always had a good thing going, Gunner. I don't want to lie to you. No, I'm not."

"So, why did you bother with the whole song and dance?"

Eddie spoke up. "Because I forced her to. She was Angelo's right-hand man and knew these streets as well as anyone else. I needed someone to keep things going while we figured this whole shooter business out."

"She was your pawn?"

"I was a little more than a pawn, Gunner. Someone needed to step up and take charge. We knew being his sister gave me a little more credibility. We put a stop to the killings. I did what I came to do and kept peace in the meantime. Things are still square with Sully. I know that was a concern with Angelo missing."

"I'll give you that one. I didn't know what to think about them hooking up with us, but it seems to be going okay. What's your position now? You going to keep up this act? I can't understand what your motivation may be to try to pull off being boss when it's not your place. And Eddie, I can't believe you'd sit back and let a skirt do it."

"I'm right here," Mandy said.

"No offense, but I don't take kindly to having my Johnson being jerked. Where do you stand, Amanda?"

Earl answered for her. "She stands where Eddie says she stands. We may have her out front, but you know where everything has always come from. Nothing has changed."

"Well, isn't that just the cat's meow coming from you."

"What's that supposed to mean?"

"I mean, don't you expect to be scooting Eddie over and taking the granddaddy of all seats, Granddaddy?"

"What are you talking about, boy?"

"The fact that your son thinks he's going to be in charge, and you are his new right-hand man."

"What?"

Gunner laughed. "I thought it was quite humorous myself. What a little prick."

"Hey now, something has seriously come unglued with Darin, but he's still my boy. You know where he is?"

"I'm supposed to call him tomorrow. Said he personally took care of the sniper and now it's up to me."

"He told you he killed Sinclair?"

"I didn't realize you were on a first name basis with the sniper."

"We figured some things out a few days ago. I just haven't had a chance to fill you in. Things got crazy with the funerals."

"Is Angelo really gone?"

"Yes. Sorry I lied to you. We needed to keep him safe. I'm sorry it didn't work out the way it was supposed to. I'm not sure where we're going from here."

"Well, I can tell you what Darin thinks about this whole thing. He said he's not coming in until I take out the fed." He spoke to Earl and Eddie as he motioned his head to Mandy.

Hunt hurried to her side. "Relax there, Big H. I'm not doing nothin' to her. I figured he lost his mind somewhere in that eighteen-year-old piece of ass. I don't know what she's feeding him, but damn...he's lost his mind, thinking I'm going to off Amanda. She may not be Vince's daughter, but she's part of Vince's team and sure as hell ain't no fed."

Mandy stood and faced Earl and Eddie. "Still think I'm off my nut? I knew someone's train of thought was heading this way. He did think he could take over with her at his side. Dammit. We talked about this practically the first day and bought her bullshit poker face."

Earl took Eddie by the arm. "This doesn't sound like him at all. You're not killing my boy for whatever his part is in all of this. He says he took out that French dude. That has to count for something."

"No one is killing anyone, Earl," Mandy reassured him. "You need to get him in here and spell it out. I can't imagine this is what Angie had in mind."

"Don't be too sure on that," Gunner said.

Mandy spun around. "Why do you say that?"

"Because I'm sure she's the one who put it in his head. She traipsed in here, acting like a fucking queen, and we were her subjects."

"She did?"

He laughed. "I don't think Darin sought her out, wanting the title. I'm sure it was the opposite. She found herself an in, and he's getting led around by his dick. Too bad he's stupid enough to think they can pull it off. This deal, not his dick. Sorry, Mandy. And sorry, Earl. I don't mean no disrespect, but you weren't here. You'd've taken him over your knee yourself."

"So, what do we do about the little bitch?" Earl asked.

"Let's not get ahead of ourselves," Hunt said. "She obviously has it in for Mandy. First things first. We don't know who else she's trying to get to kill Mandy off."

"Sully for one," Gunner said.

"Sully?"

"I hung up with him after I called you. They had already been there before they came here. Sully didn't say anything to his face, but he thought Darin was off his nut, too. He obviously isn't doing his homework if he thinks Sully would harm Amanda for any reason."

Hunt turned to Mandy. "Babe...I don't like this."

"'Babe' already?" Gunner chuckled. "You two do move fast. You can stay here tonight if you want. No one will get through. He's showing up at noon tomorrow. Want to chill and confront him, then?"

"No. We'll figure this out. I still need answers," Mandy said. "I'm not going to sit here and be bait."

"What else is still out there?" Eddie asked. "This should be wrapped up."

"There's still missing pieces as to why Sue was behind the killings."

Gunner's eyes widened. "Sue? Lonny's Sue? You shittin' me? She's as pure as the driven snow. Lonny saw to it that she never knew anything."

"She hired the assassin."

"What?" Gunner turned away, then smacked his forehead with his palm. "Wait a second. This is about her kid, right?"

"Yes."

"Damn." He sat back down. "The mob just ain't what it used to be. You broads are going batty."

Mandy's phone rang. It was James. "Excuse me, guys. I have to take this." She walked out of the office.

CHAPTER TWENTY-SIX

Mandy answered the phone with, "Is everything okay?"

"Can you talk?"

"Not really, but you have me worried. Spill it."

"Angelo is fine if that's what you're worried about. He's safe and sound in a house off the west coast. Excuse me if I don't tell even you where yet."

"That's fine. We'll hash that out later. What's wrong, then? Why are you calling me?"

"I've had a few days to pour over that book you gave me."

"And?"

"There was a very interesting piece of paper in it."

"You going to keep making me drag this out of you? I may be pregnant, but I can still flip your ass to the ground."

He laughed. "I want you to come in."

"Why? Just tell me what you found."

"You won't allow me the satisfaction of seeing the look on your face?"

"One."

"You owe me."

"Two."

"All right. Pregnancy is making you cranky."

"I'm hanging up."

"Angie isn't Vince's kid."

"Excuse me?"

"He had blood work done. A DNA test when the kid was two. She's not even his."

"But he let anyone who knew believe she was. Why would he do that?"

"Beats the shit out of me. It's tucked in with her birth certificate. He's listed as the father. I looked it up. She's still on official record as his kid."

"Sonofabitch."

"Where are you? What do you have going on? Anything I can help with?"

"I can't talk now. I'll call you back later. Looks like we have a new ball in play. Thanks, James." Mandy hung up and returned to Gunner's office. "You guys are going to love this."

She conjured up a quick lie about having a hunch and calling in a favor to the city records office.

Gunner laughed at the new revelation. "Who gets to tell the little prince? Please, dear Lord, let it be me. Stupid shit got married for nothing." He regarded Earl. "Sorry. No offense."

"She's still pregnant," Earl replied.

"Maybe," Hunt said. "Could have been a ploy to get him to marry her. My guess is she doesn't know she's not really Vince's kid."

"Or..." Mandy paced the room. "She does know. Maybe she was in on this with Sue."

"How in the hell would those two find each other?" Earl asked.

"I don't have a clue. Maybe she found out about the book and tracked down Sue to get it so nothing could stand in her way. She can't honestly think she can take things over with Darin."

"Man, I gotta call Sully." Gunner was still laughing and reached for the phone.

Mandy stopped him. "Wait. We need a game plan first. Earl? Have you even tried to call him?"

"No. I just figured he'd call when he was back."

"Try giving him a call. See what happens."

The words were barely out of her mouth when Earl's phone rang. He looked at the caller ID. "It's him."

"Don't let on that you know anything. Act normal."

"Hey, boy. About time you get around to calling me. How are things?...Tonight? Well, I'm sure that's not a problem...What news?...To both of us?...I understand that, I guess. Must be good news...Okay. See you at seven." He hung up. "Says he's pulling into town tonight and wants to have dinner at the house. He said he has great news and wants to tell me and his mother together."

"I guess he expects you to be happy about the wedding and the baby."

"Then he is a dumb ass. What now? I fake it through the meal like I'm a moron and don't know anything? My boy can read me better than that."

"You let him show up and tell you what he needs to. Hunt and I will show up an hour into things and break the news to them."

"I'm going, too," Gunner said.

"I can't have you show up at my house. You'll have my wife flip a gasket."

Mandy turned to Gunner. "Sorry. You'll have to sit this one out."

"You will come fill me in, though, won't you?"

She winked at him. "Will do. Hey, I never said thanks for trusting me."

"You and Angelo have always done right by me. Even after slapping around Sully, you had him, too. We're not new here, Mandy. You don't think we'd smell a fed from a mile away?"

She grinned. "That's why you run this leg of things, Gunner. Nothing gets past you."

It was hard for Earl to try to play happy father over dinner that night. His wife was thrilled about the news. Both the marriage and the baby. She wasn't happy to have missed a wedding but assured them she'd start plans on a reception right away.

"I don't know why you had to run off and do this, Darin. I could have thrown something together fast enough." She took Angie by the hand. "Don't think we feel any less of you, dear. Who is married a virgin these days? I'm thrilled at the news."

There was a knock at the door and Earl stood. He was relieved when Hunt and Mandy finally showed up.

"It's about time you got here. I was waiting for my wife to get online and start picking out fucking tablecloths for a reception."

"So, they shared the lovely news?"

Earl scoffed. "Yeah."

Mandy placed her hand on his arm. "News not sinking in and making you feel better, Grandpa?"

He moved his arm to shake her free. "If that no-good boy wasn't trying to take things over and become my boss, it might be a different story."

"Who is it, Earl?" His wife called.

He smirked and hollered back. "My boss."

A chair scooted back hard against the wood floor. Darin was now standing by his father.

"Amanda?"

"Hi, junior. We need to talk," Mandy said as she shoved her way in. He tried to run, but Earl grabbed him by his shirt and held him there. Earl's wife excused herself to do dishes while everyone sat in the living room.

"What are you doing in my home?" Darin blurted out.

"It's my home, son."

"You really going to pull this crap? What's she doing here?"

"She's my boss and yours."

"Well, she shouldn't be. She's not Vince's daughter. My wife is." Angie slid closer to him.

"Actually, she not," Mandy said.

"The hell she's not. You sure as shit aren't."

"Maybe not, but I have everyone backing me and no one doing anything but laughing at you."

"Bullshit."

"Darin...for God's sake. Did you really think this is how things worked?"

Angie spoke up. "Of course it is. My father was boss, and he's gone. So is Angelo. That leaves me."

"That would leave you the heir of what he left you in his will. Not the new mob queen by default."

"Do something, honey," she said to Darin, crossing her arms.

"Did you even go with her to a doctor to confirm the pregnancy?" Mandy asked.

"I don't need to. I trust her."

"Would you have married her anyway, boy?" Earl asked. "If she wasn't claiming to be Vince's kid and pregnant?"

"Of course. I don't know what you guys are getting at. I'm not using her, and she's not using me. This is the way things are supposed to be. It's what's right. Mandy has no business running things."

"So, you just order to have me killed, so you can set up and play house?"

Darin turned white.

"That's right. The one thing you need to learn is loyalty. That's earned, not bought or—" she waved her hands up and down at Angie "—bred." Mandy kept her attention on Angie. "Why didn't you have the brains enough to stay away like Vince had intended for you?"

"Because this is in my blood, and this is what I want."

Mandy removed a piece of paper from her inside jacket pocket. "You may want it, but it's not in your blood."

"What are you babbling about?" Darin asked. "She's Vince's daughter."

"No, she isn't." Mandy tossed the paper at them. Angie snatched it away from Darin. "This is a lie. My mother told me Vince was my father."

"And she told Vince the same, but he had it confirmed he isn't. For whatever reason, he chose to let your mom think he believed her. Maybe she didn't know who the father really was. Maybe she wanted to have a hold on Vince, and he didn't mind and wanted to take care of you anyway."

Tears formed in Angie's eyes. "I just wanted to belong somewhere."

"Honey, I can name a thousand places you could have called home that didn't involve drugs and semi-automatics at the breakfast table."

Darin didn't seem to care about the news. He held his wife close as she cried into his chest. "So, what now?" he asked Mandy. "You going to return the hit on me for being a dumb ass?"

"I'm not having you killed, you dumb shit. You think your father would let me in here if that was my plan?"

Earl spoke up. "I'm pissed you'd even try such a stupid stunt, boy, but you're still my son. You need to pay your dues like everyone else. Of course, you may have to eat a little crow with Gunner and Sully. I honestly don't know what the fuck you were thinking, although I do know what you were thinking with."

"You going to throw me out?"

"You're not living here with your wife. You decided to go big and get married; you need to play house somewhere else."

It was Hunt's turn to reach into his pocket and toss a paper at Darin.

"What's this?"

"The deed to Lonny's house. Consider it a wedding gift from Eddie."

Darin was obviously confused. "You're rewarding me?"

"Hardly. Eddie wanted to wash his hands of it. Too many memories there for him."

"There is a stipulation for that, too," Earl said.

"What?"

"You finish law school."

Darin threw his head back. "I told you I was done with school."

"Well, it's this or hit the road. You and your wife have caused enough trouble for everyone. You'll go where I tell you to go, or I can't say what will happen to the two of you."

Angie finally sat up. "How will we face everyone?"

"It'll blow over. You can't be responsible for what you were told your whole life. Vince wanted you to think he was your father. That's good enough for me. We don't have to tell anyone the truth. You do need to tone down the princess act a shitload, though."

She wiped her eyes. "Okay."

"Eddie and I don't want it to be known that we let an outsider come in and run things. As far as anyone will be concerned, Vince had two daughters." He turned to Darin. "And you'd best admit to lying about her being a fed to get Gunner and Sully to take her out. If Eddie hears you keep trying to push it as a fact, even I couldn't stop him from skinning you alive."

His head dropped to his chest. "Yes, sir."

Eddie was in the driveway as Hunt and Mandy were leaving Earl's home. He rolled down the back window of the limo but didn't invite them in.

"Go well?"

"As good as could be expected. You got your wish, Eddie. Looks like you're in charge."

"I never wanted it this way. It was always an unspoken thing between Vince and myself. Believe what you want, but we were like brothers. We made this what it is today, together."

"And what an empire you have," Hunt said as he shook his head.

Eddie stared at him for a brief moment then turned to Mandy. "You can do what you want. You don't need to move and change your name. We'll never come after you again. You have my word."

"For all that's worth," Hunt said.

Mandy took his hand, silently urging him to stop.

"There is only one thing I don't get," Mandy said.

"What's that?"

"What it was that triggered Sue. Why did she bother coming back?"

Eddie cleared his throat. "That one I do know."

"You what? You knew about Sue and never bothered to tell us? You lied before?"

"I wasn't sure where it would go. It could have been nothing."

"Come on, Eddie."

He shrugged. "It took time, but Vince tracked her down. Once he was out, they hooked up and made a plan."

"Why did he want to bring her back into this?"

"He wanted that book, for starters. I guess he never counted on Sue having it out for him."

"All this time you knew it was her?"

"Of course not. I just put that together after everything that's happened. It just makes sense."

"If she knew where the book was, she had to have read everything in it. She was far from the innocent player I thought she was. All the information was right there. She knew the truth about Angie. I'll bet Sue made a deal with her about keeping the secret. I have no doubt she put all of this into Angie's head. Promises of riches if they took out Angelo."

"And getting rid of you when the time came." Eddie nodded.

All the pieces finally came together.

"She knew I'd come for Angelo." Mandy rubbed at her arms as she got a chill. Eddie taking her from her home actually saved her life, whether that was his intention or not.

"I'm still confused why Ray tried to kill me."

"He must have followed us there. Maybe he cooked up something with Vince before he died. Can't say, Mandy. He's not really an issue anymore." He paused. "You want me to take care of Kermit and Axle for their part in this?"

"No. Whoever was behind paying them to beat on Angelo so I'd show up, it actually gave us a few days we desperately needed. They're nothing. No one else needs to be killed over this." She sighed. "Is this really it, Eddie? We square?"

"You're done. You sure you don't want to come to the warehouse one last time and say your goodbyes? Sully is there with Gunner, waiting on word about the kids."

"This is one goodbye I can live without."

"Anything in particular you want me to tell them happened to you?"

"Just tell them I decided I wanted to pursue other things. That I didn't want to end up like my brother, after all, and I won't ever be back." She looped her arm through Hunt's. "Tell them I went all girlie and fell in love and finally accepted that Vince was right, and I don't belong here."

"Fair enough. Have a nice life." Eddie rolled up the window and the limo drove away.

A few months later, Hunt walked into the FBI training gym in Tampa, carrying Hannah. He watched for a few minutes as Mandy sparred with James before he went over and let his presence be known.

"I thought you were giving up the rough stuff in your third trimester, babe?"

She lit up at the sight of him and hurried over, taking Hannah from his arms. "How's my baby girl doing?"

Hannah gave her mom a kiss then scooted down and ran to James with her arms high over her head. "Uncle James! What did you bring me?"

He picked her up and swung her around. "New York is running out of things you don't have, little missy."

She stared at him, smiling.

"You have me figured out, peanut. Walk with me to my locker?"

"Uh huh."

Before he left, he shook Hunt's hand. "I didn't know you were back," Hunt said.

"I didn't know I was going to be either. It's just a quick weekend thing. Can I steal you two for dinner?"

Hannah laced her fingers together and batted her eyes at her father. Hunt laughed. "Sure." When they left the gym, Hunt gave Mandy a kiss then placed his hand on her stomach. "How are you two?"

"We're fine, Daddy."

"You know you shouldn't be boxing around like that, babe."

"I was going easy on him."

"And what about the rest of the class?"

"They're a good bunch. They baby me almost as much as you do."

He grinned and kissed her again. "It's my job."

"Speaking of that, my boss asked me about you again. They really want you as an instructor at the range. Someone is keeping an eye on your scores."

"I think one Blaine back on FBI payroll is enough. Call me silly, but I like my squad car."

"And you like having your name back."

"I'm not going to lie there."

"Did you tell Hannah your news?"

"I wanted to wait for you. You know she'll be thrilled to go to Disney World this weekend. It has been two whole months. It has to be killing her."

Mandy laughed and wrapped her arms around his waist. It wasn't easy to do with her belly.

"How about we let my parents take her, and we take one last vacation before your daughter is born?" Mandy lit up. "You even say you want to go to New York, and I'll beat you, woman."

She laughed. "I wouldn't dream of it. You pick."

"How's Key West sound?"

"Perfect actually. Close but not home. I like the idea."

"I'd like to drive. Is that okay, or do you want to fly? Can you handle the long drive?"

"Give me potty breaks. I'll be fine."

"Whatever you want, babe. You're the mob boss. I mean, boss."

Four days later, Hunt and Mandy were relaxing on a beach in Key West. Hunt had pushed their chairs together and had his hand at Mandy's belly. She wasn't as brave as some of the younger pregnant women who exposed their bare bellies. She still preferred an old-fashioned maternity swimsuit, despite it looking like it was made by Omar the tentmaker.

Hunt tried his hardest not to let his eyes stray, but the skimpy suit tops and g-string bikinis were plentiful on this perfect day. Every time he worried he was the slightest distracted, he gave her belly another rub. "I love you."

"Stuff it, Blaine."

He chuckled and leaned over, giving her a kiss. Hunt noticed a gentleman take the lounge chair next to hers.

"You seem kind of distracted, babe. We're on vacation. Relax."

"I'm just wondering how to go about asking about Angelo."

"You know you're not supposed to be in touch with him."

"They owe me this, though. Eddie promised to leave him alone. It's not fair." She glanced up at him. "I'm sorry, but you know how I feel about him."

"I know. I'm not threatened by him. If you think it's safe, I'll look the other way while you pin James on the mat and try to extract the information from him."

As if on cue, James showed up next to Hunt.

"James?" Mandy said. "Why are you on our vacation, and why are you on the beach in a suit?"

James laughed as he removed his coat. "My plane was late."

"Late? Late for what?"

"After what we've all been through, I thought you wouldn't mind."

"It's not that I mind...I just don't get it."

James called the waiter over and ordered three Sex on the Beach and one more that was a virgin.

"Thirsty, James?" Mandy asked.

He just shrugged. "I've been working on that problem for you."

"Could you be more specific?"

"Sue's estate."

"You found it?"

"Not too many places to hide that kind of money when you know what you're looking for. She wasn't after the jewelry because she needed the money. That's for sure."

"So, what happens with it? I suppose finders keepers."

"You have a better idea?"

"Yeah. You let me find Angelo and give it to him."

"What makes you think I want it?"

Mandy whipped her head around. Angelo was sitting on the chair next to hers. She squealed but stayed put.

"You're a little out of commission. Allow me," Angelo said as he stood, gave her a kiss on the cheek, and then sat on her chair.

"Why are you here?"

He motioned toward James as if that were answer enough.

"Were you in Florida all this time? Did you guys lie to me about California?"

"No. I've just been here the past few days. I'll be out of here next week. Picked a nice spot in—" James was shaking his head no.

"Europe."

"You called him here?" Mandy asked James.

"It was your husband's idea."

"Hunter Blaine. I let you play mobster for a few days, and now you can lie to me? You are so in trouble, mister."

He laughed as he took her hand and gave it a kiss. "Take it out on me later."

James took an envelope out of his coat pocket and handed it to Angelo. Angelo put his hands up. "I was being serious. I don't want that money. Too many bad memories are attached to it."

James thrust it toward him again. The waiter showed up, and Angelo accepted the envelope, not wanting to create a scene. They got their drinks, and the waiter walked away without showing an ounce of concern.

"I know what Eddie gave you isn't enough to do Jack. Not by your standards, anyway. It's not like we're going to offer you anything but the right to disappear. The bank address and all the codes are there. Just take it and shut up before I change my mind."

"Won't you get in trouble, James?" Mandy asked.

"This isn't on the books. I trust you'll keep your mouth shut."

"Hey, I just work the floor. I keep my nose out of that stuff."

"Yeah, well, once upon a time, so did I, kid. So did I." James took another sip of his drink then stood. "Enjoy your vacation."

"You're leaving already?"

"Heading to the Bahamas, and no, it's not for pleasure. I don't know whether to kiss you or kill you for giving me a taste of field work again." He put on his sunglasses and headed toward the pier. "See you next time."

Angelo offered Mandy the envelope. "I don't think I should take this, Mandy."

"You know we can't take it."

"Darci was killed because of this."

"It wasn't because of that and you know it." She placed her hand on his. "Take it. Go make a life for yourself. An honest life."

"There you are, Garrett." A tall, blonde woman with her chest bursting out of her bikini leaned into Angelo and gave him a lingering kiss. "Found you, baby." She smiled at Hunt and Mandy. "Did you make new friends?"

"Uh...yeah. Denise, this is Hunt and Mandy. They're from Tampa. Just here for the weekend." Hunt reached over and shook her hand. Mandy smiled pleasantly at her.

"You going to come swimming with me?"

"In a second, sweetie. Go ahead. I'll join you." She kissed him goodbye and ran toward the water.

"Garrett?" Mandy asked.

"It was my grandfather's name on my mom's side."

"Nice to see you making an attempt at a relationship for a change. I've never heard you refer to someone as sweetie before."

He shrugged. "She was the realtor on a villa I bought in Greece. Very low-key nights. I'm liking it."

"Greece? You weren't supposed to tell us that, Angelo. I mean, Garrett."

He stood and threw the envelope on the chair then covered it with a towel. "Yeah, well, fuck 'em." He ran off to the water.

ABOUT THE AUTHOR

June, who prefers to go by Bug, was born in Philadelphia but moved to Maui, Hawaii, when she was four. She met her "Prince Charming" on Kauai and is currently living "Happily Ever After" in Minnesota. Her son and daughter are her greatest accomplishments. She takes pride in embarrassing them every chance she gets.

Visit www.junekramin.com for more releases.

Time Travel Series:
Dustin Time
Dustin's Turn
Dustin's Novel

Romantic Suspense/Thriller:
Double Mocha, Heavy on Your Phone Number
Hunter's Find
Amanda's Return (Hunter's Find II)
I Got Your Back, Hailey
I've Also Got Your Front (I Got Your Back, Hailey II)
Amanda's Got This, Hailey – I Got Your Back Hailey III
Here Today, Gone to Maui, Hailey - I Got Your Back Hailey IV
I'm on Your Side, Hailey - I Got Your Back Hailey V
Before Parker Met Hailey - I Got Your Back Hailey Prequel
Contemporary Romance:
Love You More
Come and Talk to Me
Money Didn't Buy Her Love
Devon's Change of Heart (Money Didn't Buy Her Love II)
I'll Try to Behave Myself
88s, Baby & 88s, Lady
Baby, Just Say Yes
Contemporary Fiction
The Green Flash at Sunset
New Adult
Let's Start With Forever

Visit www.beforehappilyeverafter.com for her middle grade fantasy series written under the pseudonym of Ann T. Bugg.

If you've enjoyed this novel, a review would be appreciated!